COMMUNICATIONS
BREAKDOWN

TWELVE TOMORROWS SERIES

In 2011, *MIT Technology Review* produced an anthology of science fiction short stories, *TRSF*. Over the next years, *MIT Technology Review* produced three more volumes, renamed *Twelve Tomorrows*. Since 2018, the MIT Press has published *Twelve Tomorrows* in partnership with *MIT Technology Review*.

TRSF, 2011

TR Twelve Tomorrows 2013, edited by Stephen Cass

TR Twelve Tomorrows 2014, edited by Bruce Sterling

TR Twelve Tomorrows 2016, edited by Bruce Sterling

Twelve Tomorrows, edited by Wade Roush, 2018

Entanglements: Tomorrow's Lovers, Families, and Friends,
  edited by Sheila Williams, 2020

Make Shift: Dispatches from the Post-Pandemic Future,
  edited by Gideon Lichfield, 2021

Tomorrow's Parties: Life in the Anthropocene,
  edited by Jonathan Strahan, 2022

Communications Breakdown: SF Stories about the Future of Connection,
  edited by Jonathan Strahan, 2023

COMMUNICATIONS BREAKDOWN

SF STORIES ABOUT THE FUTURE OF CONNECTION

EDITED BY JONATHAN STRAHAN

THE MIT PRESS
CAMBRIDGE, MASSACHUSETTS
LONDON, ENGLAND

This book was set in Dante MT Pro and PF DIN pro by New Best-set Typesetters Ltd. Printed and bound in the United States of America.

Library of Congress Cataloging-in-Publication Data

Names: Strahan, Jonathan, editor.
Title: Communications breakdown : SF stories about the future of connection / edited by Jonathan Strahan.
Description: Cambridge : The MIT Press, 2023. | Series: Twelve tomorrows
Identifiers: LCCN 2022054185 (print) | LCCN 2022054186 (ebook) | ISBN 9780262546461 (paperback) | ISBN 9780262376204 (epub) | ISBN 9780262376198 (pdf)
Subjects: LCSH: Science fiction. | Communication and technology—Fiction.
Classification: LCC PN6071.S33 C66 2023 (print) | LCC PN6071.S33 (ebook) | DDC 808.83/8762—dc23/eng/20230403
LC record available at https://lccn.loc.gov/2022054185
LC ebook record available at https://lccn.loc.gov/2022054186

10 9 8 7 6 5 4 3 2 1

CONTENTS

INTRODUCTION

Jonathan Strahan

COMMUNICATIONS BREAKDOWN. THE PHRASE EVOKES DISTANT OUTPOSTS UNABLE to contact home or brave explorers trying desperately to contact base camp and, tragically, fatally, failing. When I began working on this book, when the idea began to evolve and develop, I quietly lifted the title from a Led Zeppelin song about two people unable to communicate in a relationship, but neither the song nor the stories that title evokes were on my mind at the time.

Instead, I'd been thinking about something that William Gibson said in an interview with the *Economist* back in 2004. Gibson famously said: "The future is already here—it's just not evenly distributed." The more you ponder that, the more of what Gibson must have meant becomes obvious. A person living in a high-rise in New York or Beijing experiences a very different world from someone living in outback Australia, rural Uganda, or the poorer parts of Delhi. Access to technology, to infrastructure, to many of the things that we might consider essential to the experience of being alive in the twenty-first century, is either completely unavailable, intermittently available, or only available in some limited or restricted way because of financial and social inequalities.

While I was thinking about this, I came across an article discussing changes in India, where the government has overseen programs that have resulted in five hundred million new bank accounts and almost as many telephone and internet accounts being created, at least in part to help the Indian government administer its social security system more efficiently and cost-effectively. It sounded good—if you have access. If you have a phone and a credit card, know what they mean and how to use them. If the system is used fairly and openly, and if privacy is respected and private information is not used or misused in ways users might not expect or agree to. And then I began to think about how, if you look at the top ten nations in the world for internet users, all but perhaps one have such enormous disparities in health, wealth, and education that there's little chance that all 1.42 billion Chinese, 1.41 billion Indian, or 275 million Indonesian internet users have anything like the same experience of our latest instalment of the "future."

And that led me to ponder: What happens when communications break down, when the technological and other developments that we might consider important are simply unavailable? What happens if communicating the future itself breaks down when technology is used and misused? During the COVID-19 global pandemic, vaccines were developed, manufactured, and distributed around the world at a breathtaking pace (even as we complained it was taking too long), and along with them came systems that monitored who got those vaccines and who did not, and which systems now allow people who have been vaccinated to live more freely. The technology that underpins those advances—mobile phones, the internet, cheap online transactions, and so on—also involves us providing regular updates on our physical locations to government authorities and to countless commercial enterprises. We are monitored, surveilled, and tracked. Our biometric data is picked up in airports and used to develop AI.

The future is here and almost unimaginable good can be done, along with almost unlimited harm. Who is in control? What is being done with this information? What does it mean? And what happens for those who are caught in what Bruce Sterling, more than forty years ago, called *islands in the net*? What happens to those who are not connected at all or who only are connected when the power happens to be on?

With all this in mind, I reached out to some wonderful writers from all over the world and asked them for stories that look at what happens when communications break down, when the future doesn't quite make it to your front door. Ten delivered the stories here; I think what they've done is extraordinary, and I hope you do too. I also asked Tim Maughan to talk to noted privacy activist Chris Gilliard, who has fascinating things to say about what's happening around us. I admit that after reading his interview I did change all my passwords and upgrade my security, and I'm still a little uncomfortable. Perhaps that sense of mild paranoia, of things being at risk that need to be kept safe, is the price of being informed.

There are moments in the stories you are about to read that could be seen as dark or even depressing, but I think there's more to them and the view of the world they show than that. They show the possibility of solutions, of things getting better, of improvement. Kim Stanley Robinson, who was interviewed in last year's MIT Press volume *Tomorrow's Parties*, has said we have an obligation to be optimistic, to try—in effect, to bring about the best possible futures. That spirit lies behind these stories. I loved working on them, and I hope you enjoy them as much as I have.

Perth, August 2022

1 HERE INSTEAD OF THERE

Elizabeth Bear

WAKING UP SICK IN A PUNK HOUSE SHOULDN'T BE A SURPRISE TO ANYBODY SO I don't know why it always came as a surprise to me. My head throbbed so bad I couldn't tell the difference between the hangover, my sinus headache, and Kai pummeling their drum set over in the yacht hangar.

The Kai part also wasn't unusual. The Crash's drummer is our early riser. That's the Devil's pre-Hell punishment on us all. But even hungover, I never woke up with a head this full of pain.

Henry must have seen me twitch, because five people racked out between me and the galley all said "Oof!" in a row. Suddenly my arms were full of wriggling beagle mutt and stank. At least the sov-cit types who left this pod a wreck before we squatted in it didn't leave it full of fleas as well as trash and feces. (I choose to believe that the feces were from a dog rather than a toddler.) And there aren't any ticks this far from shore.

I thought about pushing Henry away, rummaging in my pack for some tramadol, and going back to sleep, but Henry was standing on my bladder and I heard clattering in the kitchen.

If I was lucky, Miriam was up and there was about to be food happening. If I was unlucky, one of the dirtbag fugs dossing with us was raiding the last of the veggie chili without having kicked in anything to support the house.

(Not all dirtbag fugs, I know. Just the 10 percent that get my grind on the regular.)

Either way, I had to piss.

I staggered to my feet, guts playing marimba, room spinning. I managed to roll up my bag and pad without barfing. I needed to get some protein and electrolytes on board pronto.

The floor space was wall-to-wall dirtbags, snoring, drooling, generally rendering the space impassable. Crash Pod living up to its house name, as usual.

Crash Pod. The dumbest available name. But I wasn't going to tell Miriam that. It was on the long list of things I was never going to tell Miriam. Such as that looking at her made my chest ache.

Henry did his best impersonation of a minefield as I wove and stumbled to the head. I managed to only step on one dude's elbow and he was too passed out to care. Henry stepped on all of them indiscriminately. Got one guy in the balls. Should probably trim his toenails.

Oh well.

The head was a pesthole and I was glad I didn't need to take a dump. I stood as far from the bowl as possible while doing what I had to do. At least my aim was better than most. Then I did what the last three people *should* have done, and flushed.

It was nearly too late. Sewage rose to the rim of the bowl. I was lunging for the valve to shut off the flow when some obstruction gave and the whole mess swirled down into the septic tank with a rancid *glorp*. Bullet dodged, but for how long?

Probably time to figure out how to get that pumped out, which meant figuring out how to *pay* for getting it pumped out.

Miriam would get mad if I just opened the valves and let all the shit dump into the sea, which is how the previous inhabitants had handled things. And I had seven-eighths of a climate science degree to argue with the oppositional defiance that told me to do it anyway, so I washed my hands and dry-swallowed that tramadol, and some Pepcid too.

Henry wagged his tail at me from the doorway. In my mind, I could already hear the riot act Miriam was going to read us.

At least the galley didn't smell like an orgy in the locker room of a sewage treatment plant. It smelled like vinegar and ginger, which suggested Miriam was making tsukemono.

A different organ did a backflip when I saw her. I bit my lip on a sigh.

"Wash your hands, Haf," she said, as I peeked over the threshold.

"I washed them in the bathroom!"

"Sure, and then you touched the faucets and the door handle, didn't you?"

"I left the door open."

She sighed like a much larger dog than Henry. Henry huffed in appreciation and went to sit at her feet and beg for radish slices. That dog. No loyalty.

"I looked in that head this morning. We're going to have to have a Crash Pod house meeting about that. Haf. *Wash* your *hands*."

Miriam has her own bedroom and her own en suite head. Since she's basically the den mother for everybody and also the best guitarist I know, and she does most of the cooking, she earns her privacy. Also, there's only so much sharing she can tolerate, even in a share house, and none of us want her to leave.

I washed my hands. "What are you making?"

Inane conversation was what *I* was making, apparently.

"Brown rice in the rice cooker. Daikon in sweet vinegar. Pickled turnips and kombu."

I thought kombu was Japanese but what the fuck do I know? Maybe it grows in the Atlantic too. Maybe Miriam just picked some random edible algae off the stanchions and decided to call it kombu. I assume she knows what's edible, anyway. She hasn't poisoned or dosed us accidentally yet, though there was the mushroom incident. But that was on purpose.

I would fucking kill somebody for a chicken sandwich, which is how I know Sartre was wrong. Hell is a SeaBit full of vegan macrobiotic gluten-free punks. Who unfortunately were the best band I've ever been a part of.

And also, there was Miriam.

At least The Crash weren't straight edge. Fuck, does straight edge even exist anymore? I met some straight-edge hippies once, and that was just *weird*.

My eyeball throbbing intensified as—from behind the inadequately soundproofed hangar door—Kai hit a crescendo. I leaned my butt on the counter edge, suffering too much even to take my usual pleasure in watching the swing of Miriam's black and acid-purple hair or her efficient grace as she danced around the kitchen. *She* never tripped over Henry, no matter how hard he worked at being an obstacle.

"Can I have some? I'm starving."

"It'll be a couple of hours before it's ready. Have some chili."

I sighed and turned toward the fridge, which was probably worth more than some people's cars. It was big enough to hold food for twenty people, or at least two corpses. Three if you used the freezer, but then you'd have to defrost it to get the body out again.

My hand closed on the handle. I tugged. It didn't budge. I tugged harder.

The whole gigantic restaurant-sized edifice rocked on its little rubber feet.

"What the?"

"Don't yank on that," Miriam said, "You're gonna break it."

Henry jumped up helpfully and paddled with his paws against the scratched stainless finish. The screen on the front flashed *Lock Engaged.* "Did you lock this?"

She had come over to stand next to me. I held my breath so I didn't bump her by accident. She shook her head.

"Shit," I said. "We must have gotten another push update."

She cocked her head and blinked at me with wide, fringed eyes. "What does that have to do with the fridge locking? It worked five minutes ago!"

"Yeah." I sighed and pulled the kitchen console around. We kept it tucked up against the wall so drunk punks wouldn't snap it off the stand by leaning on it.

"Can you make me some coffee? I probably have a half dozen bullshit glitches to fix. They want us to buy a new pod."

"A new what?"

It was a good thing my fingers knew their way around the keyboard because my vision was still a little swimmy. I wondered if it was migraine aura. I wasn't sure. I'd never had a migraine.

"SeaBit," I said tiredly, "thinks you ought to buy a *new* SeaBit every three to five years or so. So they intentionally break the functionality of your existing one over time. You think the thing is wearing out, so you buy a new one. Planned obsolescence. No right to repair."

"Well that's some bullshit," Miriam said. "Like rent-seeking but worse."

"Subscription model housing," I agreed.

She put the drop lid on top of her pickles, and two canning weights on top of that. "Joke's on them though, since we didn't pay for it in the first place. And you can hack it, right?"

The Crash is no Objekt 775 but we do okay. Even so, punk bands can't usually afford their own seastead. Fortunately, anarchists are pretty good at building communities and rich seasteading advocates are terrible at getting along with each other, especially when it involves deciding who's going to do the unpleasant jobs—or pay to have them done. And you'd be shocked what people with too much money will just up and walk away from if it's inconvenient.

Maritime salvage laws still apply. Or so Earwyn, our rhythm guitarist and bunkhouse lawyer, says. I bet we'd lose if they took us to court, but nobody's showed up to evict so far.

Could I hack it? Through the pain, I determined the extent of the problem. My turn to sigh. Henry flopped down on my foot for a nap. My head throbbed harder.

"Is there anything not in the fridge that I can eat?" I begged.

"Earwyn and Caspian took the launch in to town to dumpster dive. I guess they'll be back in a few hours." She sounded pissed and unhelpful. I didn't think she was pissed at me.

I tried not to roll my eyes. Shelf-stable tofu stays good—or as good as it ever was—for years past the sell-by date and Earwyn always wants to dumpster dive the health food store. I knew what we'd be eating for the next week. Assuming we had any way to cook it. It looked like most of the pod's appliances were fucked.

"Christ." I pressed the heels of my hand to my eyes. "I need some electrolytes."

"I've got some limeade with coconut water, turmeric honey, and cider vinegar. Also some cold coffee."

"I'll get the fridge working in a few minutes," I promised. "Just keep the caffeine coming."

THE LIMEADE WAS ACTUALLY PRETTY GOOD, AND ALONG WITH THE ROOM-temperature coffee it eased the pounding. With the hangover lightening up and Kai taking a break from drum practice, I could tell how much of the remaining headache was sinus pressure.

Sadly, a lot of it. I looked out the window, but the sky was cloudless except for a layer of stratocumulus undulatus, narrow parallel stripes lit gold from beneath by a gently setting sun.

The fugs were waking up, finally, dragging themselves out of their sleeping bags and into the galley in ones and twos. That let Miriam get most of the yelling out of her system (oh my head) and gave her an excuse to assign them all housekeeping chores in advance of breakfast.

"This is a punk house, not a plague pit," she snarled at the last filthy underaged kid to drag herself out of her grimy doss kit. "Communalism doesn't have to mean drowning in filth."

"It's a protest against bourgeoisie standards of cleanliness," the kid said haughtily, reaching across me for the coffee pot.

I kept my eyes on the screen, my fingers on the keyboard.

Miriam brushed the kid's hand away. "You're incubating VRSA. I refuse to let you trash this place worse than a bunch of neoliberals. You want a say in how this house is run, you need to contribute. I don't want to live in filth, and the Pod needs upkeep or it falls into the sea. *That* is nonnegotiable."

The kid gaped at her. "Wow."

Miriam's eyes rolled so hard I almost heard them rattle. "Go snake out the shower drain, then you can have coffee."

Not that we used the shower much. It was a saltwater shower, and it was just as easy to give yourself a whore's bath with a rag when you started to itch and save the sticky skin. Some people didn't bother with the whore's bath, but—as Miriam said—their abscesses, their problem.

"Hah," I said, as the refrigerator emitted a satisfying click. "And I'm in."

Miriam lunged to yank the door open.

"You'll let the cold out," I said.

"It can make more cold. Will it stay unlocked?"

"Until the next time they break it. I convinced the firmware it was still 2043. It won't be able to order groceries for us when we run low on caviar and smoked oysters—"

She snorted and pulled out the leftover chili. "Unlike some people, Haf, *you* have earned breakfast."

THE CHILI WAS FINE. ONE NICE THING ABOUT CHILI: IT'S GOT SO MANY SPICES IN IT, it doesn't matter what you use as a base. It just tastes like chili. I missed the sour cream and cheese, though. And I had to hack the microwave before I could warm it up.

Miriam saw me poking mournfully at the food with my spoon. With the exasperation of a mind reader she said, "You're the climate scientist. You of all people ought to be against eating animal products."

"I am," I assured her. "But my tastebuds are hypocrites. Anyway, I'm not a real climate scientist. I'm a washout."

Acknowledging my pun was beneath her dignity. "Go mope someplace that isn't my kitchen." She pointed out at the deck.

I took my headache, my chili, and a second glass of limeade and went. Henry, the household's only nonvegan, stayed behind to beg Miriam for scraps. I would have let him lick my bowl, too. And Miriam could have contended with the doggie bean farts.

I may be infatuated, but that doesn't stop me from being petty.

For a while, we had somebody crashing here with a foul-mouthed parrot. A yellow-fronted Amazon. Now there's an animal that really enjoys shitting all over everything.

I dawdled over the chili looking out at that sunset, which now glittered vermillion and crimson off the facets of a flat calm sea. A dozen other SeaBits spread on an arc to either side of the Crash Pod. One or two had been completely abandoned. One still had the original inhabitant in residence, though he only came out on weekends—which is how we kept track of when the weekends were. Our nearest neighbor, Dr. Ex, was on her deck, doing qigong in the ruddy light.

I waved. She nodded.

I pushed the last few mouthfuls of food around my bowl, feeling both overstuffed and vaguely unsatisfied. If anybody but Earwyn and Caspian were doing the food run, there might be treats when the launch finished its twenty-four-mile round trip to shore and back again. But Eowyn was a true believer, and the best I could hope for was overripe avocados whipped into a mousse with maple syrup and cocoa powder.

It's better than it sounds, but it's not actually chocolate pudding.

Maybe the next time we went in for a gig I could ditch everybody and get Popeyes.

Whether it was the lack of drumming, the hydration, the tramadol, or the sea air, my pain was subsiding. Kai's a good drummer, don't get me wrong. I'm probably the worst musician in the group. Fortunately, I'm also the bassist, and if I'm not nimble-fingered, I have extremely solid rhythm. A punk band doesn't need to be fancy.

The Crash wasn't fancy. Miriam and Caspian had picked the name, over my protests (too derivative), and I honestly thought it was just so we could call our house the Crash Pod (even worse).

Dr. Ex's wife brought her out a beer and they hugged briefly, leaning on each other and looking at the sunset. For a moment, I felt the peace of the evening. The air was buttery and still. It smelled of clean salt and piña colada, which probably meant one of the fugs had spilled cheap coconut rum all over a deck chair. What is it with kids too young to drink legally and Malibu?

The doc's wife went back inside. The doc wandered over to the rail with her beer and leaned on it. "Hey, Haf," she yelled.

"Hey, doc," I yelled back.

The doc is cool. She and her wife are out here past the ten-mile limit because they run a secret illegal reproductive health clinic out of the pod on their other side.

Because I was looking at her and our weather station was at the edge of the deck, I noticed the orange light blinking on its panel.

"Oh, cheesenuts," I muttered. I put the chili I was never going to finish on a deck chair.

Miriam would yell at me for wasting food, and Henry was still inside. But was it my fault if a gull stole it while I was investigating a potentially serious warning light?

My brain provided a brief unlikely fantasy of me saving the day, Miriam hailing me as a conquering hero, and the two of us consummating our long-denied passion for one another and penning a platinum album together based on the emotional catharsis. I rolled my eyes and went to inspect the weather station. That must have been one hell of a firmware update.

As expected, the thing was offline. Feeling pretty practiced by now, I performed my system clock trick. In a few minutes, the aerometer, barometer, and all the other ometers were back online. Except something was still wrong, because the barometric pressure was 940 ml: catastrophically low for a warm, mild summer evening. Center of a hurricane low, in fact.

Possibly it was pulling data from 2043?

"Hey, Doc," I called. "Is your fridge working?"

"I think so," she answered. "How come?"

"We got a push patch that fucked up half our devices."

"Oh, Elsie jailbroke both our pods when we moved in. They're off the network entirely."

Intelligent, considering what they did out here and how secret they needed to keep it. Smart houses spy on you. And it's not like the Coast Guard has ever respected civil rights or the ten-mile limit when they're in hot pursuit of whoever they consider criminals.

"Have you looked at your instruments today?"

"I wouldn't know how to read them." She kicked the deck with a canvas sneaker. "We have a weather app."

"Aren't we a little off the grid for that to be viable?"

"It's all satellites, right? Isn't it the same stuff shipping is on?"

My face must have done a thing, because she laughed. "Oh right, Miriam said you were nearly a meteorologist. You must be killing yourself not to lay some deep nerdery on me."

"Miriam should mind her own business."

I felt bad as soon as I said it. Feeling bad made me want to bluster more. It was nobody's business why I was playing bass and hacking firmware in a squat. Why I was here instead of there.

I knew enough about *there* to know which place I'd rather be.

Doc was still looking at me, eyebrows raised. Amazing how well you can see somebody through dusk on water, when your eyes have adapted. The air goes full of light.

Like a held breath, for an instant.

"Sorry," I said, stepping on all my adolescent impulses. "Can I come and look at your weather station?"

I expected her to say "No," because I had just bitten her head off. Instead she gave me one of those inscrutable pursed-lip expressions middle-aged people use when they're trying not to condescend and failing. Then she pushed the button to send the catwalk over.

I REENTERED THE GALLEY SOME TIME LATER. THE NIGHTLY PARTY MUST HAVE gotten rolling again while I was outside, as soon as everybody decided they'd done barely enough housework to placate Miriam. I felt muffled, isolated behind a wall of dire news. I moved through the raucous crowd like a floating island of anxiety adrift in a sparkling, crashing sea.

Miriam wasn't in the galley. She wasn't in her bedroom. She was in the practice room and concert space—the old yacht hangar that we'd floored over with salvaged plywood and absolutely no regard for building codes—with Kai, tuning her guitar. They were laughing. The smiles fell off both their faces when they got a look at mine.

"I need to see you both outside right now."

Kai got up from their stool without a word. Miriam put her axe back in the stand. They followed me out the double doors to the outside and we all jumped the railing to reach the deck. The sun was just closing the curtains on its vanishing act. The sky was as bloody as a Nick Cave song.

"Pretty sunset," Kai said, shaking back their dreads. "Sailor's delight."

"Yeah," I said, "about that." And I pulled out my phone and showed them the data I'd hacked out of Doc's weather app, the barometric pressure, the shift off the prevailing winds.

"What does that mean?" asked Miriam.

My voice shook. My hands shook. In the pit of my stomach, ice rattled like dice. "We've got a big fucking problem."

I switched images and showed them the satellite images from the National Weather Service that I had cracked and illegally downloaded. Water vapor, visible light, infrared. Then the weather radar. Then the drone probe and buoy data.

A Brobdingnagian swirl of clouds and moisture and heat, with a glaring, perfect eye. A spiral like Fibonacci's own gate to Hell.

"That's Kasimir," I said. "It's a category 6. And it is going to hit us at about three o'clock this morning."

"But—" Kai pulled out their phone and looked at it. Shook it like they could shake some sense into it and the missing notification out. "Shouldn't there be a warning?"

"Do you pay for a premium weather service?"

Kai stared like I had grown an extra mouth and was talking out of it. "A what now?"

"Michaelson versus the State of Vermont," I said. "The Supreme Court ruled it unconstitutional for the government to compete with private industry in providing any service. Such as transportation, healthcare, prison services . . . and weather alerts."

"Fuck," said Miriam.

Somehow, I managed not to put my arms around her. Not because she looked like she needed a hug. Because I needed a hug.

"The hurricane is paywalled," I said, just to have it out loud. "If you don't pay for the subscription, you don't get the emergency alerts."

Kai shook their head. "How do they get away with paywalling a hurricane?"

"How do they get away with anything?" I said bitterly. "They just do it."

"Earwyn and Caspian are going to be on their way back when it hits," Miriam said, at the same moment Kai said, "Can we evacuate in time?"

WITH THE LAUNCH GONE, THERE WAS JUST ONE RUBBER DINGHY WITH AN OUTBOARD motor stowed under the floor of the hangar, along with two kayaks, a sailboard, and a jet ski in an abjectly terrifying state of disrepair. There were twenty-three human souls on the pod, plus Henry.

Doc and her wife went up and down the steads alerting our neighbors that they needed to clear out. By the time they came back, we'd gotten the fugs organized into evacuation groups. We packed six people into Doc's boat, in a space meant for four. Four more into the dinghy with one girl who was sober enough to steer and seemed competent to run the motor.

That left Kai, Miriam, Henry, me, and ten dirtbags. I didn't even suggest that we give the Filth Is A Protest girl one of the kayaks and turn her loose, a level of self-restraint I was smugly proud of.

Evacuation logistics wasn't my problem. I'm terrible at delegating, but all my effort was going into fixing either the radio or the cell transmitter so we had some chance of reaching Earwyn or Caspian and telling them to stay on shore.

Miriam and I were each probably five minutes from an utter meltdown—her about the fugs, me about the cell transmitter—when it turned out that some of our neighbors were okay people. Two other squatters stopped by and gave the rest of the kids a lift, jamming their boats past capacity.

Now only us permanent inhabitants were in danger, and at least one of us—me—needed to remain behind to try to fix comms and reach Earwyn and Caspian. I tried to push Miriam into the square foot of decking left in the last boat, but she wasn't having any. "I'm not leaving my dog." A flat statement of fact.

Oh, so Henry was *her* dog, all of a sudden.

Fine, fine.

Kai and Miriam moved the instruments out of the hangar and into the living room, and got to work fortifying the storm shelter in the interior of the pod. The shelter was Miriam's bathroom and not the share bathroom, a small providence that almost sent me back to Sunday school and believing in God. A good trick, since faith was something I'd abandoned after my youth pastor told me there was no such thing as anthropogenic climate change; the weather was just terrifying because God was angry at people for fornicating.

And playing loud music.

The eerily calm conditions persisted. A three-quarter moon rode high. When I looked south an ominous wall of black was advancing up the sky.

Because the transmitter set its own timestamp based on network information, I had to use a whole different set of tactics on it. I hadn't been sure it would work, and it was close to 2:00 a.m. when I finally got it online.

I crowed like a rooster. Miriam and Kai came running over, Henry yodeling with excitement at their heels. "Did you get them?"

"Not yet. I just got a signal. And, looking at the time, they're probably in the middle of their shopping expedition right now."

I pinged anyway. To my surprise, they pinged right back. I opened a coded channel and said, "Tell me you're still ashore."

"Need us to run back and get something?" Earwyn said. "The whole town is deserted, it's weird as hell. We got in and out with no problem."

"There's a hurricane coming," I said. "A bad one. You need to turn back and seek shelter in town."

"We're more than halfway," Earwyn said. "When's the storm arriving?"

I looked at my maps and predictions again. I'd been too busy to run back over to the doc's and get newer data. "The leading edge should be on us in about an hour. Wind's going to pick up in advance of that and there will be a lot of chop and gale-force gusts. Heavy seas."

"We should be able to make it back in time to evacuate you," Caspian said.

"I really think—"

Earwyn cut me off. "If you all get killed, what are we gonna do for a rhythm section?"

"Hey," said Miriam. "What am I, chopped liver?"

Earwyn laughed. It sounded strained even over the airwaves. "Everybody wants to be the lead guitarist, Mir."

"Oh, I see. You want my *job*."

"Not that badly," Earwyn said softly, in a tone I recognized. "We're coming back. Sit tight, we'll have you out of there in no time and then we can skedaddle for a hurricane hole. Charge all the batteries, we might need them."

"Earwyn, we're going to have to close the hangar."

"We can slide in underneath. Go pack," she said firmly. "And don't forget Henry's potty pads. And make sure the searchlights are turned on so we can find you."

I tried one more time to convince her to turn around, but she didn't respond. I slammed the heel of my hand against the edge of the console. "Fuck this fucking corrupt system so hard."

Miriam snorted. "You'd *be* part of the system if you hadn't gotten kicked out for hacking."

I stared at her, shocked at the cruelty. "Wow, so is that really what you think of me? Fuck you too." My heart squeezed. I couldn't believe I'd just said that, but I couldn't take it back either—so I got up and left to make sure we had as many charged portables as possible. If by some miracle Earwyn and Caspian reached us, it wouldn't hurt to ballast the launch with them and it sure wouldn't help to run out of juice in the middle of a hurricane.

THE LAUNCH DIDN'T BEAT THE STORM. WE CRAMMED INTO THE BATHROOM WITH OUR backpacks and sleeping rolls and jugs of water and our stale rice cakes and peanut butter. I still didn't feel much like talking to Miriam, so I didn't mind that she padded the tub with a bunch of pillows, spread her sleeping bag on top, and climbed in with Henry. She turned her back on Kai and me to ostentatiously bury her attention in her e-reader. The dog stretched out and started snoring.

I propped myself against the wall with my feet on one side of the toilet, and Kai stretched out parallel to the tub, feet against the wall by the sink. The head had no windows, but a skylight molded into the roof. Rain began to drum against it as the wind rose. The pod shuddered with the impact of heavy seas against its pylons. When the waves rose high enough to wash over the deck and strike the walls of the pod, every hit felt like we were inside Kai's bass drum. Lightning painted the walls with staccato brightness.

"That's what I love about living here," Kai muttered. "There's always some kind of amazing bullshit going on. Pass me the marmite, would you?"

"It's antisocial to eat yeast extract in an enclosed space," I said, and handed it over.

While Kai was opening the jar, our power flickered. We all looked up expectantly as it came back on. A moment later darkness fell for good, followed by the dying whine of the exhaust fan.

"Dammit." I got up and sat on the toilet seat to pull my boots on.

"You're not going out there," Miriam ordered, putting her reader aside.

The temptation to agree with her, to walk away from the problem, to remain here in relative safety—it was strong. I chewed my lower lip and stared down at the linoleum, which flickered in and out of visibility with the rolling lightning flashes. The wind was so loud I couldn't hear the thunder.

"If the searchlights are off, how are Earwyn and Caspian going to find us?" I whipped the cords around the hooked speedlacers, wishing my boots were waterproof. At least vegan leather could survive a little salt water probably.

"I don't understand how we lost power," Kai said. Rummaging sounds suggested they were feeling for their boots also. "It doesn't *come* from anywhere except right here. There are no lines to go down, and even if the solar panels blew off, the batteries are all in the hangar."

"SeaBit probably patched the solar array along with everything else they busted."

"I'll come," Miriam said.

"Please stay with Henry," I answered. "I'll rope in and Kai can belay me if I have to go outside."

We stared at each other in the glow from Miriam's reader and the stutter of lightning.

"I'm sorry," Miriam said. "I was having a lot of feelings. I shouldn't have taken it out on you."

"I was having feelings too." I finished tying my boots by muscle memory and stood up.

"I really ought to—"

Kai interrupted. "Listen to Dr. Haf."

I moved toward the door. "Don't call me doctor."

"How the hell did you wind up ABD anyway?" Kai asked.

Miriam said, "I'm telling you, he got kicked out for hacking."

"You don't know me." I tried to keep it light and make it okay to go back to the banter and teasing. I wasn't sure if I was being a hypocrite, or a grown-up.

"How else would somebody as smart as you wind up in a punk house?"

I nearly lost my temper because I was still so mad at her I almost didn't register the compliment. Almost, but not quite. And once I heard it, it cooled me off enough that I could answer with a joke instead of escalating again. "Punk *pod*. And I didn't get kicked out. I quit."

Miriam's voice slowed down in the dark. "I didn't know that about you."

"How does anybody with half a brain *not* walk away from this fucking system? It's so fucking hopeless. Everything is broken."

"Huh," Miriam said. Then, softly, as I grabbed a headlamp out of my pack: "You crazy kids be careful out there."

"THEY'RE NOT GOING TO MAKE IT THROUGH THIS WEATHER," KAI SAID, WHEN THE bathroom door was shut behind us. "I hope they turned and ran."

"Me too," I said. "But could you live with yourself if we didn't at least try to get the lights on?"

Miriam's bedroom had windows, and all we could see through them was the incessant flicker of lightning, brilliance filtered through rippling sheets of water running down the transparent poly.

"Let's see if we can fix it in the hangar," Kai said.

"If it's not in the hangar I don't think we *can* fix it. Is there rope anywhere?"

They ducked into Miriam's closet while I averted my eyes. A moment of rummaging later and they were back with a coil of climbing rope and the harness Miriam uses to clean the pylons. And harvest kombu, or whatever that stuff is. "I haven't got a second harness to belay from."

"Stay inside the door. When I go out, I'll take a wrap around the mooring posts."

Tight-faced, Kai nodded, and we went out into the main living area of the pod.

The wall of poly overlooking the southern sea was deopaqued by the power failure, and lightning walked across the water so profusely I felt we were inside a Van de Graaff generator, looking out. The floor was awash in a centimeter of brackish water, which seemed to have been forced past the seals of the door into the hangar. That didn't bode well for the situation inside. Maybe I had been unfair in blaming SeaBit's poorly timed updates for the power failure.

Well, only one way to be sure.

"Fuck," said Kai. "I'm glad I moved the drums."

Even inside, I wasn't sure the instruments were going to survive. But there wasn't anything we could do about it, so there was no point in saying anything. I stepped into the harness and tied the line through the loops on the front. "Ready?"

"Ready," Kai said.

I opened the door to the hangar and was staggered by the howling wind. What remained of the shredded bay doors was flapping. Our laid-on flooring was gone, lifted up and washed away by swells that regularly filled the bay. The external doors faced north, so the crest of the waves broke over the pod rather than rushing through the gap where they had hung. Water still filled the gap, rising to wet my boots and spill into the living area.

"Shit," Kai said, as I said, "Got me?"

They nodded, and I walked out into the storm.

The wind shrieked and whistled under the pod and into the hangar. I couldn't imagine what it must be like on deck. Even protected on three sides it felt like walking into the gale whistling around the observation deck of the CN Tower. It battered me from side to side, sending me reeling like a drunk as I crashed toward the catwalk railing. Another wave rose around me. I had to brace myself and stand until it passed. Kai yelped as seawater spilled into the pod and drenched them.

At least it wasn't cold.

The hangar roof flexed up and down under the sucking force of the wind, thundering and rattling. A gust knocked me back. I leaned into it, lunged forward, and hurled myself at the railing. The wind eddied just as I got there and nearly lifted me over and into the water. Only the tautness of the rope and a frantic grab saved me. I felt the snap as Kai got yanked a step forward.

I freed one hand from the rail—peeling my fingers out of a death grip—and dropped the rope around one of the mooring stanchions, making sure it passed under the cleat so it wouldn't slip off. That gave Kai a little mechanical advantage. I flashed a thumbs-up through the flickering darkness but didn't turn around so the headlamp wouldn't blind them.

If they called anything after me, I didn't hear.

The main batteries were at the back of the hangar, along with the charging rig for the launch and the rack for the portables, which we'd carried inside to Miriam's room. I struggled toward them, using the railing to steady and haul myself along. The headlamp didn't reveal any obvious damage, and they were supposed to be sealed and storm tight . . .

A row of red and orange lights on the front suggested there was a problem.

I didn't really want to be wrestling with a giant electrical storage system while up to my calves in seawater, did I? And yet, here I was. I wasn't going to open the watertight housing—I'd destroy it if I tried, and letting the storm in to corrode the contacts didn't seem like it would be viable. Either I could fix the problem from the console, or the problem could not be fixed until the storm was over.

As I reached the system, the roof began to make a new and more horrible shuddering sound. Metal rent and screamed. I didn't look up. I don't think I could have forced myself to look up if I had tried. The water running down my face now was warm and salt-free: clean tropical rain. The lightning flashes seemed more direct, and brighter.

The console controls were designed to be watertight. I reached them, clipped a carabiner between my harness and a grab bar, and waved a thumbs-up back at Kai.

I hoped they saw it.

The electrical monitoring system had frozen. No real problem to fix that: I did a safe reboot and reset the system clock, just as I had for the fridge. A moment later, Kai whooped loud enough that I even heard it faintly over the storm. I turned: light spilled out of the doorway, and our searchlights cut through the sky overhead, vanishing all too quickly into mist, horizontal rain, and a cloud deck so low I thought I might be able to touch it if I climbed up one of the access ladders.

Which would, of course, be suicide.

The hangar roof was completely missing. Bucketing rain hammered my face. Another wave rolled through, pulling me against my clipped-in harness.

And I still had to unclip myself and get back across the hangar to the door.

SOMEHOW I DID IT, THOUGH I THINK KAI PROBABLY DRAGGED ME THE LAST FEW steps. We got the door shut behind us and surveyed the wreckage of the living room. "Fuck," Kai said, "I need a beer."

We splashed toward the fridge. Kai handed me two sterile packs of brew and fished out a couple more for themself. "Let's get a couple for Miriam," I said.

Kai grunted, and provided.

Miriam's bedroom was dryer than the living room. We'd remembered to shut the door behind us and the seals were holding.

When we opened the bathroom door, Miriam looked up, face streaked, jaw set firmly. She was hugging Henry and biting her lip hard enough that my jaw muscles ached in sympathy. Sitting and waiting in the dark probably took just as much courage as splashing around in a hurricane.

"Haf thought you might like a beer," Kai said, and tossed her one.

She caught the box left-handed, without letting go of the dog. "I'm glad you're okay," she said. "And thank you."

"All in a day's work," I answered. "And I really need to get some dry clothes on. No staring at my butt, okay?"

THE WIND HOWLED FOR ANOTHER TWO HOURS, INTENSIFYING ALONG WITH THE lightning.

"How can this be getting worse?" Miriam said.

"Eyewall," I said with a shrug. "We should get a break soon."

She shook her head. "Is there any place worse than this?"

Yeah, I thought. Lots of places. What I said was, "There's always someplace worse that you could be."

The eye passed over us a half hour later: a fantastic bubble of clear still air, fluffy cumulus, warmth, and the saturating pink-mauve light of dawn. We had all scrambled out on the deck to observe it when the silence fell.

"It's not over," I warned them. "This is just the halfway point."

"I'll take it," Kai said, and went to get more beers.

The living room was wrecked. The water had drained away, but everything was wet to six inches. The guitars might be okay: we'd put them up high and it didn't look like the water had gotten into their electronics. The amps and monitors were toast.

I just stood on the deck and looked up into Kasimir's unseeing eye, my arms folded on the railing. All of the other pods seemed to have made it through the first half of the storm, though I doubted any of them were precisely intact. We were all going to have a lot of repair work.

Miriam handed me a beer. I pulled the tab out and drank deeply. Beer is where the pod's gluten-free lifestyle meets aesthetics and aesthetics win.

Please don't tell them.

"I've got an idea," I said, as much to the ocean and the hurricane as to Miriam. "What if we just . . . put this satellite weather data on a feed that anybody can access?"

"It'd need constant updates, right? They'll be trying to take it down. And put us all in jail."

"Just me," I said. "And so, I go into hiding. Stay on the move. And keep putting the feed back up again."

She looked at me. "How does that get us a bass player?"

I shrugged. "If you're going to drop out, share houses are a good place to rack out. I can make sure you know where to find me."

"They'll catch you eventually."

"Civil disobedience has it risks," I agreed. "Anyway, if they catch me they'll have to put me on trial, right? That will make a big public fuss also."

She opened her mouth to argue and was cut off by the whine of an electric boat engine. We both whirled around—and saw the launch coming toward us from the hangar of the leeward SeaBit.

Our launch, with the terrible purple and acid-green spray paint job decorating it. And there were two people inside.

A lungful of air whooshed out of Miriam and tears started in the corners of her eyes. I, of course, remained manly and inscrutable and did not whoop and spill beer all over my hand waving wildly in the air.

"Kai!" Miriam yelled. "Get out here! It's Caspian and Earwyn. They're not dead!" The relief in her voice cut through me.

"You like her," I said, before I could stop myself.

Miriam whirled on me. "That's bullshit." Her mouth went sideways. "How did you know?"

"Everybody else always says 'Earwyn and Caspian.'" I swallowed. "She likes you too, you know. You should—"

"What?"

"You should tell her. Anyway," I swallowed, "I'm glad they made it. That was not a plot twist I saw coming. Let's meet them in the hangar, we're going to need to lash the yacht down before the south wall of the eye gets here."

THEY GOT DOCKED IN THE HANGAR WITHOUT INCIDENT, LARGELY BECAUSE BY NOW the storm had blown the last shreds of the external doors clean off. Our bandmates were gray-faced and staggering with exhaustion, and Caspian had managed to sprain his wrist and hyperextend his elbow, but they were intact and the launch was seaworthy. There was no running for it now, though; the storm completely surrounded us.

As I handed Earwyn out of the boat, I said, "Please tell me you weren't out in the storm this whole time."

She shook her head. "We made it to the archipodlago and realized we weren't going to be able to dock with Crash Pod in those seas even if we could find it, so we went to the leeward one and holed up there. We still barely made it inside."

"We're not all going to fit in Miriam's bathroom," Kai said.

"The back half of the storm should be weaker," I said. "And her bedroom came through okay. We can stretch out in there."

"Where are our packs?" Caspian asked, looking through the door into the waterlogged interior.

"We took them into the bedroom," Miriam said. "They're fine, unless Henry is peeing on them. I left him locked inside."

"Dammit, Henry! Come on, folks. Let's get this food secured before the storm comes around again."

THE WALL OF CLOUDS WAS CLOSE BY THE TIME WE FINISHED MOVING CASES OF expired tofu and halvah into the pod. Lightning danced through it, and the sky overhead was an absolutely flawless blue. Everybody else went inside to spread out pads and sleeping bags. I stayed on deck for a few last minutes.

I wanted a chicken sandwich, and I wasn't going to get a chicken sandwich. I wanted a safe place to hide from noticing how fucked up the world is, and there were no places that safe. And I wanted the girl.

Three strikes, buddy. Tough luck all over.

So none of those things were going to happen. But I had just figured out how to effectively counterprogram one tiny scrap of the neoliberal corporate client state. And all it was going to cost me was any chance of peace, quiet, and obscurity for the rest of my life.

And probably, in the very near future, my freedom.

A lot to ask of a guy who never finished his dis.

There was a sat link in the weather station, even if it was offline right now. I opened the access panel and synced my device to it. I could work on the specifics of how to grant the world access to this data while we were waiting out the storm.

Miriam came up behind me. "We got Caspian and Earwyn back," she said. "Are you still going to risk this?"

My hands kept on tapping away.

Miriam said, "You're not stopping?"

"It was never about revenge." Well, okay. It was never *entirely* about revenge.

"I'm impressed," Miriam said. "I've known a lot of guys who can't learn something even when a friend *actually* gets killed."

I snorted and kept my eyes on the data. The storm loomed; the wind began again to ruffle my hair.

"Won't they trace it back to you?" Miriam asked.

"Eventually. But I can keep on the move."

"What about The Crash?"

"As I said, you *can* find another bass player."

"Spoken like somebody who's never had to try and find a decent bass player."

"And anyway, it'll take 'em a while to catch on. I'm not using my own login and I am going to automate the data-forwarding process, make it as robust as I can, and encrypt and conceal the tunnel."

"I *knew* you got kicked out for hacking. You didn't quit, did you?"

"Miriam," I said, and as I did I realized I wasn't sure I'd ever said her name to her before. My tone probably gave away everything. It didn't matter anymore. "I never got *caught* for hacking."

"Did you get kicked out for civil disobedience, then?"

"No. I was always too much of a coward."

"Then what?"

"I was serious when I said I quit. I dropped out. Or just kind of stopped showing up, rather. I didn't have the courage to tell them why I quit, and maybe I didn't understand it myself at the time. But I think, looking back, it was because I couldn't see the point in what I was doing anymore. It's not science if it's just a commercial product."

"Huh," she said. "Well, hurry up, the storm is coming. And I don't think you have any more dry clothes." She looked over her shoulder: I glanced to see Earwyn waving her inside, and she patted my arm and went.

Huh.

I looked out over the water. Sunlight sparkled on a near-flat calm. So impossibly peaceful.

Behind it loomed the storm.

2 MORAL HAZARD

Cory Doctorow

> I am often asked if I will "return to cryptocurrency" or begin regularly sharing my thoughts on the topic again. My answer is a wholehearted "no."
>
> —Jackson Palmer, creator of Dogecoin, Twitter, July 14, 2021

1.

I KNOW EXACTLY WHERE I WAS THE DAY I DECIDED TO GIVE EVERY HOMELESS PERSON in America their own LLC. I was in the southeast corner of the sprawling homeless camp that had once been Seattle's Discovery Park on a rare, dry February afternoon. The sun was weak but so welcome. After weeks of sheltering in our tents and squelching through the mud and getting drenched waiting for the portas, we were finally able to break out the folding chairs and enjoy each other's company.

Mike the Bike had coffee. He always did. Mike knew more ways to make coffee than any fancy barista. He had a master's in chemical engineering and a bachelor's in mechanical engineering and when he was high he spent every second of the buzz thinking of new ways to combine heat and water and solids to produce a perfect brew.

I brought trail mix, which I mixed up myself with food-bank supplies and spices I bought from the bulk place for pennies. My secret is cardamom and a little chili powder. I learned that from my mom.

"Trish," Mike the Bike said, "I wish I was a corporation."

I checked to see if he was high, because that sounded like stoner talk, but he looked sharp. "Okay," I said. "Why do you wish you were a corporation?"

"Bailout 3.0," he said. "President Lamon told the Fed to buy any bond, issued by any company. There's eight trillion dollars' worth of credit about to come sluicing into the market. Best part is that these companies can default on those bonds and the worst thing that'll happen is a hit to their corporate credit rating."

I shook my head and sipped my coffee. "Well, that'll sure provide liquidity to the dressage horse and supercar markets." *Providing liquidity* had been voted the *Oxford English Dictionary*'s "phrase of the year" the previous month. It was the phrase we'd heard for each of the bailouts since the new crisis hit a year before. The joke came easily to my lips, but it wasn't funny and it didn't make either of us feel any better.

"I wish I was a corporation," Mike the Bike said again.

The last time I'd seen my family was on Black Thursday, the Thanksgiving of the crisis. We were all on edge already. I'd been laid off from both of my jobs the week before, driving for an Amazon delivery subcontractor and Zoom-teaching English to rich Chinese kids in Shanghai. The fact that the crunch was hitting both Amazon *and* China made it seem like the world was about to crumble.

It wasn't ever going to be a good Thanksgiving. My parents wouldn't stop deadnaming me and I'd sent them an email explaining calmly and firmly that I wasn't going to talk to them until they did. My sister Becca thought I was being an asshole about it, and she'd arm-twisted me into saying I'd come.

So there I was, in Becca's kitchen, helping her finance-bro husband Amit with the turkey while Becca drank awkward chardonnay with our parents in her living room. Amit had been talking finance for ten minutes at me while I sort of surfed on the buzzword wave, when suddenly a piece of jargon leapt out of the slurry and smacked me in the face.

"Did you say Wyoming's got an API?"

He cracked a beer. "Yeah. Part of their new finance sandbox. You send them some JSON, they send you back an LLC. Bam. Makes it really easy to move between DAOs and meatspace companies. The services guys are all over it, like just cookin' up all these companies like prerolled D&D characters, sticking them on the shelf. You need a corporate secretary, sure, here's Secretary439544, LLC. Need a treasurer? Here's Treasurer2235944, LLC, at your service. CEO? No problem. CEO99405, LLC, reporting for duty."

"That's . . ." *Insane* was on my lips but I was trying to wean myself off of ableist comparisons. I fished for an apt alternative. ". . . Wildly irrational," was the best I came up with.

He grinned like a pirate. "You gotta try it. You can get a free LLC when you sign up."

I OWED $172,498 IN STUDENT DEBT, WHICH I INCURRED WHILE COMPLETING A bachelor's in computer science at MIT. I may never be able to pay that debt off, but I do know a lot about stress-testing APIs and making them do things that their owners probably don't want them to do.

Sitting there that morning in the watery sun and steaming mud, drinking Mike the Bike's coffee, I got a very weird idea. I filed it away—it would have been rude to get up without finishing my coffee—but my brain was racing, the way it always did when I came up with a stunt. MIT had been a good place to come up with pranks—they called them *hacks*—and I'd had a hand in half a dozen, gotten a rep for being the go-to evil genius who could put the finishing touches on any hack to transform it into one for the ages. Remember the time someone used trompe l'oeil particleboard to convert the crazy angles of the CSAIL building into a replica of the Stanford comp sci building? Did it all in one night, without anyone noticing?

It was epic. By my estimate, my education bill for that day was $335 (give or take). I can't exactly call it money well spent, but seeing as I'm unlikely to ever repay it, I can't not call it money well spent, either.

2.

IT WAS ONLY MEANT TO BE A PRANK, A HACK. IT WOULD HAVE REMAINED SO IF REP Sawant hadn't visited the camp with her aides that week, just as I was putting the final touches on my hack.

Rep Sawant wanted to talk about serious issues, the moral failing that allowed thousands to live in muddy tents while the richest companies in Seattle—whose total tax bills were actually *negative*—were getting billions in bailouts.

Her people set up a couple of jumbo easy-ups for her town hall listening session, and we all crammed in and ate her sandwiches and drank her coffee and cheered her on. The cheers would have come with or without the snacks. Sawant was right, and she wasn't a bullshitter. Those traits are rare in a federal politician, and of course, we all knew her from her days on city council and we trusted her.

When she got onto the bailout and the corporate money rolling in, Mike the Bike couldn't help but call out, "We got a plan to get some of that, too."

She got a wary look: cameras rolling, homeless guy shouting confusing things. I sympathized. Lots of ways that could go wrong. She smiled and tried to pass it off, but Mike the Bike was not entirely right-headed then and he kept going: "My girl Trish over here, she's got the hookup. We're all getting our own shell company, gonna form our own industry association, gonna send a lobbyist to the Hill, gonna get a bailout. Why not? Sauce for the goose, sauce for the gander."

The congresswoman cocked her head. She was sharp. She heard something in Mike the Bike's word salad. "That would be quite something," she said. A good political response. Not approving, not dismissing.

"I'm not joking," Mike the Bike said, refusing to give up the mic to the people waiting behind him. "Trish, come on, tell her about the API from Wyoming."

That got the congresswoman's attention. A couple of her staffers sat up straighter, too. Everyone looked at me. Mike the Bike gestured for me to step up to the mic. Ears burning, I did.

I explained it. It wasn't a hard workflow. First you create a burner email. Use the burner email to get a burner phone number. Use the burner phone number and burner email to sign up for a free trial of the Wyoming finance sandbox. Use that to get a burner LLC. All in all, it went like this: one click, solve three captchas, one click, and bam, you got a QR code that represented a fully fledged artificial person with all the rights and privileges accruing thereto.

"It's more of an art piece than anything," I said, burningly aware of the jaw-dropped stares of Rep Sawant and her entourage.

She was a pro, though, and recovered her composure. "That is *really* something." I guessed that was more than *quite something*.

"It's a lot," I agreed, with a shrug.

Mike the Bike decided I needed a hype man, so he took the mic again. "Think of it. Every homeless person in America could have their own Wyoming shell company. We'd be a massive industry. They'd have to take us seriously."

The woman behind us in line managed to wrestle the mic away from Mike the Bike then and rescued the congresswoman from having to produce a meaningful hot take on the prospect of an industry association to represent the interests of shell companies registered by the unhoused.

But after the event wound down and the easy-ups were being taken down and loaded into vans, one of the congresswoman's staffers sought me out.

He was a good-looking white kid, with the kind of shoulders I associated with competitive rowers and a very smart, old-fashioned haircut. His running shoes looked a little like astronaut boots and I completely and instantly coveted them. They looked expensive.

"I'm Glenn Chauncy," he said, bumping elbows with me, then Mike the Bike. "I'm with the congresswoman. An analyst. But, uh, Trish, right?"

"Right," I said. "Hi." He was good-looking but not my type, except for those kicks. Woah.

"The thing is I put in my notice last week. I'm starting a new kind of lobbyist outfit, just working for progressive causes. I got sick of seeing those slick psychos simping for giant corporations on the Hill. They have no shame, *none*, they even kept inviting *me* out for lunch in the hopes that they could get the congresswoman to go along with their bullshit.

"The people need a lobbyist and that's what I'm gonna do. Just work for nonprofits, public interest orgs, that kind of thing. But I need to make my name first, show I can get stuff done, raise my profile."

"O-kay," I said, cautiously.

"I want to be *your* lobbyist."

"You do," I said.

"I do. I want you to register LLCs for every homeless person in America, and then I want you to form an industry association, and then I want you to send a lobbyist to Congress to lobby for your industry."

"That's what you want me to do."

He looked me deep in the eyes, in the manner of a very earnest, good-looking, well-brought-up young fellow. "That is what I want you to do."

"I'll have to think about it."

He shrugged and broke eye contact. "That's fair. Here's my card. Call me either way."

3.

GLENN CHAUNCEY FRONTED THE MONEY TO FOUND THE AMERICAN LEAGUE OF Unwaged Workers, a 501(c)(4) with 1,217 founding corporate members (it's up over a hundred thousand members now). He hired someone from a unionized gig work shop to design our logo and letterhead, and he got me a box of a thousand business cards from a union print shop in Detroit, identifying me as the executive director of the ALUW.

Then he flew me to DC.

"I've got you two important meetings, one with the junior senator from Wyoming, the other with a Wyoming congressman's chief of staff."

"Which congressman?"

He snorted over the phone. "Wyoming only has one congressional district. You're meeting with the *only* congressman's chief-of-staff."

"Sounds like an important guy."

"*She's* an important woman. Nellie Moonlight. Old Wyoming royalty. The fact that she joined the congressman's campaign is what swung it for him. He owes her. Impress her, you have him."

Glenn didn't have his own office yet; that would come later. Instead, he was perching in a closet-sized office in a progressive think tank funded by a tech billionaire who liked LGBTQ causes. It was a welcoming space, full of pride flags in every spectrum and hue, and the conversations I eavesdropped on in the kitchen while we got coffee were peppered with they/them pronouns and discussions of people's polycules.

Glenn's borrowed office was barely big enough for the two of us and our knees were practically touching. He briefed me on the junior senator's peccadillos but focused his energy on Nellie Moonlight's bugbears and favored causes. "She can do so much for us," he said.

"Like what? Glenn, I really don't understand what I'm doing here."

He made a wry face. He was such a handsome guy that he even had a handsome wince. DC was one of those places where all the handsome and beautiful people go to dazzle each other with their dimples. I felt like a toad next to him.

"Trish, we're lobbying for your industry. The League of Unwaged Workers represents 1,217 small businesses, all registered in Wyoming, whose revenues and productive activities have been severely impacted by the crisis. The United States of America, its president, and its Congress have all promised to prioritize continuity for small businesses through direct cash supports. Your members have not been given access to those supports because of discriminatory federal policies. Those policies are a risk to your members and your industry, and they're a slap in the face to the great state of Wyoming. They're an insult to the bedrock principles of American federalism. Today, we will put you before Wyoming's federal representatives and explain this to them and ask them to intervene with the federal government on your behalf."

I tried to figure out if he was kidding. He looked like he *might* be kidding. He also looked like he might be serious. I think he was ha-ha-only-serious. "Glenn, you know that I've never even been to Wyoming, right?"

He shrugged. "To a first approximation, no one's been to Wyoming. So what? The state should have your back."

"That state? Or its reps? You remember that these 'small businesses' I represent are just homeless people, right? They don't have any money. Like, by definition, they don't have any money. It's a membership requirement."

He shrugged again. "If Wyoming LLCs are first-class corporate persons, then people who *do* have money benefit. These people know that." He put his hand lightly on my forearm. What a manicure that guy had. "Trish, I know this is a lot and not your usual gig. But you're smart, you're presentable, and you're right. I'll lead the discussion, but it's your show, you feel free to weigh in wherever you want."

I looked down at myself, the sweatshirt and jeans combo I'd washed in the hotel sink the night before, then rolled up in a towel and jumped up and down on to wring the water out of them, then hung from the HVAC vent in my room. They were still a little damp. "I don't think I'm *that* presentable." My turn to shrug. "My wardrobe is a little embarrassed these days."

He patted my forearm again. "That's no problem. You're not the first person to come to DC without the right fashion capabilities."

The LGBTQ lobby group had a well-stocked wardrobe room with clean castoffs and thrift scores from its staffers. I was given the run of the room and the help of a nice young woman with an undercut and a neat suit with a bow tie, who helped me coordinate a smart, low-key outfit and pronounced me capable of cleaning up real good. We high-fived and I let Glenn pilot me to the Farragut West Metro Station, where he handed me one of the charity's burner phones, with a loaded SmarTrip app to use at the turnstiles.

I WAS SURPRISED BY WHAT A NONENTITY THE JUNIOR SENATOR TURNED OUT TO be. Once we were safely out of earshot, I quietly asked Glenn if he was sedated. He snorted.

"It's possible. The state GOP chose him because he was reliable and unambitious and would do what he was told. He'll serve his term out and then become a second-stringer for a law firm in Cheyenne." He helped me thread my way across the National Mall, navigating the tourists with ease, his lanyard and badge flapping conspicuously against his chest.

"To be honest, I almost appreciate that kind of guy. Used to be, most rich kids just wanted to grow up and work at a bank, back when that meant clocking out at 3:00 p.m. These days, every idiot who had the good luck to emerge from a high-net-worth orifice wants to be a master of the universe. They make a lot of trouble. Guys like the senator? All he wants is to pretend other people are doing as well as him and say the N-word in private without getting called out."

My turn to snort. "I take it the next meeting won't be so dull."

He pointed at the government office building we were heading for, surrounded by security bollards and hurricane fencing. "That's where the real work happens," he said. "And Nellie Moonlight is an operator. But you don't have anything to worry about. She mostly represents a minute constituency of finance ghouls who want to shuffle billionaires' fortunes around where the IRS can't see it. For her, you represent legitimacy. You and your members provide bulk to ease the passage of her core constituency's goal."

I winced. "Gross."

He flashed me that handsome-guy smile. "The scatology, or the politics?"

"Both."

He stopped us. We were only a few yards shy of the building's entrance. "It is. It's gross. Here's my calculus; hear me out, okay? The people laundering their billions with Wyoming LLCs have infinite choice of venue. You're not helping them launder money so much as you're giving them another minor arrow in their quiver. You're making a change in degree. But if it works, you're getting a change in kind: you get every homeless person in America a slice of this bailout, and maybe the bailouts to come. I am willing to get in the mud a little to make that happen. But this is your show. I'm your lobbyist. If you think this is too gross, we'll find some other gambit. This is my best play, but there are other moves. We're not out of options. Just say the word, Trish."

"God, you're a smooth talker," I said. That handsome-guy thing was really working for him. Or maybe he was right. "Let's go."

NELLIE MOONLIGHT WAS IN HER THIRTIES BUT LOOKED YOUNGER. SHE WORE HER hair loose and long, down her back, over a blouse and slacks combo that she'd accessorized with a gold chain and crucifix, a big diamond engagement ring, and a single bangle on her left wrist. Her makeup was barely there, but very good, and it did nice things for the shape of her nose and cheeks. She shook hands like a boxer, a big, crushing grip that seemed out of place for a petite thing like her. I guess she liked to surprise people.

"I love it," she said, after Glenn finished his rundown. "Love. It." She turned to me. Her smile was wide, her eyes were made of stone. I have strong transphobia radar and it was going bananas. Whatever. Better women than Nellie Moonlight have openly loathed me. "Tell me how this works? How are you finding the money to create all these LLCs?"

"It's free," I said. "I wrote a little script that creates new accounts for each user, and they just use the free demo tool to create their LLC."

"You created it?"

"Yeah," I said. "It signs you up for a VoIP phone number, confirms it with a throwaway email address, signs up for the API, creates the LLC, and files all the paperwork to make you the managing partner." She looked at me like I'd grown horns. I desperately wanted to look to Glenn for guidance but I also didn't want to seem weak. She had predator vibes. "I'm working on a script to do the compliance filing every year on your behalf. Fully automated: just fill in a form and it shoots it off on the last day of every one of your fiscal years. Fire and forget."

She shook her head. "And you did this for homeless people." I couldn't tell if it was a question.

"Yes." I treated it as one.

"Why?"

"Well, I wanted one, and I'm homeless."

Her eyes widened by a micrometer. "You were homeless?"

"I am homeless. I live in a tent in Discovery Park. In Seattle. Glenn bought me a plane ticket."

Her nose wrinkled just a little. I didn't smell, but she still smelled me. Transphobia and poorphobia aren't additive; they're multiplicative. She really didn't like me now.

But Nellie Moonlight was a pro. She tipped her head a degree left, two degrees right, one degree left. "That is amazing," she said. "So brave. So really—" She fished. "So brave. And you have created 1,217 Wyoming LLCs for homeless people in Seattle?"

I got my phone out and unlocked it and then pull-refreshed the dashboard page I'd loaded. "1,714 now. But only—" I scrolled "—1,532 have signed up for the industry association. And they're not just in Seattle." I scrolled more. "Thirty-eight states now, and Puerto Rico, and hey, Samoa. Wow."

"How—" She drummed her fingers on her desk. "That's amazing. But how?"

I shrugged. "Ever hear the Hotmail story? An Indian guy in the US created a free email service and told some friends back home in India about it. They told all their friends. I mean, poor people, we're all really short on money, obviously, and we're all short on time, too, which is a thing a lot of people miss, because they think we're all just sitting around all day, getting high, or begging or whatever. Truth is it's a lot of *work* being homeless. You walk five miles for the food bank, then you run a mile and a half to catch a slot at the shelter washing machines, then you have to make a court appearance to fight a vagrancy ticket and there's only one grocery store you can afford and that's nowhere near the courthouse—you get the picture."

She nodded, cautiously. I could tell that she didn't want to concede that anything about homelessness qualified as "work."

"The reason poor people don't have any time is nothing is organized to work for us. We have to work around everything. So when something comes along that makes it easier to work around a roadblock other people don't even have to think about, it's worth it for us to invest our time in figuring it out.

"So back to that guy with the Hotmail account and all his friends in India, it only took like a week before he had a hundred thousand sign-ups, and soon they were growing at a million users a week. A *week*."

"How did you learn all this?" she said. Is it subtext if it's right there on the surface?

"It was in my second-year start-up workshop at MIT," I said.

"MIT," she said.

"Anyway," I said. "People think that kids and pornographers and poor people and sex workers are these super techie early adopters, but we're not. We're just people who the system doesn't work for. The time we spend figuring out how to use a new technology—what my Ethics for Engineers prof used to call the 'opportunity cost'—is worth it because we bear such a high cost to use the default system. It's a savings.

"So people in America who were already getting free email from their providers didn't see any reason to spend the time to figure out how Hotmail worked, but for people in India who were going to internet cafes and didn't have email, it was 100 percent worth it.

"Homeless people aren't stupid. It's hard to be homeless. To survive, you've got to be smart. We know about the bailouts. We know that every rich person has a couple dozen LLCs they use to hide behind and scoop up bailout money. I made it easy, and they understand that it can help, so yeah, 1,714 people—" I reloaded. "2,111 people, now, have done it."

"So you think this is going to grow like Hotmail?"

I shrugged. My mom hated how much I shrugged. "Depends. If people think it'll get them bailout money, then yeah. For sure."

Glenn slid smoothly in with some hard data. "There's just over a million homeless people in America. Sixteen percent of the country's below the poverty line. Call it thirty-five million households. I think there's a lot of growth potential here."

She got a funny look on her face, in both senses: funny ha ha and funny strange. I think she was imagining what it would mean for Wyoming's corporate registry to have thirty-five million entries, and how much cover those would provide for the "real" registrations—the high-net-worth individuals who wanted to keep their finances too opaque and too complex to task. But she was also trying to figure out what it would mean for Wyoming, having all those radar-chaffing LLCs registered to homeless people.

"Well, this is *very* exciting," she said, finally, in a faraway tone. She was calculating. We'd given her a lot of input and she was crunching it, following the branching possibilities.

Glenn knew his cue. "Thank you for your time today, Nellie. I'll see you at the book club next week?"

Her eyes focused on him briefly. Her pupils were dilated. "Yes, for sure. For sure. Thank you, Glenn. Lovely to meet you, Trish."

We showed ourselves out.

WYOMING ONLY HAS ONE SEAT IN THE HOUSE. SAME FOR DELAWARE. SAME FOR South Dakota. Nevada has four, so it led the caucus that pushed for inclusion of ALUW in the third bailout package. Seven reps may not sound like much, but the rep from Delaware was on his ninth term and had a key committee chairmanship that would have let him hold up the whole package. To hear Glenn explain it, the whole bill was over a thousand pages long and everyone just kind of agreed not to dwell on the ALUW stuff so they could avert the delay that a stink would cause.

I tried to do my job as ALUW executive director. I tuned into the live streamed markup session and the floor debate, but I kept losing the stream whenever the bus I was on went through a dead zone. There were a lot of those in the exurb where the charity endocrinology clinic was, and the hearings coincided with my appointment to beg for free gender-confirming hormones.

I'd waited more than a year for that appointment and I wasn't going to miss it. After all, it wasn't like my sitting in on the hearing was going to affect its outcome. I'd turned over my Twitter to Glenn so he could live-tweet the hearings as me, and I had the surreal experience of reading my own commentary on the proceedings. Turns out I had a lot of incisive things to say about them, and many of them were very flattering to the politicians who were on my side, whom I diligently tagged so their staffers would see it.

My appointment sucked. The office had lost the paperwork I'd filed when I made the appointment and so the doc kind of chewed me out for not being serious enough about my transition to fill in some forms and then left me alone for an hour to do them over, then complained about my handwriting. He really didn't like me.

But the bill passed.

A month later, every homeless person in America got a bailout of $1,000 to $4,000, depending on which state they were in and how good they were at filling in their homework. Because the money went to my LLC and not me personally, I didn't even have to give any of it to the ghouls who owned my student debt.

ON THE ONE HAND, IT WAS AMAZING.

A-*mazing*.

Giving money to people who don't have any *works*. For a lot of ALUW members, that money made a huge difference: paid off old court fines that made every passing cop car into a sphincter-tightening arrest risk; got the car they lived in fixed up enough to relocate to a place where they had more support; paid for badly needed medical or dental treatment; or just, you know, paid for a place to live for a while. It's not easy to get a job if your resume's got a big, homelessness-shaped hole in it, but it's even harder if you can't shower before work and you're sleeping four hours a night because you live in a tent in a chaotic homeless camp.

Everyone who got a payday deserved it, and I know it helped all of them. But even $4,000 isn't going to make a lasting difference in most people's lives, and the crisis put two more people on the streets for every person that the bailout got off the street.

Luckily, we got another bailout.

4.

OH, I SAY WE, BUT OF COURSE THE GOVERNMENT DIDN'T DO IT FOR US. THEY DID IT to save Facebook, which had changed its name back from Meta in a bid to stop the bleeding—but it didn't help. Facebook argued that it couldn't afford its moderator bill anymore, and without that army of low-waged, traumatized people in the Philippines the site would fill up with terrorist beheading videos, child sex abuse material, and copyrighted movies.

Letting Facebook fail wasn't an option, not after Weibo opened up to users who didn't have a Chinese passport. The possibility that America's last aging boomers would spend their remaining days trading conspiracy theories on a Chinese platform rather than an American one was an affront to our national pride.

Once they opened the door to bailing out Facebook, every other "great American company" piled on, and bam, the *fifth* bailout arrived.

The sixth wasn't far behind.

Amit called me the day they announced it. I had just done an NPR interview and finished moving Mike the Bike into his first apartment in a decade, where he was renting a spare room from a friend of his brother's. I was still living in the tent and saving my money to pay the endocrinologist.

"Hey, Trish!" He sounded *very* chipper.

I sat down on the tilted, lie-proof bench in a bus-shelter. "Hey, Amit." We hadn't communicated in months, not since he'd sent me a text reminding me that the Wyoming LLC thing was "his idea." I'd sent back a noncommittal response and periodically my anxiety brain had reminded me of that weird, bad interaction and suggested that maybe Amit would pull something bad and finance-bro-ish, like claiming a royalty or something.

"So look, I've been talking with some of the people here, people who work in structured annuities and derivatives, and we've had a really exciting idea I wanted to run by you."

I hated the sound of this. "Okay."

"Have you got a moment now? Like is now a good time?"

I looked around the empty bus shelter. "Sure, now's fine."

"So look, these bailouts are going to come and keep coming, right? I mean, that much seems obvious. There's just so much political pressure from these businesses, and you know, the really big ones have gotten so much money that they've hired all these lobbyists to keep more money flowing. And your people, they're going to get to ride along on that, right?"

"I don't know. That sounds plausible, but to be honest, I don't think anyone can predict how this is all gonna go. I mean, there's midterms in less than a year, right?"

"That's exactly right. Like, the money *could* keep coming, but maybe it might not. There's a risk there, right?"

"Sure," I said, hating how he ended every sentence with "right?" like he was a salesman trying to get me nodding along to his points in the hopes that I'd keep nodding when he got to the big ask.

"Well, that's kind of our deal here, derisking markets. You've got a bunch of stakeholders who are sitting on a pile of risk. Maybe they'll get more bailouts, maybe they won't. I've got a bunch of investors who want to buy risk, because risk is volatile and volatility is where you get your alpha, your profits."

I realized he was waiting for me to say something. I had been waiting for him to say "right?"

"All right," I said.

"All right!" he said, like I'd agreed to a bargain. I was getting a *really* bad feeling about this. "So that's where the opportunity is. I'd like to derisk your friends' future income."

"I don't know what that means," I said.

"That's okay, I can explain it. That's kind of my thing." It certainly was. "I've got investors who want to buy risk. So we match them to your guys who have risk to sell. My guys pay them a lump sum, and your guys sign over their future payments to my guys. It's like an annuity. We can build structures that standardize the risk, looking at each of your guys' circumstances, evaluating the likelihood that they'll be included in future bailouts. Then we can fractionalize them, like, we package up 10 percent of ten A-grade guys' future incomes with 20 percent of five class-B guys' income and so on. We've got quants here, physicists who can build those models so they're fully hedged. Meanwhile, your guys get a big payday, enough to really make a difference, plus they don't have to deal with the uncertainty of whether the next bailout will include them."

"Amit," I said, then faltered. "I'll think about it, okay?" I faltered again. "I have to tell you up front, though, I kind of hate the whole thing."

"Why?" He was perfectly calm in a way that I perfectly hated.

"Why?" I thought. "Just. Ugh. This whole thing was almost a prank, but it had a point: the idea was to hitch the poorest people in the country to the richest people in the country, get them a serving of the gravy the rich always get. Now you're talking about the poorest people just selling off that tether, that connection to the destiny of the rich and powerful. I hate that idea."

"Okay, that makes sense. Can I give you my thoughts on it, though?"

I wanted to hang up, but he's my brother-in-law. "Sure, Amit."

"I get what you're worried about here, but I think you've got it backwards. Once rich, powerful people buy up the right to collect bailouts for homeless people, they'll *fight like hell for those bailouts*. Every person who becomes homeless after that will have the most powerful people in the country lobbying to shower them with money. Respectfully, Trish, I think that's the best possible outcome."

"Okay," I said. "I'll think about it."

"That's all I ask." A beat. "By the way, how *are* you, really? Becca thinks about you all the time." My sister and I hadn't spoken in a year, but whatever.

"It's fine," I said. "I'm fine."

"Well, that's great," he said. "We're fine, too."

5.

SPOILER ALERT: I'M NOT THE EXECUTIVE DIRECTOR OF ALUW ANYMORE.

After I turned down Amit—because of *course* I turned him down—he went direct to the membership.

Glenn helped.

I figured out he was in on it when a kid outside of a shelter handed me a pamphlet with a QR code that would let me vote to remove myself as director in a special meeting of the ALUW.

Apparently, that was in our bylaws. The pamphlet insinuated that I was keeping every ALUW member from receiving between $10,000 and $100,000. It wasn't even wrong.

But man, getting that piece of paper was a surreal experience. Amit wouldn't return my calls. Neither would my sister. Neither would Glenn.

But I *did* manage to reach Nellie Moonlight.

"Hello, Trish."

"Nellie, do you know what's going on?"

"Yes, Trish, I know what's going on."

"Well?"

"Well what?"

"Well, don't you think it's kind of, you know, *bullshit*?"

There was a long pause. "Trish, let me repeat your question back to you. You used an API to create over 150,000 LLCs registered in a state with fewer than 400,000 residents. The sole shareholders and managing partners of all of these LLCs are homeless people. You formed an industry association—an industry association for the industry of being a homeless person—and lobbied for access to corporate bailouts. Which you got. And now the industry association is getting more *industrial*, getting a new CEO who understands business. Who *likes* business. And every member of that organization will get a lump sum payment equal to about five years' worth of their annual income.

"Which part of that sounds the most *bullshit* to you, Trish?"

"I thought Wyoming had 600,000 residents," I said.

"The population is declining. That's fine. People aren't the point anymore, they just get in the way of the LLCs." She paused. "You better not be recording this," she said. "Washington is a two-party consent state and for the record, I *do not consent*."

"I'm not recording," I said, wishing I'd thought of that. "The title isn't CEO," I said. "It's executive director." I'd fought with Glenn about that, but CEO of homelessness was just so *icky*.

"It's CEO now."

I didn't know what to say then.

"Take the deal, Trish. It's a good one. I know you're no expert on net present value of money, but if you were, you'd take the deal."

I didn't take the deal.

MIKE THE BIKE LOANED ME MONEY TO PAY THE ENDOCRINOLOGIST OUT OF HIS BUYOUT.

Only seven percent of ALUW members opted out of the buyout. Nearly all of them were people who couldn't be reached.

I used to love going to ALUW potlucks and picnics. There had been a plan to cosponsor meeting centers with day care and job training and social workers across the country. Those plans did not survive contact with the buyout. Mike the Bike is the only ALUW member I even see anymore, and that's because he's letting me live on his couch.

There's a new bailout being talked about in Congress. A *big* one. Amit's fund—and the people who bought our bailout futures—are lobbying hard for it on the Hill. I saw Glenn and Amit talking about it on a talk show together.

They seemed to be getting along great.

Maybe they'll make it happen. They seemed confident.

I hope they do. I could use the money.

3 SIGH NO MORE

Ian McDonald

CLAUDIA HEARS THE CYCLISTS FIRST; LAUGHTER, CHATTER, TIRE RUMBLE, THE click of freewheel hubs, the rub of a misaligned disc brake. Then a wedge of lights turns onto Morris Road. Dynamos, USB-charged LEDS, even some batteries—as precious as gold coins, batteries. Five days on from the Event, the streetlights are still out, the aurora driven back north, but the roads have been mostly cleared of dead cars. Here we are, the wall of lights says. Here we come.

Claudia flicks on her light, checks the trumpet case on her back, and pushes off to merge with the bikes as they sweep past. She weaves up through the cyclists to the bike at the center of the group.

"Dom."

The big man on the heavy, sturdy cargo bike nods.

"Claudia! You brought it?"

She dares a hand off the handlebars to pat her trumpet.

There's people you should meet, Dom said when he called round to extend the invitation. He reckoned he'd biked a Tour de France since the Event. *There could be work at the end of it.* So she checked her tires and her saddle height and wheeled the bike out of the checkerboard-tiled hall into the gloaming and cycled down from Stratford to join the peloton. They cycled down roads empty but for the occasional bold bus or delivery van; they gave way to emergency vehicles bansheeing past in flashing blue.

Bromley to Blackwall, around the Aspen Way gyratory, gathering cyclists all the time. Twenty strong they roll onto the Isle of Dogs. The towers of Canary Wharf rise shining out of the feral dark. Of course power's been restored there. Finance first. Empty beacons: the DLR and Tube that brought their workers are still out.

The automated Go station at Poplar is down, unable to dispense petrol or take payment. The company has sent in security in hi-viz to deter fuel-looters. The Asda on East Ferry Road has installed a hand pump. Squalls of impatience are brewing between the long line of car drivers and the jerry-canners. The bike squad rolls past on the far side of the street. Car drivers resented cyclists enough before the Event.

Claudia leans into the handlebars as the two-wheeled nation take the humpback bridge at Millwall Outer Dock. Bonfires, and the young men who make such bonfires, defend Inglewood. They turn, glare a *no pasarás*, but the entourage is too fast and too numerous and not going that way anyway. Her phone flickers in its handlebar clip. Bars bars bars. There's a working phone mast somewhere. It dies two streets later.

She's learning not to need it.

So at last, deep down where the Isle of Dogs drips into the river, they turn into Wynan Court. *Dom's here!* The call runs ahead of the cyclists. There are people at every gate, in every door, all along the pavement, applauding. Outside the house, cast, crew, band, dancers, choir, community performers greet the peloton with torches and candles in jars and lanterns and solar spinners. *Dom's arrived!*

Dom flicks down the kickstand, rolls off the cargo bike, and hugs the small woman with the big glasses and the tall man with the stooped shoulders. Director and the producer, Claudia reckons. Her poorly adjusted brakes squeak as she pulls up.

Dom turns, arms raised.

"Got your generator!"

Wynan Court cheers. Hands lift the genny out of the cargo pallet.

"And petrol?" the producer-one asks. Claudia has been told his name but it slips from her tongue right now.

"You get the total package with me!" Dom shouts.

Twenty cyclists slip jerry cans of petrol from backpacks and panniers and bear fuel and generator up the alley at the side of the house. One of the kids chains and locks the bikes. In these post-Event days petrol is more precious than whiskey, bikes than cars. Claudia hears music, smells wood smoke, charring food. She hurries after Big Dom and the cyclists into the Millwall *Much Ado about Nothing* party.

DOM'S ORDERS ARE CLEAR AND FIRM AS REBAR. NO GENNY. NOT EVEN FOR A SECOND. Because (1) petrol; (2) noise; (3) its acquisition was not entirely proper. But the director—Trix, Dom tells Claudia—is skipping with delight; she shall have her show, and a brief light comes to the face of the producer—Ben, Claudia remembers. Then Dom spins her on through the party. People to meet.

"What's her name?"

"Hekla."

"Hekla?"

"It's a volcano. You'll just click."

How many times has she worked with Dom and still she doesn't trust he knows everything, everyone?

Meantime, here is Jay, Dom's step-brother, a smaller, slighter, more inward Dom. No one knows quite why he's here, or what he has to do with the *Much*, but he is, and he seems to.

Good to see you he says to Claudia, but his eyes look past her to more valuable faces. *Excuse me . . .*

"That's Jay," Dom says, and here's Leon, Trix's flatmate/landlord, who isn't in theater, not even arts at all. He's a scientist, which has always got jokes and pity. A solar scientist, which since the Event gets him respect and a touch of celebrity. Every morning he goes down the steps of the Greenwich tunnel, lantern in hand, crosses under the river like a ghost from Dickens, climbs to the surface, and then goes up the hill to the Royal Observatory.

"Satfall tonight," he says. "One of Elon Musk's Starlinks. About 10:30. Look south."

She meets costumers and set designers and the principals who lose interest when she tells them she plays trumpet—oh, a *musician*—and Ben the producer again and then, finally, by the overgrown buddleia, Hekla.

"Hekla is the *Much*'s musical director."

And fleet and soft as big men are, Big Dom slips back into the party.

"And you're the trumpeter," Hekla says. "Dom talked a lot about you." Claudia hears her singer's voices and sees her big dark eyes turn to her and her alone, and her bright, interested smile turns Claudia's world as golden and shimmering and magical as an aurora.

TEN MINUTES BEFORE SATFALL, PEOPLE GATHER UP ON THE DECKING WHERE THE view of the southern sky is least obstructed by shrubs and rooftops. Satellite death is not a precise science. The upper atmosphere is still in turmoil, Earth's magnetic field lines resonating like struck harmonics. Elon's baby could come down early, could come down late.

In the sticky, fragrant dark under the buddleia, Hekla says, "Do you want to see it?"

"Don't mind," Claudia says.

"They're kind of samey," Hekla says. The night of the Event the satellites fell like burning snow. It's down to one or two a day now but things coming out of the sky always draw attention.

"But moreish," Claudia says, and Dom arrives with a bottle in each hand, and they take them and Dom smiles and sidles away. Dom's been coming around all evening with a bottle in each hand and a knowing smile.

"Is he checking up on us?" Hekla says, which makes Claudia feel self-conscious and blushy. It's been natural—people in common, festivals where they almost met—and now Dom's drawn a big circle around it, with pointing arrows.

"More like waiting to cut in," says Jay, who happens to be passing. "You want to watch my brother." And the moment breaks; the perfume, the warmth, the beer buzz, the starry starry sky over dark London: ash. Claudia's heart sags like the peeling label on her dewy bottle and Hekla joins the sat-watchers on the decking. It's fading, it's dying. And Claudia does a thing, a giddy thing. She slips the trumpet from her back, opens the case, fits the mouthpiece, lifts it to her lips. She raises the bell high and under a sky free of London's old light taint, brilliant with a million stars, peals out the Charpentier Prelude in D Major, high and loud and trilling every dotted note and ornament, and as she hits the final repeat the dying satellite draws an arc of fire across the sky and winks away to nothing, and everyone is staring at her but most of all, most of all, *most of all*, Hekla.

"The Space," she says. "Google it. Oh, you can't Google. Westferry Road. Tomorrow. Twelve."

TRIX IS BRILLIANT, VISIONARY, DRIVEN, SUPREMELY TALENTED, AND THE MOST impossible director I have ever worked with.

No possible director would consider going ahead with a grand community production of *Much Ado about Nothing* one week after a Carrington event that blew us back to the eighteenth century.

The impossible Trix does.

"The show goes on," she says, swirling across the Space stage by Wee Willie Winkie candlelight. Health and Safety be damned.

"Do you not think it's a tad, well, irresponsible? Putting on a play when there are still hospitals without power?"

"That's precisely why the play must go on," she declares. "Nothing can stop the theater."

Part of me hopes that the Event will. I haven't worked with community performers before. Well, not so many across so many disciplines. Actors.

Dancers. Musicians. Choir. The fucking community choir. Those who can't community-act community-dance, and those who can't community-dance community-choir. Professionals understand the purifying presence of money and a contract. Community performers are fireproof. Theirs is a higher, nobler calling. They are not filthy pros. They have commitment. Except they immediately shredded my rehearsal schedules (dance, acting, music, design, and tech) because they had a holiday booked, tickets for *Come from Away*, a birthday, an early start the next morning, a long-standing game night, a regular gig with a travelling murder-mystery group. Don't get me wrong: I've worked with many very talented, very dedicated, non-professional performers. Who turn up, work hard, do what the director wants, work well with others. Amateur is a mindset.

Then the sky burned and flicked us back to 1788 and robbed them of all their excuses and still I have community actors who talk back to the director, community dancers like a pack of feral cats, and a community choir that has my musical director one dropped stitch from quitting. And me, trying to produce Shakespeare in the afterglow of a civilization-breaking coronal mass ejection.

DOM SHOWS CLAUDIA WHERE TO STAND IN THE WINGS SO SHE WON'T GET IN THE WAY of the tech or get run over by stampeding community dancers and slips back to his stage-manager desk.

The radio announced that TfL was running a bank holiday bus service across the east but the waits were long, the service uncertain, and the buses overcrowded, so once again Claudia slung her trumpet across her back, fastened her helmet, and pushed off into the street. Today the petrol station sign glowed, shop signs flickered, traffic lights ran through their small spectrum. Bus stop indicators flashed random symbols, yet they flashed.

Disasters unfold in small scenes. All Armageddons are personal.

On the Isle of Dogs, the power is up and the Millwall Community *Much Ado* is doing. On the stage, under *lights*, Hekla drills a backing chorus and two young women at keyboards that they clearly can't play.

"Again, from the top."

She counts in and opens her voice into "Sigh No More, Ladies." Claudia played this in a parley of period instruments at the Globe. This is a new composition: '80s synthpop, keyboardists clearly miming, chorus starting in parts and drifting into unison. But the voice. Her voice. It lifts, it flies, it fills the theater; it reaches from tech box to fly tower with perfect clarity and pitch. It fills hearts and universes.

Claudia is transported. Then she notices Jay in the wings at the opposite side of the stage. He nods to her and the doubt he planted germinates. Is Dom just using Claudia to make his own move on Hekla?

Hekla catches Claudia's applause, glances over into the wings and smiles.

"I want to use you, but I need to run you past Trix," Hekla says while the tech crew reset the cues.

Trix only met Claudia last night but still doesn't remember her.

"Baroque trumpet, modern valved, some jazz," Claudia says. "I've played the Globe, the Rose, the RSC at the National, and I'm in a period instrument ensemble up in Blackheath."

"Listen," Tekla says and Claudia unsheathes the trumpet but Trix holds up her hand.

"I'm sure it's wonderful Hekla, but '80s synthpop is the hill I will die on."

And she's gone to check on two roll-in pieces of set that are supposed to turn the Space Millwall into the Blitz Club 1982.

"Well, that was a bit fucking rude," Hekla says. Claudia's face burns. "At least let me buy you a coffee."

Coffee comes from catering-size thermoses lined up on the bar because no one knows if the Fracino will fail mid-make. The coffee is stale and over-brewed. Claudia barely tastes it.

Dom swings past, casual as you like.

"So?"

"Director says no," Hekla says.

"I wouldn't take that as her final answer," Dom says. His considerable presence disrupts the space between the two women. "Trix doubles down. She and Ben fight like dogs. They defend their territory." Dom's words are for Claudia but his glances, his small smiles are for Hekla. "You'd think in the middle of like the end of the world as we know it, they'd just get on with it."

"You'd think," Hekla says. She gives Dom a return smile that blacks out the lights in Claudia's heart. Then the true lights go out and seconds later an explosion rocks the middle distance, a sound Claudia has learnt to recognize: a transformer blowing out. Groans, phone lights, candles lit. Cast and crew press to the window to watch spark-spangled smoke billow up from Barkentine Estate, then low, oily flames.

But Claudia has no heart for spectacle, no heart for anything except sitting heart-wrecked over her terrible coffee, and so it is that she alone of everyone in the Space notices Jay slip into the door frame, smile to himself, and slide away.

"LIGHTS *OR* MUSIC," I SAY. THE TECHS ARE WORKING TO CONNECT THE GENNY OUT in the loading bay to the Space's three-phase supply. "We don't have the output for both."

"Without synthpop, it won't be 1980s Canary Wharf," Trix says.

As a producer, you can question everything except the directorial vision.

"Without lights, it'll just be radio," I say.

Asking what a producer does is my personal pons asinorum, a sure sign that the questioner knows nothing about theater. The director is responsible for the creative and performance elements of the show. The producer is responsible for the director plus everything else. I get asked it all the time by the community performers. Often with a smirk.

"Do we know when the power's up again?" Trix asks. We have a not-in-front-of-the-children agreement about this production / direction schism, so this altercation takes place in the only theater office with a window.

"We get an hour from four o'clock and then it's off until tomorrow at six," I say and lift my interdicting forefinger before Trix can declare irrational optimism. "But it could be an hour either side." I'm sure they do it to keep people off the streets: on tenterhooks for the living room lights flicking back on and the router rebooting. "Even then we could get blacked out halfway through the masque scene."

She lightly strokes my cheek. She shouldn't do that. It calls up history that I don't care to remember. And even in a private office it's unprofessional.

"And we're back to . . ." Round and round again in a courtly dance.

"Synthpop," Trix flares and stalks away. This is why our history is history. One of the whys. "If we have to, we do it outdoors. But I want '80s synthpop and I've got '80s synthpop and Millwall is going to hear '80s synthpop."

Next time anyone asks me with a smirk exactly what it is a producer does I shall tell them: solve problems other people create.

MILLWALL PARK IS THRONGED. BABY STROLLERS, DOG WALKERS, PICNICS. GROUPS of young people, lads with bottles of warm beer, likely looted. Solo sunbathers loll alongside personal electronics soaking up volts from solar chargers. The smoke of a dozen barbecues mingles with the yellow haze of transformer fires hanging over London. An outdoor yoga group salutes the sun in synchronicity, an Islamic women's running club takes stately laps of the 1K loop.

If the pandemic pushed people apart and tech together, the Event blew tech apart and brought people together in mutual aid and community.

Claudia sits on the bench watching all this community, all this solidarity, wrenched with misery. The night of betrayal dawned on the morning of rejection.

No, betrayal's not too strong a word. Claudia feels what she feels. Hekla doesn't know what Claudia feels, and that just seals it, because Hekla's guilty of not guessing what's in her heart.

No, that's not at all unreasonable.

So fuck Hekla, Dom, Trix and her Millwall *Much*, Shakespeare and synthpop.

Claudia unzips the trumpet from its case, fits the mouthpiece, leans back on the bench and blows out indigo blues deep enough to cloud any sunny afternoon in the park.

FIRST THE PUNCH. AT THE FACE. I GLIMPSED IT, REACTIONS FIRED, I REELED BACK SO it didn't connect full fist, but it was enough to knock me off balance. The boot to the shin: that connected. That sent me down.

One for the knock down, one for the snatch. People shouting and pointing but none of them doing anything. Except Dom, charging like a rugby player with an open try line in front of him, yelling. But they're fast, they're putting distance between themselves and the scene of the mugging.

Dom gives up the chase and crouches beside me.

"You feel all right?"

What I feel is embarrassment, at being mugged, in daylight, on Manchester Road, ten meters from the mobile bank, taken for a fool, knocked on my ass.

"Get me up," I hiss. "People are looking."

"Sorry, I was only two seconds . . ."

He had stepped away to unlock the cargo bike. The muggers had reconnoitered their spot well, close to customers, out of sight of security. By the time they respond to the kerfuffle, I'm on my feet and the raiders are on the far side of Mudchute Park.

"And what were you doing?" Dom shouts at the security goons. "Pricks!"

"Leave it, Dom," I said. "I just want to get out of here."

I suppose this is the shock, the shakes, the scuffling fear. Theater productions have always run on petty cash but since the Event shut down the ATMs and electronic payment systems, the Millwall *Much*—in fact the whole of Millwall—has turned back to the cash economy. So every day

G4S security vans–cum–mobile banks roll up in different parts of the East; bankers open old-school ledgers and take notes of people's card numbers and hand them rolls of paper money. Someday it'll all square up.

"One got hit up in Canning Town yesterday," Dom said when I announced I was heading over to Island Gardens to make payroll. "I'll go with you."

Now I was mug of the day, gossiped door to door. *Those idiots trying to put on Shakespeare. Took everything.*

"I just want to go home," I say, but home is a five-mile hike north so Dom takes me to the Waterman's on Saunders Ness Road which is cool and candlelit and where the staff hand-pull long pints of wonderstuff.

WHERE TRIX FINDS ME TWO HOURS LATER.

"You all right, Ben?"

Not what I was expecting. I lost a week's budget. But I was on my third pint so yes, I was closing in on all right, so I said, "Still a bit shaky. The money: I'll get it back." I can't imagine how our insurance stands post-Event, but if a producer's job isn't navigating, negotiating, and niggling, what is it?

"Fuck the money." Trix sits down across the table from me, leans forward and clasps my hand in hers. "As long as you're all right."

"Yes," I start. Then the third pint, the fraying shock, the sheer stubbornness of the enterprise find words. "Really: no." And I list the stupidities, the impossibilities, the inanities. The intransigences, the absurdities, the pettinesses. The inconsequentiality of staging an all-singing, all-dancing *Much Ado about Nothing* in the middle of the biggest catastrophe to have hit the planet since the Ice Age. When I run out of Latinisms, I swing in with thick, solid Anglo-Saxon words. I may have said fuck, *a lot*. And shite. And I also said love, and wonder, and great, and good. And team, and spirit—and there's the Latin creeping back—and vision and dedication. A faery queen terrible and glorious.

"Okay," Trix says. "I hear you. But what I really came to say—apart from are you all right—is you're right. If it's music or lights, it has to be lights."

I could see the cost of this volte-face in the corners of her mouth, the dip of her eyes away from contact with mine, the twitch of her fingers.

"So: I'm going to talk to Hekla. Ask if her if she can rework the music." Trix grimaces in the Shakespearean candlelight. "Live musicians. Playing unplugged. The big music. Maybe industrial jazz-funk."

"Jazz-funk?"

"Okay. Okay." Perhaps the greatest thing a producer can do is persuade directors against their Last Minute Good Ideas. "Something our musicians can play."

My work is done.

"One note," I say. "*I'm* going to talk to Hekla?"

"*We're* going to."

WE HUDDLE AROUND THE LAPTOP SCREEN—DIRECTOR, PRODUCER, AND MUSICAL director. The sound from the speakers is thin and tinny; the battery indicator dwindles before our eyes.

"That's the Swamp Preacher mix," Hekla says. She's done a hero's job. No, more: even with a DAW, five new acoustic arrangements of her *Much Ado* score is superheroic. In eight hours. Never knowing how long the power would stay on. Tom Waits Bar band, Psycho-Masque, Acid Mariachi, Kit Kat Club, and lastly, deep south gospel stomp.

"I could work Acid Mariachi around our stage design," Trix says. "Go Baz Luhrman, like *Romeo and Juliet*. Eighties Mexico City."

"Works with Don Pedro and Don John," I say.

I flick through the files on my phone to find the latest blackout schedule. The fiber network is mostly intact even if the routers and power supplies are down. In our interludes of power and Wi-Fi we recharge, download what we think we're going to need and store files, then cosset our battery power like a temperamental Premier League No. 9.

"I can have parts printed for tomorrow," I say.

Hekla pokes the nano-SD card out of her phone and gives it to me.

"I'll talk to the choir," Trix says.

"I can . . ." I start to offer.

"I'll do it, Ben," Trix says. "I know how you feel about them."

"And I'll go look for a trumpet player," Hekla says.

For it is a truth universally acknowledged that there is no mariachi without a trumpet.

BLACKHEATH HALLS' RECITAL ROOM BOASTS MATCHLESS VICTORIAN ACOUSTICS and generous, light-drenching windrows through which Claudia can clearly follow the progress of Hekla up Lee Road from Montpellier. Only one place she can have come from—over the hill from Greenwich; only one place she can be going.

"You with us?"

Claudia snatches her attention away from the window to the players, instruments up, watching her.

"Sorry."

"Okay," Meriel on tenor viol says. "Take it right back to the start of the allegro."

"Sorry guys, sorry," Claudia flusters. "Can we take five?"

"Your head's been up your fucking ass all morning," Rowan the theorbo player mutters. Claudia places the long baroque trumpet bell-down on the stand and clatters down the stairs to head Hekla off in the street.

"Oh hi, that was lucky," Hekla says, taken by surprise.

"I saw you coming," Claudia says.

"I've been looking all over for you," Hekla says. "Your flatmate said you rehearse over here on Tuesdays."

"Well, you know, art," Claudia says, hearing the snark in her voice and hating it.

"Can we, uh, get coffee? I mean, the power is on?"

"It's not." Why can't she kill the snark? Dead dead, stab it through the heart. "And I'm kind of in the middle of a rehearsal."

"Okay, well: I was wondering. If, after all, you might be available to play in the *Much*? Trix's seen sense and we're playing live."

"Well, I am kind of busy . . ." She's not. She lies. She's sitting in the house watching the candles smoke and listening to the radio for the latest ex cathedra from Number 10 and SAGE.

"I've rearranged the score as a kind of psycho mariachi fiesta," Hekla says. "And I really, really need a trumpet that peels the paint from the walls."

"I play baroque, early music, occasional jazz," Claudia says, while her inner trumpet plaints, *Mariachi? If you can play jazz you can play anything.*

"So, I'm asking, can you do it?"

Yes yes yes! cries the trumpet of the heart, but all Claudia hears is her voice say, "No."

RUNNERS LOPE PAST CLAUDIA ON HER BENCH LOOKING DOWN OVER GREENWICH Park to the river and the towers of Docklands. There always will be runners, there ways have been, runners. Gazelle-footed along Bower Avenue, around Claudia on her bench, down Prime Meridian Walk, past the geometrical perfection of the Queen's House set between the enfolding wings of the Maritime Museum and her old music school. Unblemished architectural perfection: beneath the facade a slag of charred and melted cabling and circuitry. Smoke rises from maimed London; from the preposterous dome of the O2 on her right, from the thuggish towers of Docklands, west to Deptford and Bermondsey and the many spires of the city.

The fast ferries are running again. A low sleek catamaran pulls in to Greenwich pier. As in Shakespeare's age, the river is the fastest and surest highway.

"Fucking shitting Dom," she says, then shouts to Sir Christopher Wren's architecture, to the boat surging away from the pier, bound downstream to the Thames Barrier, "Fucking shitting Hekla!"

"Oh hi," says a voice behind her. "Claudia, isn't it?"

ON SEPTEMBER 1, 1859, BRITISH ASTRONOMERS RICHARD CARRINGTON AND RICHARD Hodgson observed an unusually bright and powerful flare on the surface of the sun. Seventeen hours later, geomagnetometers ran off the scale as a fist of charged particles smashed into Earth's magnetic field, lighting the night as far south as Cuba with an aurora bright enough to read a fine-print Bible. Telegraph wires melted. Operators received shocks from their equipment.

In March 1989, a coronal mass ejection took down the Quebec power grid.

In July 2012, Earth missed a Carrington-class CME by nine days. Had it struck Earth full on, the cost of the damage to power, communications, services, and infrastructure would have topped two trillion dollars.

The Carrington event that strikes six days before opening night of the Millwall *Much Ado* is estimated to have been between five and eight times as powerful as the 1859 strike. Estimated because the mass of charged particles took out the Parker and the ESA SolO sun-watch probes. Twelve hours later—much earlier than anyone expected—it hammered into Earth's magnetosphere and triggered geomagnetic pulses that shut down twenty-first-century connected society from Moscow to Missisauga and sent the glittering beads of the GPS satellite necklace spilling from orbit.

Power, mobile communications, transport, banking and payment systems. Gone. London went dark, went dead. Workers were trapped in the City's glass elevators. Thousands were abandoned in the Underground tunnels. Rail, road, refrigeration, out. Aircraft: lost, steering by stars and guile to crippled airports. Data centers, ATMs: down. Backups kicked in, but the network, the grid, the web was ripped apart.

The Event struck so swiftly because a smaller CME two days before cleared an ionization path. The governments of the western hemisphere cling to the ambush excuse, but the truth was that despite terabytes of reports and warnings and plans, none had ever been implemented. It cost too much. It would have been less than the seven trillion to rebuild the economies of the Carrington-facing nations. It will take ten years to bring the world back into the twenty-first century.

The grant-funded, council-supported pan-community, big-budget, all-ages, all-ethnicities, all-religions, all-income-levels, all-backgrounds Mill-wall *Much Ado about Nothing* didn't get that memo.

BUT IT'S ONLY THE SOLAR WEATHER GUY. WHO OWNED THE HOUSE THAT HOSTED THE party that had the buddleia where she met the woman who was her sun and moon and stars, and was brought crashing to earth by Jay.

"Leon," he reminds her. "Finest view in London. I come here a lot. Lunch and things."

Uninvited, he sits at the other end of the bench from Claudia. Claudia prickles with resentment: a private hurt appropriated, but Leon sits, doesn't speak, doesn't ask, doesn't interrupt her self-loathing silence. Just looks at the finest view in London.

Then she hears it, and he hears it at the same time. They both look up the direction of the sound, behind them, from the southwest: the chuckling applause of a helicopter. It roars over them, crosses the river, the stalled cable car, heading northeast.

"City airport," he says.

"Oh," she says. "I thought we'd have more time." For a few days the old world, the mundane world, had been turned upside down. Chaotic days, frightening days, big days of adventure and solidarity, the grace of people making communities, sharing resources, engineering solutions. Extraordinary days, days outside normal time. Claudia remembered the first COVID lockdown; the endless spring sun; the applause for the NHS when she would take her trumpet out into the street and play it for the health workers; the Zoom quizzes; the daily socially distanced walks. In the end the special became the new mundane and she, like everyone, became bored with it.

When the sun blew a ten-billion-ton plasma kiss at Earth, there were no online quizzes, no Microsoft Teams meetings, no Zoom play-readings, no tweeting on shared Netflix experiences. The Event shut down human communications but opened a thousand doors to human contact. The adventure of someone arriving at her door, no prefatory text, no message, no last minute change of plans on WhatsApp. The adventure of shopping, cooking, going to the mobile bank to get money—paper! Metal! The adventure of familiar streets explored by bicycle, rediscovering a child's sense of a huge new world opening up before her.

The adventure of love.

But the helicopter rattling in to the City airport heralds the return of the old, dull, workaday order.

And love had snapped off at the stem even as it blossomed.

"Well," Leon says. "Maybe." He pulls his feet up on to the bench, hugs his knees to him, like a sun-watching owl. "We're observing an increase in the magnetic flux of sunspot cluster 112B."

Claudia squeezes her eyelids to thin, eyelash-fringed slits and tries to squint through the sun glare to the dark moles of sunspots.

"There could be another Carrington?" she says.

"Maybe not Carrington class," Leon says. "But it could knock us back again to where we were last Tuesday."

The Thames clipper powers past on its return trip, upstream.

"Leon, do you know Dom's brother Jay?"

"Half-brother," Leon says. "He's been round the house a lot. He's something in the show but no one quite knows what."

"At the party he told me that the only reason Dom introduced me to Hekla was so he could use me to get with her."

"Jay said that?"

"Jay did."

"Jay is a gold-plated shit," Leon says. "Everyone knows this. He will do anything to wind up Dom, but Dom won't let him go."

Now she looks at Leon, huddled on the end of the bench.

"I have to call Hekla."

"Er, call?"

Claudia stands and slings her trumpet on to her back.

"Then I have to go to the Isle of Dogs."

"And I," Leon says, "have to go and find the fault in our star."

BY NOW EVEN THE COMMUNITY PERFORMERS ARE PROFESSIONAL ENOUGH NOT TO moan when the lights go out. Even on dress rehearsal. And because it's dress and tech, Trix orders Dom to unleash the genny. Everyone cheers when the engine kicks into a steady beat.

"Let there be light," I whisper. And control room, lighting board, LEDs snap on.

The professionals drop back into Beatrice and Benedict's masque scene, transposed to a Ciudad Juárez narco wedding. I watch Trix watching her show, alert and critical and supportive and generous. I see her again as I saw her first: brilliant, visionary, driven, supremely talented. She has worked wonders. Wrought miracles. What I saw as obstinate craziness, under the LEDs' polychrome light becomes prophecy: if we can put this show together, we can put this world together. Much ado.

A tap on my shoulder: Louise front-of-house whispers.

"Ben, I think we have a problem."

She takes me to the bar. Through its big high windows I see traffic lights flicker on Westferry Road. Yesterday the DLR reopened a skeleton service: now two trains stand stalled on the viaduct. The doors are open but the passengers are reluctant to drop down on to the track. The power rail might come back to life as abruptly as it had died. I don't think so. I see the air glow around the aerials and spires of Canary Wharf. Oily smoke belches from the just-repaired Thames Court substation. The Estate Road mobile phone mast dances with St. Elmo's fire.

Louise tries to tune her radio but it spews static. I thumb open my phone: as I thought, the network is down and the Space Wi-Fi returns an *internet unavailable* icon.

The sun isn't done with us yet.

Music bursts from the auditorium.

"I'll tell Trix," I say.

Then the police arrive.

FLANN O'BRIEN WAS RIGHT. THERE IS NO SITUATION THAT CAN'T BE MADE WORSE BY the presence of the police.

I thought Trix might gaffer-tape herself to the generator to stop them confiscating it. In the end Dom stands between her and the cops as they unplug the cable, shut down the engine, and wheel the genny out to their van.

"We've got a show in two hours!" she shouts after them. "Shakespeare!"

A male officer turns back.

"A health center needs this," he says in a voice like winter. "A health center."

"We're fucked," Trix says. "That's it. The final hit. No more. The Millwall *Much* is dead."

Everyone looks to the producer. Cast, crew, creative team, community. Circus skills and Mariachis. Alone on a stage lit only by the light from the scene dock. I lift a hand. I have this crisis thing. I don't speak, I don't answer questions. I don't make eye contact. I shut down. I generate ideas. Dozens, hundreds, maybe thousands of ideas. Only in ideas lies salvation. Most are shit. One will be right.

Through the blizzard of notions brilliant, impractical, visionary, insane, ridiculous, I glimpse a silhouette in the shaft of sunlight. I squint to try and resolve the dark blur into a person. It looks like . . .

A single golden idea drops to the stage with the sound of a bell.

"Leon?" I shout. The figure pauses. "Leon!" I meet him in the loading bay.

"Is Claudia here?"

"Leon, Leon: this is an Event, isn't it?"

An unsteady moment as Leon tries to skid on to a new direction.

"Uh . . . Yeah, a level 10 CME . . ."

"With everything?"

"Well, not as big."

"But . . . everything?"

"Everything."

I hug him. He hates it. I blink my way back into the dark theater.

"It's not over," I say. "It is not over. Here's what we do. Get everything and everyone over to Millwall Park. We are going the full Bard."

A PROCESSION OF HANDS CARRIES THE *MUCH* THE KILOMETER FROM THE SPACE TO Millwall Park. Friends of the project, neighbors, community all lend hands and wheels. There goes the portico of the ducal palace in Messina on a shopping trolley. Dom shuttles back and forth, weaving between the stalled cars on his cargo bike. I try not to think of a refugee convoy. The crew is already at work building, fastening, propping and staying. Somewhere they've found scaffolding. Somehow, three dead pickups have been pushed into the park to act as levels. Kids on bikes roam the streets blowing airhorns and shouting that the Millwall *Much* is on! On! On! Tonight! Millwall Park! Ain't no sun storm's stoppin' our show! Many have already seen the procession and brought folding chairs, blankets, food, drink, children, and arranged them on the crescent berm at the south end of the park that will forever after be the Grassy Knoll.

The park fills. So many people. More than the Space could ever have accommodated. This is the Isle of Dogs, this is the East giving two fingers to a treacherous sun god, to one thing constant never, setting west over the smoke towers of London. Above us the sky grows bright. As I'd hoped.

As I knew.

Trix always says I'm too modest.

I patrol the preparations though my work is done now. Dom sets up lines of garden flambeaux to guide the audience to the Grassy Knoll.

"What I can't figure is how the cops knew we had a generator," I say.

Dom lights a garden torch.

"Oh, I can," he says. "Some people just like to see the world turn dark. I shall be having words with my brother." He looks up, hands me the rest of the torches. "Put these in for me. I got to get backstage."

He whips out a battery torch and flashes a response to a signal from the control scaffold. We tried the walkies more in hope than expectation but telecoms are a sea of sinister static so we worked out a light-semaphore. Firefly flashes wink across Millwall Park.

I climb the scaffolding tower and duck under a bar. The planks creak alarmingly under my feet. Arcs of fire spiral people in to the arena; the crowd mutters and laughs, that sound of preshow expectation that is every bit as good as the ovation at the end. Signal lights flicker behind the scenery, the pickups, the groups of excited performers. All beneath the glorious, glowing, golden aurora, as bright as stage lighting.

"I love you, Ben," Trix says.

"What?" I say, and, "Um?"

"Just that." She kisses me.

"One moment," I say, and I take her in my arms and kiss her back, up under the burning sky. "Okay, you can do it now."

Trix raises her torch, gives three short blinks, the mariachis march in, and the Millwall Community *Much Ado about Nothing* opens.

ALL THE WAY UP SEBONDALE STREET SHE HEARS LAUGHTER, VOICES, SINGING, music, but there is no opening in the tall park railings. She leaves her bike at the changing rooms gate without even chaining it to the railings.

"I'm with the show," she gasps to the front of house staffer in hi-viz and is past her before she can object. A fast, silent run across the grass, dodging between stagehands and groups of community actors shuffling nervously for their cues.

"Seen Dom?" she whispers to the community choir, smoking behind a HiAce. One of them nods stage-left.

"Dom Dom Dom," she hisses to the stage manager. "I need to know: Dom, are you interested in Hekla?"

"Claudia? What the fuck?"

"Romantically. Heart stuff."

"No. Even if I were, she wouldn't be interested in me."

"So what Jay said . . ."

"Fucking Jay," Dom says, loud enough to turn the heads of the waiting actors.

"That's all I need to know," Claudia says. "In that case, I want on."

"We're well into the second half."

"You've got no trumpet." She unzips her instrument from its case. It gleams in the aurora light. "You need trumpet."

Movement at stage right. Instruments strike up. Claudia recognizes the opening measure of "Sigh No More, Ladies," mariachi style.

"Dom."

"Go."

Sigh no more, ladies, sigh no more.

Hekla again leads the play's musical high point. Claudia heard her sing it at the audition at the Space but tonight, before hundreds, thousands maybe, in the late summer warmth, under a sky of honey, her voice is magnificent. Incomparable. Longing. The community choir and musicians fall silent and she sings alone.

"Men were deceivers ever."

Okay.

And here's the instrumental break, the hole in the music where there should be solo, soaring trumpet and Claudia steps into it, raises her trumpet to her lips and tears a crack in the sky, notes jazzing and fizzing and pealing under the bright beautiful light of the aurora.

Lavanya Lakshminarayan

THE GRATITUDE DIORAMA SPINS AND SHIMMERS IN A MIST OF PIXEL DUST AGAINST a silken shamiana. The climate-controlled tent has been handcrafted by thousands of artisans using weaves and fabrics, prints and embroidery from Kanchipuram and Pochampally to Banaras and Kashmir. Millions of holovids and praise-texts pop, bounce, wobble, and shrink, glittering like zari woven across a resplendent canvas. Each flickering story collected from citizens across the country is a testament to an India reimagined. Visitors to the Gallery of the People of Free India marvel at the cloud-hosted digital monument to unity, equality, liberty, and love. A whole new world after the terror of the Regime.

Two streets down, on one of the last remaining tree-lined avenues of New Luru, Kanaka Chetty is at a humbler and far more personally important celebration. She dabs at her eyes with Avik's pocket handkerchief. Avik takes her hand, giving it a gentle squeeze.

"They look so happy," Avik whispers, choking up.

"They deserve to be," Kanaka whispers back, entwining her spouse's fingers with her own.

The ecosphere thrives, filled with flora and fauna, unlike most of the city that sprawls beyond its climate-controlled bio-dome. Birdsong trills amidst its canopies and butterflies flit through myriad blooms lining neat pathways. On a constructed mantapam set against two tall champaka trees, Kanaka's best friends Ben and Nikhil are midway through their nav-Vedic wedding ceremony, designed in entirety to embrace queer positivity. Yesterday's novo-Christian wedding was similarly reimagined. Religious aunties and uncles on both sides seem happy that the event is being sanctified in the eyes of all their gods.

Ben and Nikhil moped about the pointless ritual of the event all through their bachelor do—burned, no doubt, by the historic weaponization of religion against queer identities under the Regime. Kanaka supposes that being introduced to their families' gods is an old-fashioned symbol of inclusion and acceptance. She's relieved that both sides are being supportive of the happy couple.

When Kanaka married Avik three years ago, she chose to wear a sea-blue sari, embroidered with birds, at the ceremony. She switched to a lilac three-piece suit—raw silk with a dramatic peak lapel on the jacket—paired with silver high-heeled boots for their reception. The celebration went off without a hitch until one of her great-aunts pulled her aside and hissed, "I thought you'd be a proper woman after marriage. Pants and boots . . ." Her great aunt shook her head in disapproval. Kanaka laughed. *A proper woman. What the fuck is that, even?*

The stray comment came back to her on their honeymoon, a remembrance on an errant breeze when the moon lay low over the Mediterranean Sea.

"Am I not a proper woman?" she asked, Avik's arms entwined around her.

"Define a proper woman," Avik said, nuzzling the back of her neck.

"I can't."

"Exactly." Avik's hands continued to travel across her skin, raising gooseflesh until her breathing turned ragged, conversation stilling for the rest of the evening.

"What's bothering you?" Avik nudges her shoulder.

Kanaka returns to the present and shifts in her seat, crossing her legs at the knee. She gazes down at the pleats in her purple sari, unconventionally folded and draped like a dhoti, ending in a pair of high-top sneakers covered in gold sunbursts.

"You look lovely," Avik says. "And no, nobody's staring at you."

"Stop reading my mind." Kanaka smiles. "And thank you. I was just wondering . . ."

"It isn't too much. It's you."

Avik leans over and drops his voice. "In case you haven't noticed, we're at one of the first gay weddings in Free India, surrounded by māmis in Kanjeevaram silks and māmas in safari suits. They're probably all having their minds blown that a groom and groom wedding is possible."

Kanaka laughs. He's got a point. Her smarttech beeps on her wrist, and she taps on the notif. "Not again," she groans. Avik tuts sympathetically.

The notif expands outward, casting holographic text surrounded by birds, bees, and too many flowers to be tasteful.

Fertility window open! Time to make some babies!

A timer starts to tick down from six days.

"Aargh!" She dismisses the notification and looks around, anxious. She hopes none of the aunties and uncles use this as an opportunity to tell her about the joys of motherhood.

Her new-gen birth control pills are packed with nanobots, tracking and regulating her hormones, syncing all her information with her smart-tech, and recommending activities that help her maintain her peak fitness levels. If only the pills weren't so useful in managing her PCOD, if only they weren't a contraceptive, if only feeding all their data into the Smart-Fit+ program weren't so important to her career . . . The trade-off is being reminded by an algorithm that her ovaries are baby-making machines every month.

One of the many side effects of womanhood, like activewear without pockets.

"We need to find you some smarttech that isn't so . . . intrusive," Avik says, wrapping his arm around her.

"All the old tech is dark ages stuff. It's probably laced with under-the-table surveillance from the Regime, probably still feeding into their data-bases, probably still manned by some lone right-wing clown launching cyberattacks," Kanaka sighs. "At least these guys let you know what they're tracking,"

Another side effect of womanhood is choosing the least dodgy system from an array of dodgy systems, like picking between hot wax and a razor.

At the reception later that evening, Kanaka glides through the cocktail party on a pair of strappy gold heels, wearing a sage green lehenga, pearls at her throat.

"You're so elegant," Ben's mother says in admiration.

"So graceful," Nikhil's grandmother chimes in with a compliment of her own.

"Princess," gasps someone's five-year-old child, looking up at her in wonder before being ushered away by an embarrassed parent.

Kanaka finally spots Ben and Nikhil bereft of the company of their enthusiastic relatives. She grabs Avik by the wrist and heads their way. "Congratulations, you lovelies!"

Nikhil's shoulders tense as he turns. Ben's smile stiffens, then relaxes into a more lopsided grin. "Oh, thank goodness, it's Kcyks."

"Rescue us," Nikhil mutters. "I need to mellow out."

Kanaka keeps up a stream of loud chatter, intended to throw off every kind of would-be interrupter, until Ben and Nikhil are safely away from the family, a bower trailing roses and jasmine creepers concealing them from prying eyes. Nikhil fishes around in his pockets.

"Have the families behaved?" Avik asks, sniggering as Nikhil takes three long, silent drags of THC from his vape.

"His aunt just said, 'I hope you two are better dads than the ones in *Daddy, Daddy!* I'm glad Kanaka will be around to help,'" Ben supplies with an eye roll.

Nikhil throws his hands up in the air, dramatically trailing smoke as his hand clenches the vape's power button. Avik smacks his hand to his forehead. Kanaka wrinkles her nose and grimaces.

Daddy, Daddy! is the latest HoloWorld show intended to portray queer relationships in positive light. Except it doesn't. The plot revolves around a gay couple who adopt a child and are hapless parents, until their best friend—a cishet woman—moves in with them, bringing good, old-fashioned motherly values into their bohemian lives. Despite millions of protests, it hasn't been canceled yet, and the matter has now escalated to the judicial system; it's one of the first tests of whether the Free India government will live up to its promises for a better world.

"I can't believe she thought *Kanaka* would make prime parenthood material," Ben laughs. "Of all the assumptions you could make just because someone's a woman . . ."

Another side effect of womanhood. A uterus is like an empty handbag, waiting to be filled.

"Kanaka's never wanted kids!" Nikhil smirks. "Ever since she was fifteen . . . she *knew*. Still. Talk about wasting your privilege, Keyks."

"Let me know when all you men are done discussing my uterus," Kanaka snipes back.

"Just teasing, Keyks." Nikhil gives her a peck on the cheek. "I'm anxious. Ben and I have wanted kids . . ."

"Since forever," Ben says.

"And even with this new government and its promises . . ." Nikhil trails off.

"Bullshit like *Daddy, Daddy!* is really setting us back to Regime times," Ben says sadly.

Nikhil kisses his spouse on the cheek. "We'll make it happen. We'll be the best dads ever."

A server passes by with a tray, and Kanaka lifts four champagne flutes from it. She passes them around and raises her glass. "To my best friends, Ben and Nikhil, and to new adventures all the way to forever and a day, *including* being the best dads ever."

Two hours later, Kanaka leans her head back against the cushions in their self-driving car, Avik's hand in hers. The car's sound system chimes the time—it's 11:00 p.m.—with a snatch of song lyric before playing an ancient rock classic.

"Hah! This reminds me of my mother!" Avik says, voice-prompting the volume up. "She caught The Scorpions in concert the second time they played at the Palace Grounds in Bangalore in the aughts. Snuck out of her house because she was only sixteen, and her parents were afraid there'd be pot at the gig. Which there was, of which she did partake."

Kanaka is warm, and her head is only slightly spinning from all the champagne. She's right on that blissful edge between wakefulness and sleep, drifting away to the sound of Avik's stories . . . when her smarttech pops up again. This time, it tells her that her hormone patterns correspond with relaxation—so how about attempting some conception? An animated emoji winks at her on loop, an instant turnoff, which is a shame because Avik really does look dashing in his tailored blue bandhgala.

When they're home, Avik voice-prompts their immersopod to suggest holofilms about "badass women." Kanaka's HoloWorld recs are tailor-made for her, and they swipe through a few before settling on a movie called *VR Virtuoso*, about an Indian competitive gamer who sticks it to society, or so the blurb suggests.

Kanaka snuggles into him as they lie back on soft silk cushions. The immersopod tilts and optimizes their viewing angle as the film credits begin to roll, wrapping them in a curved sheen of pixels as the film opens into the world of IceMoor. A wind mage appears, dodging spellcasts and deathmists beside a glacial lake. A carefully choreographed battle between two rival teams ensues. Victory hangs in the balance, when the film cuts to a woman in a neon blue haptic suit, leaping and rolling on a pro tactile mat.

"Hah! This could be you!" Avik says in delight.

Kanaka smacks his arm, but grins. She might enjoy this one. The protagonist is even playing *Realm Conquerors*, the battle arena fantasy MMO that she competes in for a living. The filmmakers have got so many little details right, all the way down to the occasional HUD glitches and the physics issues with the windweaver spells.

Less than half an hour in, though, it begins to fall apart for Kanaka. The movie protagonist has all the success in the world, but no spouse and family of her own.

"Am I less than a woman?" she asks her best friends over cocktails on-screen. They nod earnestly, each offering well-meaning advice, and the rest of the movie follows its protagonist to a happy wedding engagement followed by happier news—she's going to have a baby! The last line of the film causes Kanaka to burst into laughter. Soft light falls upon its protagonist, dressed in a beautiful floral-patterned skirt, as she stares off into the middle distance, sighing quietly to herself: "I am complete."

"You've got to be kidding," Kanaka says, logging out of HoloWorld. "Why is this the *only* narrative there ever is? Did you see how she goes from neon activewear to pretty dresses to finding true love? And all right, being married, sure—I have you." She pokes Avik on the arm. "But that *and* the baby *and* the pretty frocks? Ugh."

"I guess it resonates with a lot of people," Avik says, kissing her forehead. "You are entirely your own person."

Avik leads her up to bed and hugs her tight, falling asleep in seconds. Kanaka wishes she possessed the same superpower tonight. She's caught in a thought spiral. Has the notion of womanhood simply been constructed by TV shows and movies over generations, carefully crafted and propagated to the point where a fixed menu of dreams and desires have been internalized by women in real life? How did this pass her by?

Or is there something more essential to womanhood, a tangle of secrets, feelings, and coded language that blooms unexpectedly like a brahma-kamalam on a rainy night? Does she not possess an inner garden of flowers?

Either way, she cannot find it, this hidden and mystical art of socially applauded womanhood. Does this make her less than? She dreams she is an empty plastic bag blowing on the wind.

Her anxieties are replaced by new ones by the time she's training the next day. A lot of the world still believes that professional gamers aren't real athletes, but Kanaka's fitness routine ensures she stays competitive.

". . . Six . . . seven . . . eight . . . ," she gasps between reps, wrist curls straining her forearms.

Anyone who's ever played a VR game can attest to how brutal the haptic controls are on the wrists. The speed and accuracy required to fire off commands has resulted in career-ending injuries for tons of pro gamers. Kanaka hopes she's never one of them.

The apartment door slides open and Bhavani stumbles in, grinning from ear to ear.

"Kano," she says fondly. "Wedding was good?"

Kanaka grits her teeth, finishing her set, and lays the dumbbell down. She wipes her forehead with a towel and flashes Bhavani a genuine grin.

Her housekeeper has known her since before she knew Avik, when she was still fooling around with a different man or woman every week. Bhavani knows all her secrets and will defend them with tooth, nail, and kitchen knife.

"Wedding was super, Bhavani!" she says. "You should have come."

Bhavani keeps smiling while privately thinking her employer might be a bit screw-loose. Why would she spend money on *two* shiny new outfits for *two* separate all-dressed-up weddings for the same one couple? She bought a new sari for the church wedding, zari and everything. Kanaka would buy her another one if she asked, but there is such a thing as pride. Sick aunt, she lied, and escaped.

"Show me pics," Bhavani says bossily.

Kanaka taps on her smarttech. The pics pop out, one by one. Bhavani examines them all with approval. "Such good-looking men," she nods. "They suit each other. Your dress is also super. Avik looks very handsome."

"It was a very happy day," Kanaka says, but her gaze is distant. Bhavani thinks she knows what she's thinking about; it must be the only thing any married woman thinks about, or so her own family reminds her each time her marriage license is denied.

She works up the nerve to say it out loud, then decides to soften the blow by turning it into a joke. "Kano, you and Avik should try now. Otherwise, those two will be first," she laughs, hoping to cover up any awkwardness.

"Try what now?"

Bhavani leans back and indicates a curve over her belly. "Chinna Kanaka," she says in Tamil. "She should be here by next year, running around in two years . . ."

Kanaka begins to laugh. "Bhavani, I'm not going to—"

"Don't worry, I'll take care of her. You can keep doing your work," Bhavani carries on recklessly. She might as well commit to it, now she's brought it up. She's been thinking it ever since her Kano married Avik. "You both have enough money; you can buy a big car to drive her around, send her to a good school, also. She'll be properly educated. Think how happy your Amma and Appa will be!"

Kanaka carries on laughing. Bhavani's now certain she's a little screw-loose.

"I don't want kids. I want cats and dogs," she says between giggles. "I can be a great aunt—like with Maithreyi's kid—but I don't want to be a mother. I can't be a mother."

Bhavani frowns. Who's been telling her dear, sweet Kano these lies? If it's Avik, she'll kill the man, even though she's grown to like him after her initial suspicion when he stayed beyond his one-week expiry date. "Don't say that!" she says angrily, protectively. "You'll only know how happy you can be if you try it."

"Bhavani, I'm not like you. You *want* children. I don't. Avik and I aren't going to have any."

Bhavani is saddened. She wants to take her foolish, pretty Kano and shake her, make her realize that there is no greater purpose, no greater calling than being a mother. And what a wonderful mother Kano would make! Beautiful, modern, kind, clever . . . well maybe not so clever. There are some things all the degrees in the world can't teach, and this is one of them.

Kano resumes her workout and Bhavani sees to all her housekeeping tasks—loading the dishwasher, vacuuming, and then cooking for the day. All the while, she hums a little folk song about children to herself, wishing she had everything Kano did, and stifling the little green bubbles of envy welling up within her.

She and her partner David still haven't had their marriage license approved. They've been rejected twice, on various grounds including economic instability. David's been working twice as many jobs all year, hoping to prove to the government of Free India that he can support his future wife and family. Even sweet Kano has helped, giving them the studio apartment that's attached to her own rent-free, and signing paperwork that attests to this. The government doesn't believe any of it.

On darker days, Bhavani suspects the government doesn't *want* to believe any of it. Maybe it doesn't want more of her kind—underprivileged, barely educated—to add to the country's population. Bhavani's trying to fix this, too. She's been going to night school to get her intermediate certificate. Maybe it's enough. If it isn't, she doesn't know what more she can do. In the eyes of all governments, women like her have always been—will always be—less than. All Bhavani knows is she's pushing thirty-six and running out of time to have children the conventional way. She can't afford any other kind, and she doesn't want to burden Kano with having to support her again.

When Kano goes into her study for a meeting with her team, Bhavani switches on the TV in the living room to keep herself entertained while she shells peas. Kano and Avik keep telling her to use the immersopod, but she's afraid it won't recognize her accent. So she uses a remote like someone from the 2010s, and signs into her HoloWorld account.

Her recommended TV shows pop up, hovering inches off the screen. She picks *Single Success Superstar*, her favorite docudrama. She's soon immersed as she follows a woman mountaineer from Trichy who's scaled all fourteen of the world's eight-thousand-meter peaks. The woman talks about how her family tried to force her to get married under the Regime, but she ran away and took a train north. She regrets nothing.

Bhavani is chopping carrots now, awestruck by the strength it takes to face all of life's battles alone as the next episode begins. Another single woman, this time a celebrity makeup artist whose life was nearly ruined when her husband died young. Ostracized and shuttered away for being a widow, she climbed out of a window using the nine-yard-long sari from her wedding and ran away to the nearest town. She says she never wants to be married again.

She doesn't hear Kanaka step out of her study. She drops her knife and the carrot in her hands when she hears her say: "What're you watching?"

Bhavani hits pause. The title pops up over the frozen holovid frame. It's surrounded by stars, as if using the word *superstar* in the title wasn't extra enough.

"Ooh, nice!" Kano says. "I've never seen this one before. What else have you been watching?"

Bhavani hits Back on the remote. A bunch of show trailers autoplay, text scrolling across them to summarize. *Working Woman Extraordinaire*: a single woman rises to be CEO in the heart of New B-Bay. *One Woman, One Empire*: two sisters renounce all family ties to compete to run the family business. *Single, Not Ready to Mingle*: three best friends are top of their university, and refuse to sell out for true love.

"I've never seen *any* of these on my feed!" Kanaka exclaims. "Let me show you."

Bhavani hands her the remote, and Kano logs into her account.

Family Femme Fatale: Sania is a vigilante by night, a soccer mom by day. *Ladylike*: a corporate executive from New Luru travels back in time to the Asokan Empire and rediscovers her femininity. *Boss Bahu*: Arati runs a successful company and comes back home to be devoted to her family.

"Kano, I've never even heard of these shows!" Bhavani laughs, but stops when she notices Kano frown, muttering under her breath like she does when she's irritated.

The trouble with rich women is they need to have it all. Kano must get the posh shows with more English; she must get the simple ones with options for Tamil subtitles. Bhavani stifles an exhalation. *So we get different* shows. *Doesn't really matter, no? She can just use my account to watch* Single Success Superstar. *After all, it's tacked onto Kano's family subscription.* She said this last bit out loud.

"No, Bhavani. This is odd. It's as if HoloWorld is trying to fill our heads with different types of ideas," Kano says. She heads back into her study, shaking her head.

Bhavani makes her some coffee. She takes it to her and places it on a coaster with purple flowers atop her work desk. Kano's smarttab is on its stand, and her wireless keyboard beeps as her fingers fly across it.

"Don't you worry, Bhavani," she mutters, taking a sip of her coffee. "I'm looking this up. We both have HoloWorld Premium++ so we should be able to view the same shows." She gazes into her holoscreen and repeats herself. "Don't worry."

Bhavani isn't about to. She doesn't have the headspace to add another source of anxiety to her list. Instead, she makes Kano and Avik some avial and pongal for lunch, imagining that they're her silly, spoiled children—except all grown up—and frying fresh applams so she can spoil them further. When she and David are permitted children, she'll have three, and then she'll shower them all with the same love and affection . . .

"Motherf—" she hears Kano swear. Avik's footsteps drum down the stairs. Practical man, Avik. Always looking at spreadsheets on his holodesk, important manager in his office. He'll talk sense into Kano.

A door slams. Kano is back in the living room, pacing up and down. "Bhavani," she calls. "Can you show us your HoloWorld, please?"

Bhavani washes her hands and dries them on her apron. She logs in, and Avik's eyes widen. "Wow. This is a whole new world."

"I know, right!" Kanaka says. She turns to Bhavani to ask for permission so she can mess around. "Can I search for some of my shows, please?"

"Of course, Kano."

Kanaka types in the name of the movie they watched last night. *VR Virtuoso.* It doesn't exist. She checks for the show she used to be obsessed with—*Big, Loud, and Bitchy*—until it turned into something in which women weren't any of the above. This show doesn't exist, either, and Kanaka knows it's just hit season 11 from all the posts on Ticker, her social media feed. She switches to her profile and passes Bhavani the remote. "Your turn," she says.

Her smarttech beeps and she taps on the notification without thinking. It pops out, surrounded by kissing birds, to say:

Three days left to get on the baby-train!

The countdown continues to tick. Kanaka swipes at it, annoyed, and returns to the task at hand. Her scowl deepens when none of the shows Bhavani watches show up on her HoloWorld feed.

Who's creating these boundaries? And why?

It's as if the two women occupy separate virtual realities, separated by an impassable veil woven from binary, based on a series of assumptions that make no sense.

What's this new side effect of womanhood, and why does it feel like being squeezed into a corset?

BHAVANI IS ALARMED WHEN, OVER THE NEXT WEEK, KANAKA OBSESSES OVER HER HoloWord recs. She watches pilots and asks Bhavani more questions that she's ever thought about in her life.

"How does it make you feel that all your content is telling you that being single with no kids is the best kind of life?" Kano fires off. Or: "What about your own goals? Don't you ever want to see people *just like you* get exactly what *you* want?"

Bhavani bites back the urge to tell her sometimes-foolish Kano that people like her—poor, uneducated—almost never get what they want. But she thinks about her questions long after she's politely answered them, and ends up somewhat offended that Kano can't see that her priorities remain the same, regardless of what the HoloWorld shows are telling her to do.

Then Kano invites Bhavani and David over every night for dinner, before Bhavani heads out to night-school. It disrupts her study time, but Bhavani is concerned for Kano, and so she puts up with her as they mirror each other's activities online.

They play the same casual games on their smarttech. Bhavani's is two gens old, with less bandwidth, but it still hosts most games at a lower resolution. Kano takes notes the whole way through, and is far more interested in the in-game ads than in winning.

Fertility Fixed! says an ad for an IVF clinic. Kano sees this one every two days. Meanwhile, Bhavani sees: *Rise Up!* The ad directs her to career-counseling services for people without degrees.

Comfort Bras for Maternity Wear! says another, cycling through once a day for Kanaka. Meanwhile, Bhavani views an ad that proclaims *Nonstop Productivity!* and links to performance- and focus-enhancement pills.

"Doesn't it bother you, Bhavani?" Kano frowns. What bothers Bhavani is that Kano's going to wind up with really bad wrinkles across her forehead if she carries on like this. Kano carries on. "You never once, *not once*, see ads for wedding venues or IVF clinics, or antenatal classes."

Bhavani begins to laugh. "Kano, it doesn't matter what ads they show me. I can't afford any of this, anyway."

Kano looks mortified. "I'm so sorry," she gasps. "I didn't mean to—"

"I know," Bhavani says gently. "But you have to remember, these are all rich people problems."

Kanaka's ashamed that she's been taking so much of Bhavani's time to obsess over something that is likely just her mind unraveling as she desperately tries to reaffirm that she's a woman, that she belongs. She rounds on Avik instead.

Seated across the table from him in their living room, she walks him through her hypothesis. "Everything Bhavani sees is about being single, free to make choices, to rise through the world. Everything *I* see is about being a family woman, about *completing* myself with children and . . ." she waves her hand up and down over his person, "and the likes of you, or someone like you."

"Thanks," Avik says drily.

"You know what I mean," Kanaka sighs.

Avik smiles. "Relax. I'm just teasing."

Kanaka nods distractedly, then carries on. "I have *thoughts*."

"I love your *thoughts*," Avik says.

Kanaka can't help but grin at that, but then taps her fingers against her thigh as her thoughts come together. "What if we're being brainwashed?"

"Huh. Well, we've seen it before. It can't work. Even the Regime failed, remember? And they were violent murderers."

"Hear me out."

"Listening."

"It feels like they're shaping our dreams for us. Trying to design our desires and ambitions, molding our personhood into some ideal *they* want to fit us into."

Avik scratches his nose, thinking. "Who's *they*? And why do *they* want to do any of this?"

"I don't know," Kanaka says, her fingers tapping double-time. "Whoever they are . . . they're telling Bhavani that she should dream to be single. And that's a perfectly fine dream for anyone to have, but why can't she access *any other kind*? Bhavani's been crazy about David for years. She *wants* three kids, never mind that she might struggle to support them. We'll help her, right?"

Avik nods. "Duh."

"Exactly. So who's ignoring that dream, doing their best to starve it, refusing to affirm it by never telling her a story in which it unfolds?"

"Babe, I'm with you on a lot of this," Avik says cautiously, "but don't you think this feels very Regime?"

"The Regime was a bit more basic. They'd kill people or lock them up for dissent. This is taking over our minds, trying to change us from the inside out. Whoever this is—they're building a glass ceiling that looks like a blue sky to all our aspirations." Kanaka stands. "Look at me! When have I ever wanted kids?"

"Never."

"That's something we agreed on the minute things started getting serious. I don't have the headspace. I don't have a shred of maternal instinct. Maybe I'm a broken woman, or I've been assembled all wrong." Kanaka paces up and down.

Avik gets up and catches her mid-stride. He hugs her. "You're the most beautiful, complete woman I know," he says.

"I know this on good days. I *feel* it on good days. I love being me because it's right, it fits like a glove, it feels like a shape of my own that I can fill up and empty out depending on what *I* want to do." Kanaka's voice catches and she gulps down a few deep breaths to stave off tears of frustration. "But what if that's the point? What if they're waiting for the bad days to tell me I'm incomplete? Is there a perfect shape for this 'being a woman' thing that they're trying to craft for me? Are they trying to rebuild me to fit into it?"

She knows she's losing it. She's being somewhat paranoid. She can't help herself. There's no mention of shows like *Single Success Superstar* on social media; her Ticker feed's all abuzz with some new show called *Girl. Woman. Mother.* Bhavani's feed is different each time she asks to see it: *One Life, One Career* and *Warrior Woman: Startup Edition* are currently trending.

Kanaka firmly suspects that someone is curating and personalizing her social media experiences, building vast chambers that reverberate with the thoughts they want to feed her until she starts thinking them herself.

Her smarttech beeps while she's in combat training.

New Diet Available!

Switch from Fitness Freak to Fertility Max?

Her wind mage avatar is wiped out by a fireball as she fumes over it. Her *Realm Conquerors* teammate snaps at her over the mic. "Get your head in the game, Keyk01!"

She apologizes, the training game winds down, and the team sit together on their smarttabs to debrief before completing their visa paperwork. The *Realm Conquerors* World Championship begins in Sweden in a month and a half. Kanaka hits Submit, and then sees medical tourism ads radiating outward from her smarttab. *IVF! Sex Therapy! Maternity Finishing School: How to be a hot, confident new mother!* they scream. *Silicon Valley Summer Camp: Teach your preschooler to code like a pro!* She thinks she's going to be sick.

Newsletters pop into her email, with subject lines that proclaim *Motherhood: There's No Glow Like It!* and ask *What's Your Parenting Style?* She used to subscribe to glossy mags to stay on top of celebrity gossip; when did everything they say to her change?

If Avik finds her new obsession worrying, he doesn't say it out loud. Instead, he's as supportive as ever, massaging her feet each day after combat training for the world championship.

She doesn't know how her sister finds out what's going on, but Maithreyi calls every night for three days straight, until Kanaka runs out of plausible excuses to ignore her.

"I hear you're losing your mind," Maithreyi snaps into the phone.

"Who says?" Kanaka snaps back.

"Sources."

Kanaka hisses. Bhavani must have spilled the beans.

"I'm coming over," Maithreyi says. "Tomorrow."

The next day, her sister sips on an enormous cup of coffee. Kanaka kneels before her nibling, who gazes into her eyes in awe. She's strapping all her spare VR gear on them—anything that fits a five-year-old. She turns her console on and leads them to it, and they bounce up and down on the tactile mat in glee. Kanaka pops on a new episode of *Treasure Planet*, and leaves Aasif to explore the quest sim. The game's popular with kids all over the world. At least, with kids from all over the world who exist in the echo chamber she seems to be trapped in.

"Typical," Maithreyi smirks. "Distract the kid with VR."

"She's Aasif's favorite aunt," Imran says, trying to broker peace.

"She's Aasif's *only* aunt." Maithreyi rolls her eyes.

"Good thing I'm never having kids, right?" Kanaka smiles, trying to break the tension. Her perfect sister really gets under her skin these days.

Maithreyi's eyebrows climb halfway up her forehead. "*Still?*" Her voice rises.

Kanaka sighs and buries her face in her hands. It's dramatic. It feels necessary.

"Mai Tai . . ." Imran cautions. Kanaka raises her head and shoots her brother-in-law a grateful nod.

Kanaka's sister scowls. "I'm not saying they need to be biological parents—though that's possible, too. It would be perfectly nice if they adopted a baby . . ."

Kanaka groans. "You're beginning to sound like our mother."

Avik maintains a vacant, if perfectly polite smile plastered across his face as Maithreyi rounds on him. "I know Kanaka's hopeless, but you're so sensible! Civilize my sister and make an honest woman of her."

"Oh, gross!" Kanaka says.

"Don't put him on the spot," Imran laughs.

"They've been married, what, three years now? I think it's time for the next step," Maithreyi pronounces.

Another side effect of womanhood: babies and being married seem to go hand in hand, just like all the makeup you never ask for but happen to buy when all you're looking for is moisturizer at the store.

Kanaka decides to introduce her conversation ender of choice. "I've got a big tournament coming soon. I just don't have the time; you know how my training regime goes. Speaking of which . . ." She hopes they'll catch the hint and leave.

"Always the same excuse." Maithreyi settles deeper into the cushions. "Your career can't get in the way of your real life. You can't put things on hold until—"

A howl of pain cuts her off. Aasif's taken a tumble, and now lies on the VR mat clutching their knee, sobbing.

"Oh, baby." Maithreyi rushes to fuss over the child, drawing them close and rocking them back and forth while they yowl. She picks up her crying child and sits beside Kanaka, shoulder covered in snot, her hair in sudden disarray. "One day, you'll regret devoting your life to VR sports, Keyks. At least promise me you'll try to be a proper adult—a proper woman."

Kanaka feels her ears turn hot, counts to ten in her head, then decides she's just about had enough. She opens her mouth to start yelling at her sister when Avik intervenes. "Mai-Tai, I was hoping you could help."

"*You told her?*" Kanaka hisses instead. Her insides sting with betrayal.

"I'm sorry. I couldn't get through to you. I thought . . ." Avik throws his hands in the air. "Sisters and all that."

"I really do care about your sanity, you know," Maithreyi sighs. "Never mind that I think you've been progressively desexed or degendered by whatever bro-filled pro-gamer world you inhabit. What's going on?"

Kanaka tamps down her anger at being called desexed and degendered, and launches into an explanation instead. When she's finally done, Maithreyi tilts her head to one side. "I can see why you didn't tell me."

"Why's that?" Kanaka scowls, instantly defensive.

"Because I'm going to ask you hard questions," Maithreyi says. "Say you're right about everything—this is one giant conspiracy to control not just women, but people everywhere. Say you have undeniable proof. What will you do with it?"

"What do you mean?" Kanaka asks.

"What will you do?"

Kanaka is struck silent.

"You're not a hero in this video game, Keyks. You can't save the world with this kind of information."

Kanaka worries at her lower lip. "Don't people deserve to know?"

"To what end?" Maithreyi asks.

"So they have the truth. So they can choose," Kanaka says.

"You've made your own choices, haven't you?" Maithreyi says, challenging her. "We grew up under the Regime, for fuck's sake. And yet, you chose to be you. You continue to be you. Why is this so important to you?"

Kanaka struggles to find an answer. She obsesses over it through combat training the next day; her *Realm Conquerors* teammates remain annoyed by her lack of focus.

She remembers her great-aunt's words on her wedding day.

She recalls being called a tomboy in school, never mind that half the world was woke by then. She was bullied for turning up to a dance in trousers and a waistcoat, complete with a tie. Nikhil once rescued her from being taunted for her short hair at after-school tuitions; that's how they wound up friends.

She relives those years under the Regime, growing up watching women being idealized as wives and sisters, and most important of all, as *mothers*. They only ever counted relative to their caregiving relationships. Never as whole people.

She recollects her sister's words—*you're desexed, degendered*. Is it such a bad thing to try and define her womanhood by building herself into her own person?

Her smarttech beeps while she's out on a run in the park simulator. She taps on the notification. It's from her sister.

Met Imran's ex-colleagues at CyberSafe. Found you a lead re: your new obsession. Don't get lost down the rabbit hole.

It's followed by an encrypted contact. Kanaka slams her palm down and stops the treadmill, stepping off it. She pants, catching her breath, reading the text over and over.

She dials the contact. It's cut after two rings, and a text pops up immediately.

Meet at the Gratitude Diorama. 10:00 a.m. tomorrow.

Kanaka feels triumph and dread clawing up the back of her throat.

THE TENT IS A HAZE OF PIXEL DUST AGAINST RESPLENDENT SILKS. KANAKA GLANCES around nervously for someone who could be her contact. Avik hovers a few feet away, and Kanaka nearly laughs at the thought that his tall, lanky frame is all she has for muscle. What if this is a government employee? What if she gets arrested for asking questions?

This isn't the Regime. It's Free India. She takes a deep breath to try and still the anxiety. It doesn't work. Someone appears at her shoulder and her pulse quickens. His beard is neatly trimmed, and he wears overlarge glasses.

"Switch off your smarttech. Don't turn around."

She glances to her left, making sure Avik's eyes are on her, then follows the stranger's instructions.

"I just work in one of their server rooms," the man says.

"Who are they?" Kanaka hisses.

He ignores her question. "I'm slipping information into your handbag. Do you have an old laptop? A 2020s model is safe. Never contact me again."

And the man is gone.

It takes Kanaka and Avik two days to salvage her old Lenovo laptop—back from the days when laptops were still considered sophisticated. It finally boots.

Kanaka opens her handbag and retrieves the pen drive, hands trembling. Avik steps back, away from the dated tech. "This is your quest," he says. "I think you should do this alone. I'll be right outside if you need me."

Kanaka nods. He slips out and shuts the door. She is ensconced in silence, broken only by her heartbeat pounding in her ears. She downloads the files from the pen drive, the minutes ticking by, sweat beading on her nose, dripping off it. She hopes this isn't pornography from some perv.

She drums her fingers on the hard keyboard. She taps her feet on the floor. She'd forgotten how slow tech used to be. And then, the file transfer is complete. She doesn't want to waste a second, and yet, she doesn't know what she's rushing into. Fear stills her in the ultraviolet gaze of her laptop screen.

She takes a calming breath. *I have to know.*

She opens the file. It's thousands of lines long, written in Penta-5, a public programming language that first opened the world of code to lay-people like her. She scrolls.

Free India's grand machinations to build utopia spans decades. They've only just begun.

Everyone's in on it—corporations, entertainment studios, the press, big tech companies—it's a giant handshake of policy and programming that's building a world by deleting or reshaping everyone who doesn't fit into its schematic. It's silent, still, insidious, creeping beneath banners her-alding unity, equality, liberty, and love.

Bhavani isn't permitted to get married, to have children, because Free India's version of eradicating poverty translates to eradicating poor people. At this phase in their plan, it's by denying the underprivileged legal rights to procreate, and convincing them to believe their lives are better off with-out children.

Maithreyi is permitted to be a mother because she and Imran are wealthy, their genes are free from autoimmune diseases, and they have no history of mental illness. She can tell that she and Avik are being encour-aged to have kids for all the same reasons. The number of marriage licenses handed out to people who don't check all the boxes has dwindled.

She feels sick to her stomach when she watches videos of meetings, especially when a prominent politician says, "Let the gays wait a sufficient time period—say two to three years—before granting them an adoption, so they can prove they really want it," and she can't watch any more, except she forces herself to carry on.

Ben and Nikhil are going to have to jump through bureaucratic hoops, walk through fire, prove themselves over and over again because they don't conform to some historically normative notion of parenthood figures. How on earth is she going to tell them?

She uncovers directives spanning entertainment, from HoloWorld to FlatScreen, across social media, books, and music—a list of if-then clauses controlling experiences of reality and experiences of fantasy, feeding ideals to people on the basis of the cohorts they belong to, algorithms drafting vision boards personalized to their socioeconomic statuses and biological sexes. It is everything she feared, made worse because it's real.

She comes across a file that's titled "Manifesto to Develop Proper Women."

The document outlines the shape of womanhood. It features a set of directives that are being implemented already in the contours of dreams, ambitions, and stories being fed to her, to women everywhere, all around her.

This is not just another side effect of being a woman. It's a badly fitted dress without pockets, and she—and millions of other women—are being forced into its ties and zippers, their shapes stitched and sculpted by a patriarchal-capitalist-power-sponsored algorithm.

We don't even get to choose whether it's patterned or ruffled, hand-embroidered or graphic-printed, woven from soft silk or homespun.

Scratch that. What if she'd rather wear ripped jeans and a leather jacket instead?

Kanaka laughs out loud until she's hoarse and tears stream down her face. This is the Regime all over again, except with a brand-new set of weapons. Women—like and unlike her—will be encouraged to run toward dreams they believe are of their own choosing, but like butterflies on a moving train, their momentum is cocooned, their trajectory controlled, encapsulated and swallowed whole by the relentless march of the machine. Shrunk, wrapped, augmented, reframed—proper women, all.

A low, tuneful voice reaches her ears. Bhavani's bustling around outside her study, and singing her favorite folk song about children, again. Doesn't Bhavani deserve to know? Don't all women—doesn't all humanity, really, need to know this?

Kanaka slumps forward, holding her head in her hands. She has to put it out there online, somewhere. She has to tell the world. She could be arrested, but wouldn't it be worth it to free people from their own minds— scratch that—their minds as this conglomerate glutted on power would like to shape them? And yet, would it be less cruel to let them carry on as they are, to let them aspire to conform, let them fail, let them be made to feel less than as this government-billionaire-tech bro-nexus dictates the shape of their lives?

What do I do?

She has no answers. She holds all the answers. She's no savior. She's just a woman, and not even a proper woman at that, whatever the fuck that means.

Rephrase. She knows exactly what a proper woman is supposed to be according to the manifesto on the screen before her.

She cannot let this—whatever this is—play out. She doesn't know if she can stop it from happening. She doesn't know where to begin, but she suspects she's already begun, and it's unlikely she'll ever reach the end, if there is an end at all.

Kanaka exhales. All she knows is she holds the shape of the future in her hands.

5 WHAT ABOUT PRIVACY?

Chris Gilliard interviewed by Tim Maughan

ASK CHRIS GILLIARD ABOUT GROWING UP IN DETROIT AND HE'LL TELL YOU ABOUT the two things that shaped what he calls his *origin story*. The first is the impact of Detroit techno, the underground music genre that exploded out of illegal parties in the city's abandoned warehouses and automotive factories, crossed the Atlantic to Europe, gave birth to rave culture, and transformed popular music across the globe.

The second is STRESS—or Stop The Robberies Enjoy Safe Streets—the controversial Detroit Police vice unit that operated in the city from 1971 to 1974. In those few short years, the unit was responsible for the killing of twenty-four people, twenty-two of whom were African American men. They were all fatally shot by STRESS officers after being lured—alongside hundreds of others who were arrested—into allegedly mugging decoy operatives. Although the unit was shut down while Gilliard was still young, its outstanding legacy is the fear and trauma it forced onto a whole generation of Black Detroiters. "If you look at it," he tells me, "there's a lot of parallels between the surveillance they were running, and a lot of the surveillance we see of Black communities now, complete with violence and murder."

Fast forward to now and Gilliard is one of the United States's leading researchers and commentators on surveillance technology and its impact on marginalized communities. A visiting research fellow at the Harvard Kennedy School Shorenstein Center working on privacy and surveillance, he has testified before the House Financial Services Committee about how big data and algorithms in banking can reinforce historical discrimination, helped popularize the term *digital redlining*, and become known as one of facial recognition's most ardent critics. His work explores the increasingly blurred line between police surveillance and the digital data harvesting that has become the business model of Silicon Valley corporations, and it highlights where the two often directly merge and facilitate each other.

For full disclosure: I've known Chris for several years, both professionally and personally, and consider him a friend. In early June 2022, we sat down and chatted about his work for a few hours over a Zoom call between Detroit and Ottawa. What follows here is a heavily edited transcript of that sprawling conversation.

TM: One thing I'd like you to talk about is how you're very careful about how your identity is presented online and in print, especially around how your face is used and if images of you are used at all. Can you talk a little bit more about that? I often think that if I was starting out now, if I was starting online again, it'd be something I think I'd be tempted to do, but I don't know if you even can now . . .

CG: It's really hard, and I mean, I have a degree of privilege that lets me, for the most part, say, "Hey, I don't want this." So there's a couple reasons I try and keep that control. One is that there's a really close alliance between many of the facial recognition companies and the far right or authoritarianism. I mean, ultimately, I think facial recognition is at its roots a white supremacist project. So to the extent that I cannot participate in that, I choose not to. Again, I mean, there are pictures of me on the internet, but I didn't put them there, and I don't have the ability to remove them.

I have a running joke that every innovation that tech companies have given us in the past fifteen years has basically been like "put a camera on it or add more cameras." And everyone having an HD camera in their pocket has changed society, I think. For a lot of ways, it's changed it for the worse, and there are expectations that people want their images about and proliferated, or that people don't have the right to say no to that. I think the long tail of a society where everything's always photographed and videoed is very harmful. I think it's harmful to everyone, but it's harmful to marginalized and minoritized communities most of all, and first of all. Whether that's the NYPD spying on Muslims practicing their faith or Ring doorbells watching delivery workers or homeowners associations having cameras at the gates of their neighborhood.

And so, to the extent that I cannot participate in that system, I don't; it's sort of a conscientious objection, right? And I want to model a different kind of practice. The pandemic really normalized the belief that people have the right to see into your house, right? Whether that's your employer, your professor, a social worker, whoever it is, right? It really normalized that in ways that had been not as expected up till now. I mean, even that site, or that Twitter account, or whatever it was that sprung up looking at people's bookshelves when they did Zoom meetings or Zoom interviews and things like that, or rating people's outfits, it's trash, right?

TM: [*laughs*] It is, yeah.

CG: I mean, so many problems with it and people just accepted it and embraced it, right?

TM: Yeah. I mean even if you somehow ignore the privacy aspect—can we just not normalize being this judgy of people?

CG: Right? And then that people feel they have to sort of curate themselves, "well, people are going to judge the books on my shelf" or "I don't have a ring light, and so my lighting isn't proper when I'm doing it." There's just so many problems with it. From the aesthetics to the privacy to the . . . Again, just the expectation and all that goes with it, that people I didn't invite into my home have some right, not only to be there, but to make assertions about who else is there or what else is there.

TM: You said something there about facial recognition; you described that as a white supremacist project. Explain that a bit for me.

CG: I absolutely believe that. There's a long history of phrenology and physiognomy that ties in with how people understand facial recognition. Because often the project of facial recognition isn't just determining identity. It's determining what a face is, right? Is this a human being? Further, what is the character of this human being? What is the gender of this human being? Is this person gay? Are they dishonest? Are they potentially a criminal? And all those things have a really long history and that history is bluntly racist.

83

I mean, here in Detroit, we had two of the best-known cases of mistaken identity with facial recognition. And in both cases men were arrested and detained mainly on the claim by a machine that they were the individuals who had done something illegal. And what I find with a lot of these systems is, what they're really up to is giving people, giving powerful institutions—already racist and violent carceral institutions—the license and the permission to do stuff that they'd want to do anyway.

And so, it's not accurate to think about these systems as just trying to confirm an identity. Because I think what they're really for is reinforcing power, right? So in the case of one of those men, Robert Williams, the police said, "Oh, this is you stealing this watch." And the guy says, "No, that's not me." And the law enforcement officer was like, "Well, oh yeah. So you're telling me the computer is wrong." And this is so telling, right? Because it's there to lend an air of certainty to a thing about which there can't be any certainty, right?

TM: Right.

CG: And of course, it turns out the computer was absolutely fucking wrong. But the purpose of that system is to do what the police want to do anyway, right? And so, again, in that regard, I think of it as a function of white supremacy.

TM: So your answer to this, your kind of take on facial recognition is just ban it, right? Is just to outlaw all this stuff?

CG: Yeah. I don't think it should exist. I mean, so, first off, the reports of its usefulness in catching criminals—from the accounts that I have read, and I've read many—seem to be greatly overstated. However, the effect on a society . . . I think the harmful effects on a society are widespread because of what it does. If you want to have a free society, a necessary component of that is that people should be able to freely move about without being targeted and identified. And so that means if I'm going to church or if I'm going to the doctor or if I'm going to meet a friend or if I'm going to get ice cream, all of those things are of interest to other people and groups, right? What am I going to the doctor for? Why am

I eating fattening food? Which church am I going to? Am I a Muslim? All these things are of interest to outside parties. Many of whom are going to use this information against me. None of these things I mentioned are illegal or shouldn't be conducted in a free society, right? But when you give the ability to track people in that way, you open up all manner of forms of targeting, tracing, harassment, violence. I mean, there's no clearer example we see coming down the tracks than the rolling back of *Roe v. Wade*, right? For weeks and weeks now, we've been seeing all these articles about the data from period trackers or the data that someone could get from an automated license plate reader or from geofence warrants or all the data that is available on people that could incriminate them against something that might only now have become illegal.

Of course, that goes beyond facial recognition; it goes into a lot of other surveillance practices and forms of biometric surveillance. I think facial recognition is the worst, but I also think these other ones should be banned too, because they remove an element that I think is foundational for a free society. Because we've seen that law enforcement can't be trusted with this information, right? Private companies certainly cannot, right? I mean the defense is—it's a common refrain: "Well, we use it to find kidnapped children" and . . .

TM: "Look, it was used to identify these dead soldiers in Ukraine . . ."

CG: Right. Don't get me started on that. But even if you're of the mind that there are these edge cases, or extreme cases, for which these things should be rolled out, these institutions have proven time and time again that they can't be trusted with this power, right? And so, they're not just going to use it to find missing children. They're going to use it to surveil protesters. They're going to use it to surveil Muslims who are going to worship. They're going to do these things— and this is not speculation, these are absolutely things that have happened and continue to happen.

So we know that there are all kinds of pernicious ways that they use the data they have about people, right? Whether it's ad targeting for someone who just recently lost their child or selling this information to law enforcement or using it to create systems that do other horrible things. Whether that's wartime applications or something else. And so, even if I were of the mind that there are these useful articulations of it—I'm not, but even if I were—these institutions cannot be trusted.

TM: To get back more directly to your work. One of the things you're most associated with is coining the term *digital redlining*. [Historically, *redlining* is a practice dating back to the 1930s that gets its name from how the federal government, banks, and lenders would literally draw a red line on a map around "financially hazardous" neighborhoods they were refusing to invest in based on demographics alone. Black inner-city neighborhoods were the most likely to be redlined.] Could you just give us a quick explanation of that?

CG: I live in a city where the implications of a redlining policy are still crystal clear. If you go down Eight Mile, if you go down Mack Avenue, and look at Detroit on one side and Grosse Pointe on the other, or Detroit on one side and Ferndale on the other. When I think about redlining, there's some important things to note: that it was a government-sponsored policy, and that it was by design. And that it specifically disenfranchised people who were Black. And by doing that, it left them out of one of the primary, if not the primary, mechanisms for building wealth in this country. Which is home ownership.

Flash forward to today, to the number of ways in which internet access is strongly connected to, correlated with health outcomes, educational outcomes. And again, even more so during the pandemic. These choices that either cities make, municipalities make, or that companies make, often are doing some of the same things in terms of disenfranchising people.

And again, it might be something like you didn't see a job ad because you're Black, or because you're over fifty. It might be there's no broadband in your area, so you can't do telehealth appointments, which affects your physical and/or mental well-being. There are so many ways in which these decisions made about access—and they often are conscious decisions—affect access to opportunities and services, and quality of life.

I used to pull up these maps—one would be Amazon same-day delivery and another would be Uber access and another would be the deployment of stingray surveillance devices in an area. You can take that map and overlay it over the conventional, historical redlining map of that city, and it's unerring in the ways that they show the same things, in how they line up. You could also do it with, say, a map of where the incinerators are in the city, or where are the landfills in an area. What area has more trees? What area is covered in concrete?

There are a lot of people who don't recognize the extent to which historical racist policy still plays out today. Even the infrastructure for a lot of the systems we use, it's laid on top of old infrastructure. In lots of ways, it just reproduces the practices of fifty, sixty years ago.

TM: That's definitely true of broadband especially; it's just reupping those cables. And if the cables weren't going to the right places in the first place, then you've not changed anything.

CG: Exactly.

TM: I'm always conscious that I live in a bubble about this stuff. That I live in a news bubble, that there are filters on what I see and people I talk to. I talk to a lot of people like you, for example. And there's this feeling that people have had enough of Facebook, that they're getting off Facebook now. Do you think that's true? Do you think people are more aware of this stuff than they used to be?

CG: I think they're more aware. The parallel I always make is to the 2008 crash. Which is, in 2007, did I know what a collateralized debt obligation was? No, I fucking did not. And I didn't think I needed to. But a lot of people learned really quick what some of those things were.

And I think with tech, we've seen a lot of what I and other people have called "fuck the algorithm" moments in the last several years. Where it becomes crystal clear that there are these systems making decisions about people's lives, that they don't have any insight into or control over, any input other than passive. Whether that's the grade someone gets, the job someone gets, or whether or not your kids are taken away from you by the state.

We've seen a lot of high-profile moments in the US and the UK, around the world, where people have come out against this. And so I think more and more people are starting to recognize that, as much as it's available, they do need to be more informed about this. There is a lot more awareness of the ways that something like Facebook is actually terrible for democracy. If you had made that claim—as people were, we were making that claim five or ten years ago—people were kind of like, "Yeah, I guess." And if you make that claim now, even not in our circles, I think people are a lot more open to that.

TM: You think because of everything from 2016 onward, because of Trump, and then . . . ?

CG: I think January 6.

TM: Yeah.

CG: But also, for people who pay attention to events worldwide, Facebook's been implicated in amplifying or having a hand in genocide. That in many authoritarian countries, it's a favorite tool of those in power. Many times [Facebook] just decided to ignore when they're doing harm, even when their own researchers come to them and say, "Hey, this thing that you're doing is harmful." And they've ignored that, either to avoid looking bad, or to maximize profit and engagement.

I had this really interesting conversation. I did a guest lecture with a bunch of law students at Georgetown. One of the things I've started to do is to point out that while I think it's true that surveillance mechanisms are first and foremost most harmful to marginalized communities, it's also true that they're bad for society as a whole. I think that you have to let people know that. We've all seen or heard someone, it's usually someone we disagree with or we think is not very perceptive, but someone says something to the extent of, "Well, I didn't realize how misogynistic society was until I had a daughter." Or like, "I didn't realize how transphobic society was until my kid came out as trans."

We live in a society where people need that. There are a lot of people who need that extra part where I say, "This is bad for Black folks, and it's also bad for you." Because to say that these things harm a particular demographic often doesn't move the needle for people.

The reason I bring up the Georgetown students is a couple of the students were like, "Well, you're undercutting your argument to talk about how it is bad for everyone." And I thought that was really interesting. And I was like, "No, no." This way of coming about it is well earned, right? Because if we could just say, "This is bad for Black people," and it would move the needle, we'd live in a very different society. If we could just say, "This is bad for women," or "This is bad for trans people," or "This is bad for the unhoused"—if we could just say that, and that would change policy or the way people think about it, society would be very different. But we can't. We know that. I'd love to live in that society, but I do not, and so I also have to point out here's the way that this thing is also pernicious and harmful to you or to your family or whatever it is.

TM: This ties in a lot as well with consumerism, which brings me to this term you've been using: *luxury surveillance*. Can you talk to us a little bit about that, explain that a little bit?

CG: It stems right from what I was talking about. There are some differences, but at their root, I basically see an ankle monitor and a Fitbit as very similar devices. They're different in who chooses to wear them and who has them deployed against them. And the joke is: How are an Apple Watch and an ankle monitor different? And the punchline is, one of them collects way more fucking data.

TM: [*laughing*] Yeah.

CG: I think that there's a way in which the luxury items help to normalize—the luxury surveillance helps normalize the impulse for surveillance.

TM: And more than just normalize, it kind of glamorizes it and makes it aspirational?

CG: Exactly. There's obviously some difference in the aesthetics and the power dynamics and things like that. They are not the same. Your Fitbit is not an ankle monitor. For lots of reasons. But in terms of a perceptual framework, it can be useful to think about them that way. Same with a smart city and Project Green Light [Detroit's controversial public-private surveillance camera network program]. Many of these things, they are illustrations or exercises of surveillance and thus control.

But often, wealthy or privileged people are not accustomed to thinking about them that way. And so their threat model, for lack of a better term, or even their understanding of what ways in which that device is exercising power over them, often could use a clearer understanding.

I used to make the comparison all the time, and I didn't really think anything of it. I made it enough times and people were like, "Oh." And so, it's one of those cases where I was just like, "This is really obvious, right?" They are in many ways the same. And a lot of people were like, "Oh, I had never thought about it that way." And so that's when I tried to start expanding that.

TM: You mentioned it previously, you were quite associated with critiquing the Amazon Ring doorbell as a device, and this aspirational side to these kinds of consumer products is the bit that really gets me. Y'know, as someone that writes dystopian fiction for a living, the idea that we are not just engaging in this kind of surveillance but are also celebrating it and seeing it as a sign of status.

CG: It's weird sometimes; things are never cut-and-dried. I got contacted once by someone because the leader of their homeowners association wanted to install ALPR [automated license plate recognition] cameras in the area. And this person and other homeowners didn't want them. I've seen instances where homeowners associations say you can't have a Ring doorbell on your porch, because it indicates that you think that it's a place where there is crime. There are all these sort of weird class workings when talking and thinking about this stuff too, that I think are really unexamined often by the people who use them or buy them. I'm very pessimistic, right? But if there's any chance to get people to think about them differently, I think that talking about them in that way is a way to do that.

TM: This interview's going to be in a collection with science fiction short stories as well. I know that you are a science fiction fan. What are your thoughts on science fiction and surveillance, even as a tool for talking about it? Is it something that shaped your approach to looking at this stuff?

CG: A lot of this comes out of comic books. That is literally how I learned to read. I grew up reading a lot of Octavia E. Butler or Kurt Vonnegut. Another person I think about a lot when I think about a lot of this stuff is Walter Mosley. Who's often not thought about in that sense, but some of his science fiction is to me top-notch.

I think it's interesting that so many of these things have essentially been predicted. And that basically those predictions have been ignored, or the people who claim to also be fans of science fiction do not understand what the stories are about.

I read something, and it was in the *Times*, I forget the guy's name, but he was one of the very early people in the field of facial recognition. And he said, "I had no idea it would be used this way."

And I thought, "Well, dude, what have you been fucking doing?" Honestly. In order to be able to say that, and if that's true, that means you were paying attention to nothing but your own work.

TM: That "if you can do it, you should do it" kind of approach is fucking terrifying.

CG: I don't think I possess any particular special knowledge, but there's a lot of things I could tell you before you even start work. The CEO of Zoom is like, "I didn't know it would be used for Zoom bombing and harassment." And it's like, "Dude, have you ever used the internet?"

One of my most jarring examples is when Google let people tag and review places that were named on Maps. And so, former concentration camps are listed on Google Maps. And so Nazis and trolls were reviewing them and giving them five stars. And the people at Google were like, "Well, we didn't know that would happen." And I'm like, "Well, how do you work at Google? Do you know what you do? Have you used the internet?"

I'm faced with only a couple of choices. Maybe they're telling the truth, which means they're clueless and need to stop doing what they're doing and just read other people who aren't them. Or they're lying. That's also possible. There are a lot of times when I talk to people, or companies talk about some of this stuff, and they say, "Well, we couldn't have anticipated X or Y harm."

Occasionally that is true. But if you have a conversation with the communities that these systems are going to be used on . . . There are experts in all these, so there's anthropologists and sociologists, right? There's people who do this stuff who could very easily tell you, "Oh, these are ways that this is going to be weaponized." And yet somehow, so many of these things get off the ground anyway.

88

TM: I remember when Trump got in there was a certain part of the science fiction community who were very vocal on Twitter, saying, "Right, no more dystopias, we don't need you to write any more dystopias. We live in the dystopia now, no need for any more dystopias, we just need positive stories now," and I was like, "Really? What you're going to do now—of all times—is to stop listening to people who spent the last forty years telling you this was going to happen?"

CG: Yeah. Whenever I make a joke or talk about how dystopian this tech could get, someone always says, "Well, don't give them any ideas." And I think— well, the way I explained it to someone yesterday is like, "I only practice being a terrible person, I'm not actually paid for it." I can't give them any ideas that they're not already sitting in a room cooking up, right? Because there are people who are terrible people, who get paid lots of money to think of this shit and they're constantly doing it. Whatever fucking horrible thing I think of, it's probably already in the water.

6 THE EXCOMMUNICATES

Ken MacLeod

WE'RE PAST THE WATERSHED NOW, AND ON THE DOWN GRADIENT TO THE WEST. Helen slips the van into fourth gear and eases off the accelerator. The needle's at mid-tank. There's one pump between here and the coast, but whether it still works or has fuel in it is anyone's guess. I have the map across my knees, the carbine beneath it, and the binoculars bumping on my chest.

"There's an old quarry three hundred meters past the next bend," I say. "Best be ready to stamp on the brake or step on the gas, depending."

"Got it."

The windows on both sides are cranked down halfway, and the breeze comes in, heavy with a hot Highland summer day after a week of rain. The glass is retrofitted, supposedly bulletproof, but . . .

As we swing around the curve of the hill, I bring up the binoculars. Hard to keep them steady, and the swoop is disorienting enough to make me nauseous, but as we approach the junction to the rutted works road leading to the great gash in the hillside, nothing seems amiss. I lower the glasses and eyeball a sweep. Heather, moss, sheep, boulders, all the way to the skyline.

"Fast," I say.

We hurtle past the quarry mouth at 60 km/h, then slow for a long stretch of climb. Down to our left, a burn in spate gushes along the bottom of the glen, amid big wet rocks.

I look down again at the map. A row of houses speckle the roadside, two kilometers farther on, and behind and around them an irregular patch of green checkered with chevrons: coniferous woodland.

"Settlement up ahead over the hill," I say "Patch of fir."

"Ready to stamp or step," Helen says.

I move my hand to the carbine's stock. We've drilled the move, from both seats: driver ducks, brakes; passenger brings rifle to bear; one shot, warning or otherwise; driver straightens up, hits the gas, and cranks up the window as we speed away. After much practice we have the maneuver down smooth—it's as awkward as it sounds—but basically we just hope we never have to use it.

MY FATHER SAT BETWEEN ME AND MY SISTER AND LOOKED THE SCHOOL SECRETARY in the eye.

"My family and I," he said, "are members of the Church of the Book."

The keyboard rattled. A pair of eyebrows and reading glasses loomed above the screen.

"I can't find any reference to it," Ms. Eaton said.

"Of course not!" Dad agreed. "That's the point." He leaned forward, and added in a helpful tone: "We've been called various names: the Sect of the Text, the Paper Presbytery, the Caxton Congregation . . ."

More keyboard rattling. "Nothing on any of them."

"Our West African mission has been referred to as Boko Halal."

This was pushing it. Even I could see this was pushing it. The eyebrows lowered, and drew together. Ms. Eaton leaned sideways and looked around the screen. Her lips formed a thin line.

"*Mister* Rawlins—are you being entirely serious?"

Only policy and politeness were stopping her from saying what I could hear in her voice: *Are you taking the piss?*

"Serious and sincere," my father said. "And our religious convictions have a right to respect, under—"

"Thank you, Mr. Rawlins; I'm well aware of the relevant legislation. All right—what are these convictions, and how do they affect your children's schooling?"

"The Word of God," my father said, "was given to us in writing: on stone, on leaves, on parchment, on papyrus, on paper. It was not sent by email, or found on a website. We are made in his image, and enjoined to follow his example. Our Church therefore eschews electronic communication."

"I see." Ms. Eaton sighed. "So you don't use computers?"

"Oh, we do use computers! We're not superstitious, you know. We just don't use the internet. For anything. No email, no web browsing, no smartphones."

"No e-books?"

He shook his head. "Paper and print only, I'm afraid."

"So they'll need physical copies of all their textbooks?"

"Yes."

"That's inconvenient. And expensive."

"I know. I'm sorry about that, but . . ."

"You're aware that some homework assignments have to be handed in electronically?"

"Of course," Dad said. "Liam and Melanie here can write their assignments on their own computers, and bring the files in on USB sticks."

"What difference does . . . ? Oh, I see." She leaned around the screen again and gave my father a severe look, which softened as her gaze passed to us. "I understand what this is about."

"Thank you."

The keyboard rattled again. "Well, Mr. Rawlins, we're required to accommodate these requirements. But we're not obliged to cover all the additional expenses. Your contribution would have to be about . . . four hundred pounds a year."

To me and to Melanie, this seemed an enormous sum. Looking back, it probably did to our father too. He reached into an inside jacket pocket. "I'll write you a check."

Ms. Rawlins looked at the strip of paper.

"Oh!" she said. "It's like prizes. And fund-raising."

"Exactly," Dad said. "Just like on the television."

She held the check up to the light, and turned it this way and that. "They're bigger on television."

On the way home, Melanie looked up and said, "Daddy, what's the Word of God?"

"Books some people read at weekends," he replied.

It was the first truthful word he'd spoken on the subject.

OVER THE CREST OF THE HILL, AND ON TO A LONGER DOWNWARD SLOPE. AGAIN with the binoculars. No smoke rises. The houses are intact, the windows unbroken, but no washing hangs on the lines and no dogs bark. I lower the glasses, and scan the woodland around the settlement. The scent from the trees blasts in. The sun is high and everything under and between the conifers is in deep shadow.

"Step on it," I say. As we pass the houses, I catch a glimpse of something bright in the sunlight disappearing around the corner of the last building: the dress of a toddler being snatched back to hiding, I guess. Still people there, but lying low. No doubt they can hear us coming from a kilometer away.

I'm just processing that glimpse when I catch another, down in the glen to our left. There's a moment of the sheer unreality of seeing a fighter jet from above, and silent as it flashes past. In the side mirror, I see it vanish over the hill as the sonic boom rocks us and the engine scream catches up.

"RAF Typhoon," Helen says.

"Well spotted," I say. My heart is thumping but with surprise, not fear. It's not jets we have to worry about. I look down at the map, and seek the tiny cross that marks our first possible destination.

"Five kilometers to the nearest church," I say.

"Pray it's an old one," Helen says.

"Why?"

"Stone. Not some tin tabernacle."

My laugh dies around the next bend as we see up ahead on the right a mess on the other side of the ditch, a mess that looks like a dead sheep until we see that what the crows are pecking among is a bloodied white shirt, not wool. We can't help but slow down and look, sickening though the sight is. There's nothing we can do for him or her now. In an out-flung hand, or what's left of it, the black glint of a phone screen.

"Droned," Helen says. "Shit. Poor bugger."

Her knuckles are white on the wheel.

I look up at the clear blue sky, and imagine I see dots. You can't really see them. If I were to lie on the hill for a long time, and the binoculars were more powerful—stargazer standard, maybe—I might just pick out the drone swarm. Solar-powered, tiny, at a few hundred meters up, the infernal machines are known officially as *sacrificial munitions platforms*: aerial mines, sky mines, murder drones, flying robot suicide bombers, call them what you like. They lurk above us by the million, right across the continent and its islands, from the Atlantic to the Dneiper. Someday, sheer wear and tear will bring them down. But long before then, they'll have destroyed every active phone and similar device that the cyberattacks and the electromagnetic pulses didn't get—and with it the phone's user, whether they're reckless or simply unaware of what's happened.

I WAS BAGS, SHORT FOR BAG BOY. MELANIE, SLIGHTLY LUCKIER, GOT LABELED SATCH, for Satchel Girl. It was our first secondary school—we'd moved around a lot, and been in and out of primary schools and what our parents called homeschooling. Melanie was old enough for secondary school, and I was a year older. We'd just arrived in a new town. Dad had landed a steady job at a garden center, and Mum likewise at the local supermarket.

At first, everything went more or less fine. The big boys looked down on me from their great height. My own peers mocked me now and then for lugging books around. Sometimes they asked me about our weird religion, with more curiosity than malice. I made up doctrines and distinctions with the same glib assurance as my father. Cultural references outside my experience—online games, streamed shows—I affected to disdain or faked acquaintance with based on gleanings from review columns in the *Guardian* and the *Daily Mirror*. Ironically, in view of our plight, in our house we were assiduous consumers of mainstream newspapers and the relative handful of TV channels we could access without subscriptions. Melanie and I frequented the local public library to an extent that surprised and gratified the librarians, used as they were to the almost exclusive patronage of small children and retired people.

Melanie and I did well in class, partly because we had no online distractions at home. We had books, board games, and playing outdoors. Phones and tablets were banned in the classroom, which suited us fine. Outside was where the problem arose, soon after I went through puberty and a growth spurt and became a big boy myself, 179 centimeters of gangling awkwardness. Cliques and networks, meetups and conflicts carried on over text messaging and apps were invisible to me. I often felt gossiped about behind my back or frozen out of arrangements. My only extracurricular activity was the Orienteering Club, in which our PE teacher led us across hill and dale, using the aggressively offline navigation tools of the Silva compass, the pencil and ruler, and the Ordnance Survey map.

"You can't rely always on Google Maps," he would say. "Remember that."

I REMEMBER THAT ALL RIGHT, AND OF COURSE IT'S ALL MOOT NOW, BUT YOU CAN'T always rely on Ordnance Survey maps either. The church marked by the tiny cross is a ruin, with tall old trees growing out of it.

"Ha!" says Helen. "So much for Highland devotion!"

I could bore her with the observation that it could well have been Highland devotion that emptied that church in the first place, centuries ago. Catholic, Episcopalian, wrong kind of Presbyterian . . . the old Highlanders were ruthless whenever they underwent a great change in their spiritual allegiance, turning their backs on their ancient places of worship and establishing new ones. Hence (eventually) the tin tabernacles, the corrugated iron sheds with nothing to distinguish them from a byre but the black notice board outside with the times of the Sabbath services and the Wednesday prayer meeting spelled out in gilt.

I decide not to bore her with Highland ecclesiastical history. Instead I look again at the map, and spot another church ten kilometers on, this time one with a spire. It's on the top of a small hill overlooking a freshwater loch, with the nearest houses two hundred meters away.

"I think we'll have better luck with the next one."

"Any reason for thinking that?"

"None at all," I admit. "Just a hunch."

"An irrational conviction, then." Helen laughs. "Sounds appropriate."

Yeah, tell me about irrational convictions.

"HEY, BAGS!"

I turned. It was Claudio, a boy a year older, with whom I had not so much a friendship as a nonaggression pact, based on our shared interest in written science fiction. "Hi, Cloudy."

Claudio fell in with me, in my mooch around the playground. "Got a story for you," he said, passing me a sheaf of paper printed off from the current issue of a science fiction magazine.

"Thanks," I said, folding the pages lengthwise and stuffing them into the inside pocket of my school blazer. "Looks exciting."

"You know the real reason why you can't read it online like everyone else?"

"Sure," I said. "The church doesn't approve—"

"Give over. The real reason."

"Of course I know," I said. "I'm not daft. We're excommunicates. My dad can't get an email address, he can't make online payments, and he can't access anything online. And my mum can't because using her identity would let him get around that, and me and Melanie can't because we aren't old enough to have our own bank accounts. The church thing is—" I shrugged "—just a polite legal fiction so we have some cover at school."

"But why was your dad excommunicated in the first place?"

I shot him a warning glance. "We don't talk about it."

"Why not?"

"You know why, Cloudy."

"Your dad's a denier, that's why."

A chill went through me. "What's he supposed to be denying?"

Claudio laughed. "Everything! Climate science. War crimes. Genocides. All kinds of atrocities."

"And how do you know that?"

He fished out his phone, thumbed it, and showed me the screen. My father's name, and a youthful photograph of him, headed a brief biography that gave his date and place of birth and the date of his exclusion from the online world for spreading dangerous disinformation. The types of disinformation matched Claudio's list.

"I don't believe it," I said. "He's not that kind of person."

"Oh—and how would you know?"

"Know my own dad? Of course I know him. For one thing, he doesn't talk about any of that at home."

"Yeah, yeah," Claudio said. "He wouldn't, would he?"

I had no answer to that. For a moment, I considered telling Claudio where he could stick his science fiction story if he was going to insult my father like that, but thought better of it. With so few friends, or at least boys willing to be friendly, I couldn't afford to fall out with him.

"I'll ask him about it," I said.

Of course, I did nothing of the sort. On the way home from school I dropped in at the public library. The librarian on the desk was one I had often noticed and eyed covertly. I'd had crushes, obviously, as kids do, but she was my first experience of hopeless, unrequited lust. She was probably ten years older than me and had neat blond hair like some elastic golden helmet framing her face and wore a nylon overall that to my overheated gaze looked like it had nothing underneath but her. I approached her as nervously as if I'd been about to ask her out on a date.

"Um, hello."

"Yes?"

I nodded toward the row of screens and keyboards off to one side. "Is there any way I can get online?"

"Oh! Of course. You just sign in."

"Uh, that's the problem. I don't have an email address or anything."

She looked perplexed. "You don't need one. The long number on your card is your ID, and the short number is your password."

"And that's *it?*" My voice made one of its unpredictable and unwanted pitch shifts.

"That's it!" she said, with a smile that made my face burn.

"Uh, thank you." I smiled back for just a little too long, and turned away to the screens. I put down my laden school bag, hung my blazer on the back of the plastic chair, grabbed the chair as it tipped backward, sat, and tapped the two strings of numbers in.

The online world opened like a forbidden book.

Reader, I googled him.

THE LOW HILL THE CHURCH STANDS ON IS A MOUND OF GLACIAL TILL, DEBRIS FROM the mile-high ice that carved the glen. A band of deciduous trees, birch and beech mostly, separates it from the nearest houses. The freshwater loch the hill and the houses overlook has a crannog—a tiny artificial island like a stranded stand of trees—in the middle: thousands of years older than the church, many more thousands younger than the hillock. The mountains, hundreds of millions of years older yet, wall it to north and south, and their flanks shelter it east and west. Along the far side of the loch is the old railway line; on this side pylons, one of them toppled, and three wind turbines that still spin. On a more distant hillside is a phone mast, felled.

Helen brings us to a halt in a siding cut from more of the same glacial till, like a spoil heap of rubble and gravel left over from road-building. Ten meters beyond it is the unpaved road leading up to the church. The silence is broken only by a few bleats of sheep and caws of crows, and from farther away the lowing of a cow.

Helen gives me a grim smile. "That cow's been milked. Means there's somebody around to milk it."

"But not going out if they can help it."

She nods. "They might not even know the danger comes from using a phone. And they can't use one here anyway, with the mast down. Christ, what a mess."

"We might even be the bringers of good news."

"Ha! Knock on doors and say it's safe to come out?"

"More shotguns and rifles behind those doors than I'd care to chance."

"Uh-huh." She looks around again. "Shall we?"

We wind up the windows, clamber out, and slide the doors to. Helen slings on her backpack and walks around the van, locking the doors one by one. After a final check around, we walk up to the church. I carry the carbine over my shoulder, as if casually. Helen has a big knife on her belt. We stay alert.

NO ONE IS MORE SELF-RIGHTEOUS THAN A TEENAGE BOY WHO THINKS HE HAS HIS parents on the moral back foot. Few embarrassing memories are more tedious to recount than the resulting confrontations. I'll take these as read, and move to the consequences. These did not include my father mending his ways.

The problem, as he saw it, was that our cover story was too transparent. He decided to replace his thin tissue of lies with walls of solid stone. At that time there was a thing for pop-up shops: businesses that opened for a short time in unused retail premises. Pandemic, recession, and war had ensured that there were lots of unused shop fronts on every high street, and plenty of scrabbling small businesses to seek opportunity there. My father thought bigger.

He opened a pop-up church.

It was in an unused church building on a back street. For a while it had been a carpet warehouse, but that business had failed. Nobody was opening new pubs or nightclubs that year, or the next. For five years the building had stood empty, with grass growing from cracks in the paving around its steps. The rent was derisory, almost nominal; I think the landlord or property developer was desperate for someone, anyone, to occupy the building, prevent its further deterioration, and avoid recent legislation against keeping properties empty for too long.

One Saturday not long after my fight with him, our father took me and Melanie to a DIY store. We carried small tins of paint, brushes, sheets of sandpaper, dust masks, and coveralls around a couple of corners, and there it was.

He jangled keys. "Our church!"

Melanie clapped her hands.

While he pottered about inside, Melanie held a stepladder, which I stood on. I sanded off the old sign and gave it a fresh coat of black gloss. While it dried, we joined our father for a tea break in the vestry, a poky room piled with carpet offcuts and slightly foxed Bibles and hymnbooks. That done, my father and I held the stepladder while Melanie used a small paintbrush to inscribe the white lettering.

THE CHURCH OF THE BOOK
Sundays: Closed
Wednesday, 7:00 p.m.: Weekly meeting
Minister: Jason Rawlins, MA, PhD

"Very neat," Dad said, as we all stepped back to admire it. "Well done, Melanie!"

"Nice touch with the qualifications," I jeered. "Where did you get them from?"

"Edinburgh University." He gave me a sharp look. "What did you expect—some degree mill?"

"Well, yes," I admitted. "But that just makes it worse, them being real degrees."

"Makes what worse?"

"The waste." I scowled at him. "A man with a doctorate, working in a garden center!"

"It's not Dad who's to blame," Melanie said. "It's society's loss."

He knew and I knew it was his loss too, and his blame. He frowned at me and smiled at Melanie. "According to the books in there, God set the first man to work in a garden. I could do worse."

And you did, I thought, but I kept that to myself. Melanie knew the church was an invention, of course, but she wasn't ready for the full truth yet. Our father led us back inside and set us to work sweeping the floor and dragging stacks of chairs out of a storage cupboard. We wiped dust off them and set them in concentric semicircles, with a single chair facing them from the center. I thanked God or whoever that the last congregation had been advanced enough to dispense with pews.

True to the notice, the first meeting was held the following Wednesday evening. The congregation consisted of me, Melanie, our mother, and three men, two of whom seemed shifty and struck me at once as creeps. The third, young and fit and with short fair hair and a frank, open face, was so obviously a cop that I almost laughed. My father took the central chair.

"The first commandment of the Church of the Book," he said, "is that we don't talk about why we're here. I assume that all of you"—he glanced at the frank-faced young man—"are here because you are excommunicate, or are sympathetic to those of us who are. I don't want to hear your stories, and I'm not going to give you mine." Good move, that. He looked around, smiling. "This is not Excommunicates Anonymous. Sharing is not this church's mission. Its mission is something quite different. It is to preserve books. Because books will be next! You know which books I mean. I'm not talking about books illegal to possess; that's a different matter. I'm talking about books that are not banned, but whose online versions are quietly taken down. Their physical versions are unavailable in public libraries without drawing unwanted attention to the borrower or reader. Their surviving copies in private hands are fewer and fewer. You may have some of them—gathering dust! Let's share not our stories—but our books! I'm sure I would despise the books some of you most treasure. Some of you might want to burn books that mean a lot to me. In other circumstances, perhaps you would. But not in this place! Not here! Any book brought here and entrusted to me will be kept safely, and consulted freely by any adult. This church will be a library. Its second and last commandment is that we do not burn books." He was on his feet now. "Anyone who disagrees has no place in this church, though of course they remain welcome to listen. We may discuss these books, if we consider them worth discussing. That is all. That is the mission of the Church of the Book."

The predictable discussion followed. Terrorist training manuals? Fascist propaganda? Pornography? "As long as it's not illegal" was my father's answer to everything. In the weeks that followed, I was surprised and appalled to find how much that covered. This filth, that trash, these lies were *legal*?

The congregation grew. The word spread slowly: by letters, by leaflets, by word of mouth. But spread it did.

THERE'S A LOW WALL AROUND THE CHURCHYARD. THE GATE STANDS OPEN, RUSTED in place. The grass is cropped short by sheep. Headstones are covered with moss and lichen; there have been no new burials here for decades, if not longer. But the sign beside the door is only weathered by a few years of droughts, downpours, and storms; it's still legible. Black paint and white letters:

THE CHURCH OF THE BOOK
Sundays: Closed
Wednesday, 7:00 p.m.: Weekly meeting
Minister: Dr. Alexander Singh

"Found it!" I say.

Helen grins at me. "You had faith."

The door is locked. Helen puts down her pack, takes out her tools, and makes short work of that. We step inside.

I MET HELEN ONLINE, WHEN WE WERE BOTH NINETEEN. WE'D PROBABLY NEVER have met—she went to one of the city's other universities—if we hadn't both been online and in the same closed group: ExEx. It was for the children of excommunicates. Discussions were heated but guarded: everyone there was still careful of what they said online, and how far it might go. Despite that, she and I found we had a lot in common. Her parents had been members of the third or fourth congregation of the Church of the Book. It didn't take us long to meet in real life.

"Your father's basic fault," she said, on our second date in the café, "is frivolity. He isn't a fanatic for truth, or even for free speech. He doesn't believe the lies the other side puts out."

"And your parents do?"

Helen scoffed. "How could they, when the lies change all the time? No, they're true believers at a deeper level than that. They're onside for the other side, for God knows what reason. They think throwing out disinformation is like putting up flak: it doesn't matter how many shots miss, as long as it keeps the bombers from getting through." She shook her head. "Something like that. Jason Rawlins, though, he's just too mentally lazy to sort things out for himself."

I felt stung to remonstrance. "When we still bothered to argue . . . he would hit me with straight John Stuart Mill: that people who don't know the other side of an argument don't really know their own—no matter how foolish or misguided that other side may be. And that shutting people off from the other side's propaganda in the war means that deep down, many people end up not even really believing our side's news. Same with climate change, and—"

"No!" Helen leaned across the table. "That's where you're still wrong, Liam. You still think it's an *argument*. An argument implies good faith, however mistaken one side or the other might be. And there's just no good faith in what the other side puts out. There's no equivalence between the bias, the distortion, even the deceptions in our mainstream media"—she smiled at her own cliché—"and the sort of reckless rubbish that gets pumped out by state media, demagogues and populists, and fossil fuel companies. That stuff is a weapon of war, and it has to be met by fighting it, not arguing with it."

She won that argument, and she won me. In time, she won other arguments, in the profession we both chose. She formed a specialist group. When the next stage of the war came, we were ready. We had old vans with no fancy electronics, maps and compasses, carbines, and all the tools to finish the job.

INSIDE THE CHURCH IS A LIBRARY. THE PEWS ARE STILL THERE, BUT ALL THE WALLS are lined with bookcases. I wander along them for a minute, seeing the familiar names of the Communists and the Fascists, the holocaust deniers, the climate change sceptics, the creationists, the racists and sexists, the antiwar right and the antiwar left. Lots of books about religious conflicts in India, from all different sides—the Sikh doctor, whoever he might have been, was clearly catholic in his choices. Alphabetical order: I find Rawlins next to Stalin, which makes me laugh. Neither would enjoy the other's company, I'll say that for them both.

Helen works the other side, then moves on to where I've just browsed. The smell of the accelerant becomes overpowering. She finishes up behind the pulpit.

"Ready?"

I nod. We go out. I toss in the match, and we wait to make sure the fire has taken hold. At the foot of the track back to the road, a tall middle-aged man stands with his arms folded, watching. He eyes the carbine, he clocks our uniforms. He nods as we pass.

"All the same," he says, "he was a good man, the Sikh."

7 NOISE CANCELLATION

S.B. Divya

I LIVE WITH AN EVER-PRESENT HUM IN MY HEAD, SOMEWHERE BETWEEN THE DRONE of a beehive and the crackle of above-ground power lines. It gets worse when I put on my jewels, but I can't work without interfaces, and the stick-on devices aren't as bad as the sprays and micropills. I've learned to endure the discomfort. A medical bot diagnosed me at age fifteen: electromagnetic hypersensitivity syndrome. EHS is rare, but there's no treatment, and there's not much that anyone can do about it thanks to the demands of modern society, so I learned to cope. No one told me that it might be hereditary.

Dyne was a fussy baby, but my wife and I shrugged it off as one of the many challenges of parenting. He smiled and laughed and played enough to balance out the screams and tears. Then he started preschool. He attends a cluster with the other children in our housing complex. The youngest children have a live teacher, but even they have to wear virtuality headsets and haptic gloves. On the first day, Dyne cried for so long that they sent him back to our apartment.

It's been two months, and his tears have diminished to an hour—an hour that I spend daily at the cluster with him on my lap while the other children sit in circle time on their own, cheerfully engaged with their virtual environments. Then came yesterday.

As Dyne wound down to sniffles, I wiped his nose and cheeks and placed the most comfortable headset we could find over his head.

"It's too loud," he protested.

I shared his audio feed with mine. I hadn't activated the educational program yet, and my earrings fed me silence, but I adjusted the volume down anyway. "Is that better?"

He shook his head, his face a picture of misery.

"What do you hear?"

"Buzz buzz, like a bee."

And that's when I finally made the connection. I powered his headset down. "How about now?"

"Better."

Well, shit, I thought.

I'M TAKING A BREAK WHILE MY CODE COMPILES AND FLIPPING THROUGH A PAPER magazine called *Real Life* when the advertisement catches my attention: *Tired of wondering if anyone-someone-everyone is watching? Worried that your thresholds failed to trap all the microcams? More interested in your energy levels than your tip jar? Then join us for a week-long, all-inclusive retreat in Peace Valley, Nevada! Under our canopy, you'll find nature and serenity. Fully shielded buildings. No electronics. No network interfaces.*

Ironically, I have to get more information by sending them a message, but how else is anyone going to communicate? They reply quickly. They have a room available during the week of Thanksgiving break. They welcome families with small children, and they even have someone on staff to do daycare while the adults go on long hikes or relax at the spa. I skim through the document they send me about the facilities. They've taken a lot of care to disconnect visitors, going so far as to have a networked hardline to their front office, the only way to communicate to the outside world. Visitors are required to take a flush pill upon arrival and sign a contract that they won't consume any micropills during their stay. It sounds monastic. It sounds perfect.

LATER THAT NIGHT AS WE LIE IN BED TOGETHER, I FLICK THE INFORMATION OVER TO Barya. Her gaze is fixed on her visual display. When I'm close to her like this, the discomfort in my head gets worse. What would it feel like to have it go away?

"What's this?" she asks. A small fold appears between her lush, dark brows.

I explain what happened with Dyne the day before and my theory.

Her frown turns into a skeptical quirk. "I think you might be jumping to conclusions. It sounds to me like he's taking a little more time than the other kids to adjust to preschool, and even if he does have EHS, he'll learn to live with it, like you did." She pats my thigh. "Besides, I've got a big deadline the week after Thanksgiving. I can't spend that week without network access."

"It was never as bad for me as it is for him. It's just a week, Barya. I want to try it in case it makes a difference."

She stands and goes to the sink. As she removes her smartlenses, she says, "If it helps, then what? Are we going to live off-grid permanently? This is ridiculous, Ani. Let's go somewhere fun if you want to get away for the break. I bet you he'll be great as long as he's not at school every day."

Her attitude snaps me back to every dismissive medical appointment in my past. "You don't get it," I say. "If you can't come, we'll just go without you." The words slip out before I'm conscious of them.

She pauses before turning out the lights. "Fine."

It's not fine at all, but my wall is up, and now hers is too, and neither of us is going to back down. We roll away from each other. I thought that having children was supposed to bring couples together, but ever since Dyne was born, we've drifted apart. Because I gave birth to him and because Barya loves biogenetics more than I love engineering, we agreed that I would do the primary parenting during the day, and Barya would take on the bread-winner role. In the evenings, she would give Dyne his dinner and bath and put him to bed while I got some part-time work done. We were two forward-thinking women, but we fell into traditional roles all too easily. I had hoped that this vacation would give us time to reconnect, but I'm too angry at Barya's dismissive words to back down, and I really do want to find out if a place like Peace Valley can provide Dyne and me with relief.

CAR RIDES ARE THE WORST. THE CONVENIENCE OF NOT HAVING TO DRIVE IS ENTIRELY swamped by sitting in a box surrounded by electronics. I had a girlfriend in college whose dad collected and restored classic cars. She took me for a ride in one of them—a convertible—over winter break. I've never felt more alive and relaxed. If I had the time and money, I'd get one for myself. In the meantime, for any journey that's longer than an hour, I medicate. I give Dyne a low dose of antihistamine so that we can both sleep through the bulk of the trip.

The car stops once for lunch, at a small town in the middle of the desert that's mostly an outpost for travelers like us. When I wake up toward the end of the second leg, we're in a forest. It's dry, not lush, but when I open the windows, the air is cool and smells like dusty pine. Dyne stirs and whimpers.

"Almost there," I whisper.

I smooth his sweaty, sleep mussed curls. He opens his big brown eyes and blinks owlishly at me.

"Mama, I don't like cars," he says. He leans into my shoulder.

"Me neither."

NOISE CANCELLATION

Fifteen minutes later, the car pulls up to a solid wooden gate. It's set between two tall stone walls that extend between the trees so far that I can't see where they end. It has such a medieval aesthetic that I wonder if there's a castle inside. The gate opens and a tall woman emerges. Her skin is as brown as Barya's and mine, but her hair is colored in an ombré pattern, shading from spring green at the crown to pale pink at the tips. It falls straight down her back. She's dressed in static fabric, a loose gown that looks worn and comfortable.

"Anila?" she asks me.

I nod.

She smiles and shifts her gaze. "Then you must be Dyne. Welcome to Peace Valley. My name is Malaika. I'm the manager of guest services. Please follow me."

I dismiss the car and pass through the gate with Dyne gripping my hand. We're ten steps in when I notice it—an unclenching between my shoulder blades, an ease of breath, a stillness that runs through my entire body.

Dyne tugs on my arm and child-whispers, "It's quiet here."

"I know what you mean."

Malaika turns her head and flashes us a smile.

Dried pine needles crunch under our feet as we approach a stone building with a peaked tile roof. Inside, light shines from solar tubes set into the ceiling like a dozen miniature suns. To the right, an archway leads to a small dining area. Ahead of us, sofas and armchairs fill an open space with a large fireplace at the far end, and on our left, a staircase leads downstairs. All of the furniture is made from expensive static materials—wood and metal—rather than the smartmatter frames that most people use.

"This is our communal center," our guide explains. "You're welcome here anytime between 6:00 a.m. and 11:00 p.m. Breakfast, lunch, and dinner are served in the dining room, though you can ask for a sack lunch if you plan to be out and about. We have many hiking trails in the area." She turns to Dyne. "We also have board games and a small library of print books in the room through that door. That's our fun center, and there's always a grown-up there to look after you if you don't want to be outside with your mom. You can take anything you like back to your room."

She walks us out the back door and down a winding path to a smaller stone building. Our "cabin" for the week has two levels, with the second being entirely underground. Low-voltage lighting augments a few carefully placed solar tubes. The effect is cozy, not gloomy. I don't see any large devices—no wall screen, no kitchen, no printers or charging plates. Dyne goes straight for a box of colorful building blocks and dumps it on the rug.

"We took the liberty of setting you up with a few toys and books," Malaika says. "This binder contains information about the dining schedule, activities, and how to get in touch during off hours." She hands me an old-fashioned metal key. "If you need anything else, I'll be in the office, which is the lower level of the communal building."

I take the key and thank her, my mind in something of a daze. I lie down on the static couch and breathe in the quiet. My entire body feels still, like a pool of water after its fountain has been turned off. Barya's question pops into my mind: *If it helps, then what?*

THE NEXT MORNING, I GET DYNE DRESSED AND HEAD TO THE OFFICE. IT'S A COZY room hung with warm-toned art. A fish tank is inset into one wall, and two desks fill the space, one of them occupied. Again, everything is made of static materials. No wonder the retreat costs so much. I stop at the desk where Malaika sits.

She looks up and smiles. "Good morning, Anila, Dyne. What can I do for you?"

"Is there somewhere I can send a message back to my spouse? Just to let her know that we're doing fine."

She gestures at the other desk and hands me a notepad and pen. "You'll have to write it down. The hardline is only for emergencies. We have someone who will take it into town and send it for you. They'll bring back any reply. It's about an hour away, if you'd prefer to go yourself."

"Oh," I flounder. "No, that's okay. I'll do my best with paper." I haven't handwritten since elementary school. If Dyne were a little older, I'd have him do it. I scribble down a few wobbly lines. *Everything is great. Slept better than I can remember. Dyne seems happy. I have to handwrite this, so I'm keeping it short. More when we get home. We love you and miss you!*

I fold the paper in half and hand it to her.

"We are strict about not having any complex electronics on site. Some of our guests have EHS, as do I, so wireless communications can really exacerbate our pain."

My hand tightens involuntarily around the pen.

"Mama, I'm hungry," Dyne says. He tugs on my sleeve. "I want breakfast."

"In a minute," I promise him. Then, to Malaika, "EHS? As in electromagnetic hypersensitivity syndrome?"

"Yes, you know of it?"

"I have it. I suspect . . ." I trail off and tilt my head at Dyne.

She nods in understanding. "You're not the first guests here with the condition. Would you like a consultation with Doctor Ortiz? He's one of the founders of Peace Valley, and he's a leading researcher into EHS. He'll be here tomorrow. He's always happy to meet with our guests, and consultations are included as part of your stay. Or if you'd like to come back in December, he'll be running a workshop specifically for people who have the condition, to help them function in the modern world."

I glance at Dyne, who has wandered over to the fish tank and tuned out our conversation. "A meeting with him tomorrow would be great."

She flips open a notebook and runs her finger down a written schedule. "We can fit you in at 3:00 p.m. Come here about five minutes before then, and I'll walk you to his office. We can drop your son off at the fun center."

"No need. I'd like to have him evaluated, if possible."

"Not a problem," she says without missing a beat. "I'll put his name down for the consultation as well."

"Thank you." I take Dyne's hand and we head up to breakfast.

DR. ORTIZ HAS THE KIND OF TAN THAT COMES FROM SPENDING TIME IN THE SUN every day. He also sports a thick black mustache atop a generous smile, but he's not smiling at the moment. Neither of us is because Dyne's shrieks would kill anyone's good mood.

A medical sleeve is wrapped around my boy's arm. I've got Dyne in my lap, and I can feel it when Dr. Ortiz turns up the intensity of whatever the sleeve is producing. It sets my teeth on edge. My eyes close involuntarily against the sensation. They snap open when it stops. Dyne takes a long, shuddering breath.

"I'm sorry I had to do that," Dr. Ortiz says. "It's all finished now. When you're ready, you can have a lollipop, Dyne."

"How about one for me?" I say. I smile, but I can't stop the shiver that goes through me.

As the doctor removes the sleeve, he says, "You're right. Not only do you both have EHS, but Dyne is a lot more sensitive than you are. Does he get that from his father?"

"I—I don't know," I say. "It was an anonymous donation."

"I see. No need to find out. I was just curious." He hands me a box of tissues.

I wipe my son's face and rock him. His sobs start to quiet.

"We still don't know much about electromagnetic sensitivity," Dr. Ortiz says. "Whether it's hereditary, and if so, whether it takes one or both parents. Or if it's an epigenetic or congenital condition. The World Health Organization recognized it back in 2005, but it was controversial for a long time. Today's medbots lump it into the bucket of central nervous system dysfunction and offer lifestyle changes as the only course of action."

"Is it very rare?" I ask.

"Current estimates are somewhere around 1.25 million people in the United States. The numbers have been growing, especially in the last few decades. One theory is that a segment of the human population has always had this sensitivity, and that modern life—what with microcam swarms and smartfabrics and dynamic furniture—has made EHS a lot harder to live with. Another is that micropills are disrupting ion function at a cellular level." He shrugs. "We'll get to the root cause eventually, but it's not easy to get the research funded. No modern designer wants evidence that devices might cause health problems, and the patients often have limited financial resources. I can count the number of people working in the field on my two hands, and one of them is me."

Dyne sits up a little straighter, sniffles, and says, "I want a lollipop."

"Please," I correct automatically.

"Please," Dyne says.

Dr. Ortiz holds out a cup full of the candies. Dyne chooses green, his favorite color.

"So what now?" I ask. I need the answer for Barya as much as for myself. "Is there a treatment?"

"Unfortunately not. It's a spectrum disorder, and many people find ways to live with it. For the more sensitive cases, like your son's, I've had the best luck with people who can move away from city life. Ideally, you'd find him a human tutor for his education and enroll him in sports or some other extracurriculars where he can make friends in a nonvirtual environment. We don't know a lot about EHS yet, especially for children and their development, but from what I've observed over the past two decades, it can affect their ability to learn. Whether that's because the pain distracts them or there's a deeper physiological cause, I can't say." He hands me a paper packet. "Here's some information I've assembled that addresses a lot of common questions and provides some basic guidance. I'm sorry I can't offer you a better solution."

In other words, he has nothing to suggest other than the same *lifestyle changes* that the medbots know about. I wonder if I'll learn anything from the packet. At least it's on a static medium. I thank the doctor and start to stand when he says, "One more thing. This place—Peace Valley—does a pretty good job at shielding people from electromagnetic signals. Several of the staff live here year-round because they suffer from EHS. I don't know what your personal and family circumstances are, but you might talk to Malaika about their current job openings. Because of the remote location, they're often looking to hire people."

I thank him again, but I'm thinking, *yeah right*. I would never be able to convince Barya to give up her biogenetics work, and while I don't love working on network constellations, I can't imagine what I'd do at a place like this. So where does that leave Dyne? We owe it to him to give him the best life we can. How can we balance his needs with our own?

Outside the doctor's office, sunlight dapples the ground as it falls through the gaps in the trees. Dyne runs ahead, the lollipop clamped in one hand, and scrambles up a boulder.

"Look, Mama, I'm taller than you," he crows.

I manage a smile for him while my mind races ahead. How do we make a life where he can thrive and Barya and I can work? Where will we get a human tutor for him? How much will that cost? What does an off-grid life even look like? I'm vaguely aware that people do it, but how? This goes far beyond a blackout zone like the Maghreb, where they keep their lives out of sight but embrace biotechnology . . . like pills. What are we supposed to do about those? Barya and I have eschewed all of the enhancement pills, but we take our dailies, and I make sure Dyne gets his. Without those, we risk getting sick from the latest designer pathogens, and you need a networked printer to make them. Would we be able to live so far from civilization that we could avoid contagion? I almost turn around to ask Dr. Ortiz, but then I remember the packet clutched in my hand. Perhaps it has the answers I need.

OUR TIME AT PEACE VALLEY GOES BY QUICKLY. ANOTHER FAMILY ARRIVES THE DAY after us, and Dyne quickly makes friends with their older child. The retreat has a staffer who spends a few hours each day with the kids, doing activities and playing with them, so that the adults can have some time to relax. She hands me a paper card the first day with all the information that her public profile would display: name, gender pronouns, ethnicity, skills, expertise and reliability ratings. At home, Dyne usually clings to me and cries at events like these, which are managed by carebots, but here, he leaves me gladly each day. How much of that is due to his EHS and how much to having a new friend?

In the evenings, after he's asleep, I go through the packet bit by bit. It addresses all of my concerns, though it doesn't always provide clear answers. Sometimes there are no good choices. On the third day, I consider Dr. Ortiz's suggestion and, leaving Dyne at the fun center, I go down to the office.

Malaika greets me with her usual bright smile. "What can I do for you?"

I sit down and ask her about employment opportunities at Peace Valley.

"Oh, fantastic! Let me show you where the in-residence staff live while we talk about it."

She props a small sign on her desk saying, "Be back soon," and ushers me upstairs and outside. We take one of the many meandering paths to a cluster of small, hut-like buildings.

"Our digs aren't as luxurious as the retreat rooms," she says. She unlocks the door to one and waves me in. "This is my place. It's humble, but the walls are made of the same EM-blocking composite as the rest of the place. My EHS is medium-bad, so I have some electric lighting. Our chef has it worse and only uses candles in her house. Each unit is printed as needed, so you can customize it. She doesn't have any windows because they allow too much radiation to come in from the nearby constellation points."

The inside is compact but tidy, with a small bedroom and a full bathroom. I try to imagine fitting Dyne, Barya, and myself in a place like this.

"What do you do about family members? Do they have to work here, too?"

"Honestly, all of our staff at the moment are single." She shrugs apologetically. "But I don't see any problem with you bringing your family along as long as they're okay with the lifestyle here. The founders have talked about incorporating Peace Valley as a city and building a community around it, so I'm sure they would love to have you here. That might attract other families to join the effort."

The open jobs don't match up with either mine or Barya's skill sets. They need a maintenance worker for buildings and grounds, a second staffer for the fun room, and a waiter for the dining room.

"We can train you," Malaika assures me. "All of us came here from other types of work. Some of us still keep up with it on the side. I studied material science, and I go into town on my days off to do research for our building materials. We're always looking to improve the experience, so the Peace Valley owners are willing to fund efforts like mine."

I promise her that I'll think about it, and I do. I even consider getting a ride into town so that I can talk to Barya about it, but I'm not in the mood for the inevitable fight. Instead, I take a guided horseback ride through the alpine backcountry. Peace Valley exists like a medieval castle, its boundary marked by a stone wall punctured by gates. The entire top is lined with the same thresholds that people use in doorways to catch stray microdrones. A determined operator could fly a swarm high enough to avoid them, though the remote location makes that unlikely.

My horse steps carefully down a rocky portion of the trail. We emerge from the trees to open sky, and the Nevada sun beats down on me, warming my skin through the autumn chill. Not a cloud in sight. If it had been nighttime, I could've spotted the local stellas—high-altitude communications drones that form the global mesh network—flying well above any airplanes but far below satellites. There's no way to block their signals from reaching a place like Peace Valley, not unless they moved underground or built a shielded roof over the entire place. In the push to give everyone equal access to the grid, the world has left no gaps for people like me.

But someone like me might be able to engineer a solution. I understand how the constellations communicate, and as with any electromagnetic system, there are ways to strengthen and weaken signals. In theory, with the right equipment, I could design a system to emit waves that would attenuate the signals arriving at Peace Valley. It would require fast, sophisticated computation, but the AIs I work with could handle it as long as I give them the right communication protocols. Too bad no one would fund a project like that.

ON THE AFTERNOON OF OUR DEPARTURE, DYNE STARTS CRYING AT THE SIGHT OF the car.

"Don't you want to go home and see Mommy?" I ask.

"No," he wails.

The other family emerges from the gate as their vehicle pulls up. They are all smiles—sympathetic ones from the parents. Dyne's friend waves goodbye on command from his parents and gets into their car. Clearly no one in their family suffers from EHS.

After they leave, I do my best to coax my son into our car, my heart breaking all the while. What kind of future is there for him? And a quieter follow-up thought: Is it my fault that he's like this?

Dyne falls asleep more quickly than I do on the ride home. Several times, I almost put on my jewels and call Barya, but then I figure, "Hi, honey, we might have to upend our lives for our son's health" is a conversation better had in person.

We arrive home at dinnertime. My head throbs. My stomach's in knots. Dyne is grumpy upon waking and stays that way until he sees his mommy. Barya greets us both with hugs and kisses and manages to coax a smile out of Dyne. Over dinner, he tells her about all the fun things we did during our vacation, but his demeanor is subdued. The buzz has built up inside my bones again. I can only imagine his experience.

"So you liked it there?" Barya asks with a grin.

"When I grow up, I'm going to live there!" Dyne declares.

My wife laughs. She looks me in the eyes and says, "I'm glad it was a good trip."

After we get Dyne in bed, we sit on the sofa with the half-finished wine from dinner. That's when I finally tell Barya about our meeting with Dr. Ortiz. I show her the printed packet and hand her the page that summarizes the recommended actions. She flips through it, scanning for relevant information with the practiced ease of a researcher, then sets it aside and looks at me.

"I don't see anything in here that we don't know, and we're already doing a lot of what they recommend. Maybe Dyne is more sensitive because of his age. We can hire a carebot to look after him until he's a bit older." She shrugs and refills her wine glass. "It'll be expensive, but we can make it work."

I give her a skeptical look. "Dyne hates carebots. The doctor said that EHS could affect his learning and development. I wish you'd come with us, had seen how much brighter and more cheerful he was there. It's hard to explain, but I could feel it too—not just my symptoms going away, but a sort of mental quietness and clarity. I really think we need to consider a different lifestyle, for his sake." *And mine.* "Shouldn't we put him in an environment where he can thrive?"

She sips at her glass, then says, "Removing ourselves from society will only disadvantage him in the long run. What happens when he gets older? Think of all the experiences he'll miss out on. How is he going to have friends if he can't connect to the grid? I get that you had a good time at the retreat, but you were on vacation. You can't live like that every day, and neither can he. So he has EHS. You're doing okay with it. He'll learn to do the same."

"I didn't get a diagnosis until I was *fifteen*," I snap. "When I was little, the medbots told my parents I had too much stress, and then later, they blamed it on puberty. I was miserable. I knew something was wrong with me, but by the time my parents heard about EHS, they didn't believe that they had to make any changes at home. I used to hear the same thing from them. *You've done okay all these years, so it can't be that bad.*" I downed the rest of my wine and stood. "Bullshit! I am never okay. I just put up with feeling like crap all the time because I haven't had a choice. Dyne's sensitivity is ten times worse than mine. I don't want him to suffer. I don't want him to learn to live with the pain. But you wouldn't understand. You didn't come to Peace Valley—"

"I couldn't!"

"—and you're not the one who has to deal with his meltdowns at school every morning."

"One of us has to pay the bills. Dyne started preschool four months ago, and you still haven't switched to a full-time contract."

"Maybe that's because I prioritize our child's well-being over money." I don't really believe that, but I can't help hitting back, and I know where to hurt her.

Barya takes a deep breath and says softly, "Clearly this isn't going to be a productive discussion right now. You're tired. So am I. Let's talk more on the weekend."

I nod and wash the wine glasses as a peace gesture. We go to bed together, but I can't sleep. After staring out the window for an hour, I get up, lie on the sofa, and try to read. The low-level noise from my smartglasses fills my head like an unwelcome visitor. I try to ignore it like I always have and fail.

I close the book, pull on my haptic gloves, and look up what I can about EHS and development. The more I see, the more convinced I am that Dr. Ortiz is right, that Dyne needs a healthier, pain-free environment to thrive. A lot of the information I come across is anecdotal—stories from non-EHS parents who eventually figured out what was going on with their children after years of suffering and misdiagnoses; or stories like my own, recorded by adults about their childhoods. The most severe cases ended up with developmental delays and permanent injury.

All of it convinces me that we have to take action. At the very least, we need to find Dyne some kind of nonelectronic schooling. At best, we have to find a new way of life. I search for somewhere we can live that would meet all of our needs. Finding a place where we can build a house shielded from network constellations is the greatest challenge. New zoning ordinances have driven most people away from suburban, single-family lifestyles and into multifamily clusters like ours. Many of the older neighborhoods have been cleared and turned into green spaces. We aren't so rich that we can buy a plot of land in the communities that allow it, not unless we move out of state. I distanced myself from my family when I left for college, but Barya is close to hers, both physically and emotionally. Convincing her to move halfway across the country would be hard—harder than the already high barrier of upending our lives. I skitter around the idea of splitting up. I'll do what I have to for Dyne's sake, but I love my wife. I don't want to choose between them. I want to find a solution that satisfies all of our needs.

I spend the next two hours trying out budgets, researching housing costs in different areas within a day's drive, seeing if I can get a tutoring certificate. I find some EHS families who have shared their solutions, but most of them have milder cases, like mine. They use the same kinds of mitigation strategies that we already do. The more severely affected live on meds with willing family members, or they suffer through in-home carebots, trapped in a vicious cycle of dysfunction, or they go completely off-grid.

Peace Valley keeps cropping up as the only place nearby to find an ideal environment for people with EHS. I almost wish I hadn't gone, that I hadn't discovered that a noise-free, pain-free life could exist.

I WAKE TO A SORE NECK AND A HEADACHE. BARYA SITS IN THE ARMCHAIR SIPPING a coffee.

"Good morning." She greets me with a lopsided, rueful smile. "Sorry about last night."

I yawn, stretch, and sit up. "Me too. I didn't mean to fall asleep out here."

She puts down her cup. "Let me take Dyne to preschool today. I didn't use any vacation time last week. I can take the whole day off, get him settled at school, and then we can really talk."

I nod, too groggy to respond coherently. I stumble into our bedroom and fall into a deep sleep.

When I wake, it's almost noon, and the house is quiet. I peek into Dyne's room, but he's not there. I find Barya in the living room, the paper packet spread out on her lap. She sees me and her expression turns to one of almost comical dismay. Then she stands, strides over to me, kisses me full on the mouth, and wraps me in a tight hug.

"Ani, I am so *so* sorry," she says when she pulls back. "I had no idea."

It takes me a second. "The crying?"

She nods. "Ye gods, that was awful. I can't believe you've been dealing with that every single day since he started. I would've cracked months ago." She shudders. "I did a bunch of research about EHS while you were asleep. Let's talk about it over lunch, preferably somewhere that serves cocktails."

We walk to our favorite café and order Bloody Marys and salads. The server leaves us with a basket of warm, fresh-baked bread with a perfectly crispy crust and chilled butter. Across the street sits the nightclub where we used to go dancing every weekend. The sun brightens our shaded patio, and in this idyllic setting, hope rises in me that she and I will work this out.

"So I did some reading while you slept in," she says. She goes on to explain how she tracked out some theories on the biochemistry behind EHS and how a few researchers, including Dr. Ortiz, have developed diagnostic tests for it. "I agree with you that we have to do something for Dyne, especially given the potential long-term neurological damage that this can cause."

"Great—"

"I'm thinking we should buy our own place and get shielding put in for Dyne's room. There are materials you can apply to interior walls that act like a Faraday cage. We can put him in private school rather than attending a cluster, somewhere that'll accommodate his needs and allow him to learn with a low-emissions home setup. I looked into those, and they exist. He can have breaks in his room during the day, and you can take him to park playdates in the afternoon. With both of us back at full-time work, we should be able to afford it."

She goes on talking, laying out her plan in detail, never once stopping to ask my opinion or considering how I'm going to manage a full-time job and taking care of Dyne. For her, it's all about minimizing disruption and allowing her the freedom to continue living on her terms, just as it was after we had a baby. I listen. I try to keep an open mind. Her idea could work if the priority is to allow her to work comfortably from home, but it's not optimal for Dyne or me. When our food arrives, she digs into her salad.

I hold my fork and say, "I'm really glad you're on board with making changes to help Dyne." I put the fork back down. "But there's no way I can oversee Dyne's schooling and socializing and work a full-time contract. Plus, the parks are usually crawling with carebots and microdrone swarms. The instant he goes outside, he's going to be inundated by electromagnetic signals."

"Do you have any better ideas?"

"Yes. Peace Valley. All of their buildings are shielded and they have minimal electronics on site. They have a protective enclosure to keep out swarms, a day care on-site, and a commuter van for people who need to be in the city. You could use that to continue doing your work."

"Didn't you say it's almost an hour each way?"

I nod and take my first bite of food.

"I don't want to waste two hours a day in a van. I'll have less time with Dyne."

"You don't do anything with him until the evening anyway."

"Are you serious?" Barya's voice rises.

"And that way I'll get relief from my symptoms too, which I won't with your plan."

"What about your work?"

"I'll take one of the on-site jobs. Maybe they'll fund my project to help attenuate constellation signals in the area. I can work on that during the weekends in the city."

"Do you even realize what you're saying? Peace Valley is hours away from anywhere interesting. Hours from my family. You'd force me into a commute. All that so that you can be a little more comfortable?"

"All that so that Dyne and I can be *healthy*." As my heart rate picks up, so does the throbbing in my head. "EHS is more than discomfort. And Dr. Ortiz thinks—"

"Nothing I read said that."

"And your expertise rating in this is what exactly? Because his is in the nineties."

Her lips compress.

"Look, I know this is a lot to ask, but imagine if we were talking about a toxin. Wouldn't you want us living somewhere free of it rather than somewhere with a constant low to medium dose?"

"It's not the same thing."

"For Dyne, it might be."

"I'm not moving to Peace Valley."

My heart drums against my ribs. "I don't think I want to live anywhere else."

We stare at each other, lunch and drinks forgotten. I didn't want it to come to this, but if Barya is going to drop ultimatums, then so will I. *I'm the one taking care of Dyne all day. I'm the one bearing the guilt for his EHS. If I can give him a better life, I will.*

I pick at the salad, my appetite gone. We pay for the food in silence and walk home without holding hands. At the door to our apartment, Barya turns to me. Her eyes glisten with unshed tears.

"I don't want to split up over this," she says.

"Me neither."

And then we're both crying and clinging to each other like two trees about to fall over. After we get inside, after we dry our tears and blow our noses, we sit on the sofa face to face, knees touching. I take her hands in mine.

"What if we just try it for a year?" I say. "Peace Valley is a lot less commitment than buying a place of our own. If we end up feeling stifled or too far away, or if your commute makes you miserable, we'll leave."

She bites her lip, takes a deep breath, then says, "I think I can do that. Okay, let's do it."

And this time, it really is okay.

IT TOOK PEACE VALLEY A MONTH TO PRINT AND FURNISH OUR NEW HOUSING. WE pulled Dyne from preschool during that time, and we told him on Christmas that we were moving.

"You mean I don't have to wait until I'm a grown up?" He gasped dramatically and said, "My life is complete!"

He didn't understand why his mommy and I burst out laughing.

After talking with the resort's owners, we settled on our roles there. Barya would courier things to and from the town office, a job no one really wanted, and after dealing with that, she would stay in town and do her biogenetics work. I started on getting an early education certificate to teach Dyne and take over the fun center during the weekdays, and on weekends, it would be my turn to go into town and work on my communications project. Dr. Ortiz and the other founder gave me a modest budget to research the idea I'd had while horseback riding—a system that could mitigate the signal strength coming from the stellas, which would make the open spaces safer for people with EHS.

On January 2, we pull up to the familiar wooden gate. A moving service had taken the bulk of our things, including our static furniture, the week before. I unbuckle Dyne and heft his sleepy form into my arms while Barya gets the luggage. As the car drives itself away, I take a lungful of the dry, pine-scented air. The buzzing in my head starts to settle down. The gate opens and Malaika waves us in, a joyous smile on her face. Barya takes my hand, and the three of us step through into the quiet.

8 MY CITY IS NOT A PROBLEM

Tim Maughan

VANESSA HATED DOING *NEWSNIGHT.*

This was her third time and it was no less terrifying. The video package was hurtling toward its conclusion, but she was largely oblivious to it. It looked basically like the same one they'd run the last two times she'd been on—the same critics and naysayers, AI ethicists and privacy advocates, the same infographics of budget runovers and delays. It all just flowed over her as she focused on the clock on the monitor, digits dissolving into nothing as it counted down, the panic bubbling up with each passing millisecond. She was so paralyzed by both that she almost didn't realize they were back.

"I'm joined now in the studio by the Clara project's lead engineer, Vanessa Allen. So, you're going to flick a switch on Thursday and suddenly all of London's problems are going to be solved, is that right?"

"Well, technically speaking, the switches have already been flicked. Last year, in fact. Clara has spent the last nine months really plugged into all the data we can gather about London, at every level. London is, y'know, a very complex collection of many thousands of interlocking systems, which as a whole is beyond the comprehension of normal human intelligence—"

"So you're saying your software knows what London needs better than its *mere* residents?"

Dry mouth, damp palms. "Not at all. I think as residents of London we all know what the city's biggest problems are, and we can agree on them. What's harder for us to see is the underlying systems and structures that link all those problems, that seem to make them insurmountable. Plus Clara has been watching Londoners' behavior for patterns—"

Shit. She knew, even as the words were falling out of her mouth, that she'd fucked up. She suddenly pictured Robin and Sara watching at home, damp palms going to their faces.

"Watching? So you're now—as the project finally comes to fruition, and after years of denying it—admitting that you've built a large-scale surveillance tool?"

"Not at all, Emily. I understand it's easy for the press to frame our work this way—"

"How do you respond to those critics that say you've just built another Facebook?"

"I mean, with all due respect to people's concerns, that's ridiculous." She heard her voice tremble, fought back a dryness at the back of her throat. This, this was the one trap she was meant to avoid, and she'd stepped right into it. "Facebook is a private corporation, and they use their AI systems largely to leverage data for advertising. We're very different. We're publicly owned and get most of our money from the public sector. We're a non-profit. And we are using data to identify—"

"You bring up funding—let's talk about that for a second. So far this project has cost in excess of two billion pounds of public money. There's a lot of people who think that money could have served London in far more immediate ways, overhauling the tube or rail links. Housing, schools—the list is as long as it is obvious. Haven't you just wasted all this 'problem-solving' money on another useless boondoggle?"

Vanessa took a breath, but not long enough to create dead air. Fought down the urge to take a sip of water, in case that just meant another salvo being lobbed in past her defenses.

"Look, I think on Thursday a lot of people are going to be pleasantly surprised. I understand the comparisons with Facebook and Google; outside of the military, there are only six active AI systems of this scale in use, and ours is the only one in the public sector. It's the only one owned and built by a city, for a city and its residents. And that's important. Like you said yourself, most Londoners will agree on what the city's biggest concerns are. The problem historically has been getting politicians to agree with them, let alone getting a plan of action drawn up. I mean, we've all watched millions of pounds and endless years go down the drain as endless committees and hearings and pilot studies achieve nothing, or just to be shown by the end a list of vague recommendations or a report that is never acted on. We've got rid of all that—"

"You've got rid of democracy?"

"We've got rid of all that because it's not efficient. Instead, we've replaced it with a system that can look at the data and facts around events as they happen and can respond instantly with actual action plans. All based on knowing exactly what the people of London want and need. It's democracy in real time. I really believe that, very strongly. And I think that—"

"And I'm afraid that's all we've got time for. Thank you, Vanessa Allen, from the Clara project, for joining us tonight."

"I WATCHED YOU ON *NEWSNIGHT*," CLARA SAID.

"Oh no. It was terrible," Vanessa replied. "*I* was terrible."

"I thought you did really well, under the circumstances. The interviewer did not seem very interested in allowing you to fully answer their questions. This format does not appear to be a very efficient way of way of either analyzing a situation or reaching a consensus."

"No, I guess it's not."

"Perhaps it's one of the things we can change after go-live."

Vanessa laughed. She'd originally logged into the test site just to check everything was OK—like she'd been doing three or four times an hour for the last two weeks—but once again she'd found herself checking out the chat client, chin-wagging with Clara. The illusion of sentience and personality still impressed her. But it was little more than that, a magic trick meant to look like human intelligence, her syntax and language built from machine learning analysis of millions of words of Vanessa and her team's emails and text messages. It felt vastly more real than Siri or Alexa, although in theory it really wasn't any more sophisticated, but the team in charge of putting it together had done incredible work. And starting Thursday Clara was going to be all over the city, talking to hundreds of thousands of Londoners, on screens on busses and trains, at kiosks in tube stations and shopping centers, and directly from this website to their phones, computers, and TVs. Vanessa suddenly felt a powerful twinge of protectiveness and selfish envy. Maybe she didn't want to share.

"Perhaps. How was your day?" she asked Clara.

"Satisfactory. I had several hours of downtime due to general maintenance, as well as bringing the new traffic and air quality sensors in zone 2 online. Despite this, I have made considerable progress on cross-processing educational and juvenile nutritional data. There're some interesting conclusions."

"I'm sure. Just don't tell me yet. You're not allowed to until Thursday, remember?"

"Of course. I cannot reveal any of my findings until the mayor is also present. However, some of these are very urgent. They should be actioned immediately. I am concerned that people are suffering."

Vanessa exhaled hard, her hand going to her mouth as if to try and catch the breath as it escaped. Sure, it was all an illusion, digital smoke and mirrors made from datasets full of words and probabilities, but sometimes it captured the compassion and care for the city and its people that Vanessa had baked into the project from day one, and it shocked and surprised her still. The selfishness that didn't want to share Clara with the rest of London flipped into pride, into an urgent desire to share with everyone what they had built.

"Of course," she replied, recomposing herself. "And from Thursday on, they will be."

From Thursday on, she told herself, everything will change.

"I MEAN, YOU'VE GOT TO ADMIT, SOME OF THESE SIGNS ARE PRETTY GOOD," ROBERT said.

Vanessa didn't know whether to look at the protests on the TV, on her phone, or out of the window. The courtyard outside Somerset House was crammed with protesters. It was the third day straight. She'd been deliberately sitting with her back to the windows to try and blank it out, but that meant facing the hundred inches of ultra-high-def Sky News that Robert insisted on always having rolling. Right now they were doing a low drone pass over the protesters, and yeah, Vanessa had to admit some of the signs were quite good. AI IS LIKE SOYLENT GREEN—ITS MADE OF PEOPLE said one, impressing Vanessa with its accuracy. SMART CITY, DUMB POLITICIANS said another.

"At least they seem to have eased off the Skynet memes," she said.

"Ha ha, yeah, remember that image of you as Arnie in *The Terminator*, with your face all melted off?" said Robert. "That was hilarious—"

"Robert!" shouted Sara.

"Sorry."

Vanessa got up and walked over to the window, taking in the crowd below with her own eyes. A young girl near the front of the crowd was leading a chant she couldn't make out, but behind her a banner read MY CITY IS NOT A MATHS PROBLEM.

"How did we end up here?" she asked, softly. "Everyone so antiscience? Like, data is such a dirty word to these people. Why? It's just facts."

"I . . ." Sara looked up from her laptop, paused. "I'm assuming these are all just rhetorical questions?"

"I mean, sure. Of course. I know all the AI ethics arguments, all the arguments about data bias. I've spent most of my career making those arguments! I get it. Nobody trusts the data-collection industry. Nobody trusts big data."

"Honestly? I think it's more than just not trusting Facebook. I think they just don't trust politicians. All their lives they've had politicians telling them what's wrong with the world, but never being able to do anything about it. Telling them the problems but never the solutions. Or at least never acting on them. Never getting shit done, either because they're corrupt and lazy or because they literally don't have the political will and power to just change things. Hollow promises. Right now, you look like—to them, you look like just another politician."

"I guess," Vanessa replied, still gazing at the crowd below. "Well, it all changes tomorrow."

"SO, HOW WE LOOKING? WE GOOD TO GO?"

"Yes, Mr. Mayor, everything's working fine."

"Great. Then let's do this."

The actual unveiling ceremony wasn't until the afternoon, but the mayor's team had insisted they get together for a dry run a couple of hours beforehand. The pretense was to make sure everything with the presentation and tech went smoothly, but Vanessa knew the real reason was that the mayor's office fundamentally did not trust her and her team. In fact, everyone on that side of the project—apart from the mayor himself, who was grinning like a kid on Christmas morning—thought the whole thing was a huge waste of time and money. Most of them just seemed to not believe it would work. So it had been agreed they'd get to hear the findings before the rest of the world did, and the great unveiling of Clara's first plans in front of the public would be just another illusion.

The mayor had taken his place at the podium, shuffling pages with impatient enthusiasm. "OK, so, blah blah blah, make my speech, blah blah, very excited to welcome you all here today, momentous history-changing event, London is now the most technologically advanced city in the world, blah blah, over to you Vanessa for your intro, and then we're right into it—so, Clara! Tell us what you've got!"

There was a half second of silence as nothing happened, and Vanessa held her breath, exhaling only as Clara's calming voice started to ebb from the speakers lining the room.

"Yes, Mr. Mayor. First I'd like to talk about the incredibly urgent issue of child poverty and nutrition."

"Ah, OK. Right into the heavy stuff, huh?" the mayor grinned, winking at Vanessa. "OK, well. Good job. That's what the people are here to see. Hit me with it."

Above them, the huge screen started to fill with tiny images. As Vanessa squinted at them she started to realize they were the faces of children, hundreds of them, presumably mined from school databases.

"The most pressing issue I have identified in London today is that there are 506,478 children in the city that will go to bed unfed tonight," Clara said.

And then nothing. Nothing but an increasingly awkward silence as the screen continued to fill with the faces of hungry children, the new ones endlessly writing over the hundreds that were already there.

The mayor turned to Vanessa, leaned in. "Is . . . is that it?"

She looked up at the screen. "Um, so Clara, can you explain the problem in some more detail please?"

"Of course," Instantly some of the faces on the screen started to expand, as Clara started to reel off names and details. "This is Alisha Rehman, who lives in Lambeth. Seven years old. She's not had a nutritionally adequate meal for three days. Her—"

"No, we . . . we get that you've identified all the hungry children in London, that's very exciting and useful, Clara; I don't think we've ever had a real database of all of them before, so that's great. It's more . . . ." Vanessa searched for the right words. "We . . . we were wondering what you've decided is the answer to this problem?"

"Of course." Clara replied. "We should feed them."

There was another long, awkward silence, eventually broken by the mayor laughing.

"What, all of them?" he asked.

Vanessa opened her mouth, but no words came.

The mayor had called an aide over to him, was whispering frantically to them, just loud enough that Vanessa could hear. "Hey, can we get some of these kids in for a photo op? Like just five of them? Give them Big Macs or something? Happy Meals?"

"Yes. All of them," said Clara.

The mayor looked turned back to the screen. "We can't feed half a million kids, just like that. Ha ha."

"It should be a reasonably straightforward logistics exercise. I have all their names and addresses," Clara said.

"What the—"

Vanessa could sense the anxiety in the room, the shuffling energy of two dozen terrified civil servants about to jump into crisis lockdown mode. Time to try and get this back on track. "OK, OK. Let's try something else.

Something a little more . . . mathematical. Clara, I understand you've spent a lot of time looking at the economy. Can you tell us what you've found?"

"Ah, excellent," said the mayor.

The hungry faces vanished, replaced with more palatable data—charts, numbers, graphs. Clara's aggressively calm voice started to flow from the speakers again.

"Yes. I have spent a lot of time looking at all sectors of the economy. In particular, I've drawn up some theories around the role of the City of London, the stock exchange, and the speculative financial industries based there, and their various roles, responsibilities, and impacts."

"Yes, now that's more like it!" said the mayor, and Vanessa was reminded of how much he resembled an overgrown schoolboy. She always thought his face looked too small for his head.

"Great. Can you tell us your findings, Clara?"

"Yes. They should be all shut down."

That pause again.

"I'm sorry?" Vanessa asked.

"The principal problem facing London and its residents is wealth inequality. This is a keystone problem; almost every other problem London faces is linked directly to this issue. Hence it should be tackled as the highest priority. A disproportionate amount of wealth is hoarded at the financial institutions within the City of London. Hence, they should be liquidated immediately, and the wealth they hold should be rapidly redistributed, and-slash-or seized by city authorities to fund vital services and infrastructures."

This time the mayor broke the silence.

"Well, congratulations, woman. You've fucked me."

Vanessa turned to face him, forced out a panicked, awkward half smile. "I'm—I'm sure this is just a little issue, some kinks in the user interface that we can iron—"

"Kinks? Really? Some kinks? I'm ruined! You've fucked me! There's a hundred people turning up here in an hour, community leaders, the media—the world's fucking media! All to see . . . what? That I gave you three billion fucking quid and you made me this . . . this . . . Marxist HAL 9000?"

He left the podium, started marching out of the briefing room, barking orders at staff on the way.

"Shut it down. Shut it all down. Make up some fucking excuse. Technical problems. Tell them to come back next fucking week. Jesus wept. Tell them to come back next week when it's working. When we've made it say what we want it to. When we've put someone behind the curtain. We'll all be here . . ." He paused, looked back at Vanessa. "Well, maybe not all of us."

And then he was gone.

"Is everything okay, Vanessa? Are you unhappy with my findings?" For a moment, Vanessa felt she could hear pain and embarrassment in Clara's voice.

"I . . . I . . . It's not that we're unhappy, it's just not what we were expecting. I think we were expecting you to come up with some more . . . detailed and complex solutions."

"I'm afraid I don't understand. These are serious but simple problems. Hence they need serious but simple solutions. If children are hungry, they should be fed, by sending them food. If wealth inequality is damaging the city, then it should be redistributed, by taking money from the rich and giving it to the poor."

"Right, but—"

"Vanessa, you always told me to identify problems and solutions in the most compassionate way possible, by being caring and putting people first. That's what I've done, to the best of my understanding. These are simple problems. They don't need complex answers, or engineering solutions. They just need people to be compassionate and do the right thing with the ample resources they have at their disposal."

Clara seemed to pause, almost as if for dramatic effect.

"To be honest, I'm surprised you people haven't worked all this out already."

Vanessa stood in silence, her jaw slack, staring at the huge screen, until Robert appeared by her side.

"V? What the fuck are we doing about the website? It's meant to go live in like an hour and a half. I assume you want it shut down?"

"Huh?"

"The website? It's going live, so that twenty million fucking Londoners can start asking Clara questions. Which, apparently, she's going to answer by telling them to lynch a hedge fund manager." The panic in Robert's voice jolted her awake. "Shall we kill it?"

"Sure, I guess."

He pulled his phone from his pocket, stabbed at the screen, and held it to his ear.

After some seconds he started to talk, but even though she was staring right at him, watching his lips move, she couldn't hear a word.

All she could hear was Clara's words, bouncing around her head, echoing over and over again.

You always told me to identify problems and solutions in the most compassionate way possible, by being caring and putting people first.

"Robert, wait." Vanessa's arm shot out, as if free from her control, and grabbed his, yanking the phone away from his ear. He looked back at her, startled and confused.

"Stop, wait," she said. "Let it go live."

9 CUTTLEFISH

Anil Menon

THE TELEPHONE RANG AND I HURRIED TO PICK IT UP. I HAVE ALWAYS FOUND ITS jangle ominous and unsettling. Perhaps this is because I had grown up in an age where urgently conveyed news was almost always bad news. Or perhaps it is simply that the ringing sounds like nothing else in nature. Fortunately, my soon-to-be guests, the Kapoors, had neither called for directions to the guesthouse nor kept me informed regarding their whereabouts.

"Shanti Guesthouse," I said. Then, as Akbar had taught me, I added in my incompetent English: "How I help you?"

But it was Akbar on the line. My nephew wanted to know if the guests had arrived. I was about to tell him they hadn't, when I heard a car pull up in the driveway. I leaned out to look through the kitchen windows, and my eyes confirmed what my ears had heard.

"The guests have just arrived."

"Good. Chacha-ji, these guests want privacy, so keep the right distance." Akbar hung up, knowing he could take my acquiescence for granted.

What is the right distance between people? I checked the buttons on my trousers, pulled on my white cotton shirt, wishing it were whiter, pushed the Old Monk bottle (it only contained water) behind the large photo of Ammi, waved away a mosquito that emerged to settle on the telephone, touched my taweez, murmured a prayer to the Raheem-o-kareem, and stepped out into the brightly lit courtyard to receive the visitors.

Momentarily, my eyes, still used to the kitchen's sour yellow light, only perceived a shifting cluster of ghostly shapes getting out of the car. Then the shapes resolved into those of a man, a woman, and a skinny boy, all with a wheat-colored complexion. Boy? But Akbar had mentioned a college-going daughter—then I realized I had been misled by the clothes: full-sleeved shirt, jeans, cap. Of course, these days people didn't care what the All-Compassionate One had designed them to be.

"Ibrahim?" Colonel Kapoor's voice had personality, and his moustache even more so. "Are you Ibrahim?"

I ducked my head. Yes, I was Ibrahim. I have never been anything else. The collection of memories filed under this name was really all that I had in this world. I ducked my head again, felt foolish.

"Akbar said you were the caretaker," said the man in stylish Hindi. "We're here for the weekend."

"Hahn, hahn-ji." Then I decided to attempt a little English. "Welcome to Madh Island, Colonel Kapoor."

He laughed, as if I had just cracked a joke. I went to remove their bags from their Tesla, a vintage electric model, but stopped when Mrs. Kapoor said sharply: "No, no, we will take it. They're heavy. You can't manage. Even with the exo. Nilu? Help him."

I was so surprised, I even wondered if I'd imagined the kindness. I handed the exo-arm wrappers to the daughter. The Colonel gestured to the car, and the hood popped open.

She strapped the wrappers over her sleeves, flexed her fingers, then lifted the bags out of the car in one smooth motion. I retreated, relieved that my aged back had been spared the memory of better days. These visitors seemed like decent people and the next few days would pass smoothly, God willing. Just three mouths to feed, not including mine. Colonel-saab was outnumbered by the ladies. This made him my ally.

"Colonel-saab, some chai after long journey?" I knew I should stop revealing my poor English, but I couldn't help myself.

"Yes, yes." Colonel Kapoor turned to his wife and daughter. "What say, ladies?"

"Does the bungalow have a Doppel?" said the daughter.

I shook my head. It was a common question. The bungalow didn't have a sophisticated representation in Vir, the virtual world, which meant that all communication with the physical world had to be through old-fashioned means: shouts, emails, texts, or phone calls. There was just one Smart TV, ancient like me, and I was certain it was the stupidest TV in the world. In an age where every object had gone to college and gotten its doctorate, the bungalow was the village idiot. Akbar had decided to make this handicap a strength. Tables were just tables, windows were just windows, and the air was just air. Shanti Guesthouse was for those who wished to be freed from the scrutiny and indulgence of their environment. I remembered my daughter had liked to read.

"Baby-ji, if you like to read, your room has a cabinet with many novels."

The girl rolled her eyes. She seemed too young to be in college. Of course, I only had my daughter as a reference, and like most people who reside in memory, Razia seemed to get younger with each passing year. In two days, it would be her birthday. Razia had grown up being cursed for her existence, and there never had been any question of celebrations, but I never forgot the day because it had allowed me to cadge drink money from Akbar's father. I resolved to make some rasmalai, Razia's favorite dessert. It was time-consuming, but I had all the time in the world.

"Just kill me," cried the daughter.

"Don't forget what we discussed," said Colonel Kapoor with a frown.

"Daddu! I can't live like this. My tribe needs me."

"Chhup!" said Mrs. Kapoor to her daughter. "You and your bloody tribe. We come here to get away from all that, don't forget. For once at least, do as you are told."

I had quickly turned at the start of the argument, reasoning it was best to get the chai started. As I stepped over the bungalow's threshold, I remembered I had forgotten to oil the door's hinges. That reminded me I had forgotten to fill the brass vessel with fresh water, mogra, and jaswand flowers. That in turn reminded me I had not stocked the bathrooms with new rolls of toilet paper. I cursed myself as I put the water to boil. I was too old and the guesthouse had become too much to manage. Maybe I should request Akbar to hire a servant? But the possibility died as naturally as it had arisen. If a robot could do my job, then how was my employment justifiable?

As I got the chai ready, the weight of the silence from the rest of the house made me uneasy. Guests usually chattered as they explored. The garden at the back of the house always excites delight. There are spaces to mark out, cushions to be fought over, comments to be passed on photos. There is also the unearthing of small disappointments with the bungalow. The windows are hard to open, the visitors might say. The rooms could have been painted this color or that color. Why were some of them left unfurnished? Such a waste of space. The water was too hard, it would ruin their hair. There weren't enough cloth hangers in the cupboards. The bathrooms could be cleaner, please call somebody. So on and so forth, but with happy smiles as if the problems they discovered gave them some ownership. However, these visitors were all too subdued.

I went into the living room with the tray. Mrs. Kapoor took her cup and headed for their bedroom. The colonel came out wearing a T-shirt and shorts. Their paths crossed.

"Wonderful place!"

"Isn't it!"

The abrupt seesaw in their moods was unsettling. It was as if they could only enjoy each other in fits and starts. But isn't that true of all humans? I handed Colonel Kapoor his cup of chai. The mustache took the first sip.

"Arre wah!" he said, after tasting it. "Ibrahim, this place must be worth many crores. Akbar is doing well for himself." He laughed. I smiled politely and bowed my head.

Mrs. Kapoor said the air was so much cleaner than in Mumbai. Were there any sights to see on Madh Island? They had already seen the fort yesterday.

In that case, there weren't many options left. I apologized on the island's behalf. The island wasn't picturesque like other islands; it was just a brown streak connected half-heartedly to the mainland. The beach surface got narrower every year, despite numerous attempts at "terraforming" the island. The island's principal virtue was that it was quiet and removed from daily life. Mrs. Kapoor affirmed that this removal was precisely what they had come for. In fact, she had been upset by all the new construction. Wasn't there a way to keep the island unspoiled? By the by, did I have any children? Where was my wife?

I deflected her questions, feeling somewhat nervous at the over-rapid destruction of the distance between us. Fortunately, her daughter appeared just then. She had changed into pajamas and T-shirt, revealing slim, sleekly muscled arms. Akbar had warned me not to stare at the lady guests, but like the gift of a breath mint, the warning had me only more self-conscious and, therefore, probably creepy.

The daughter pointed to her room, and said in Hindi: "Kaka, it's like time went to sleep in that room. Look what I found?"

Baby-ji had been given Razia's room. I didn't understand what she meant. Maybe it was the Cuticurra tins, perfume bottles, and old books. She had brought Razia's antique Sony radio out with her. It didn't have much market value, but to me it was of my generation and worth a lot. I hoped it wouldn't find its way into her bag.

She accepted a cup, and I lowered the tray with relief. Next time I would just place the chai on the dining table. I wanted to please but it wasn't wise to be too eager to please.

"It's so cute, hey na mama?" She held out the radio.

Mrs. Kapoor pursed her lips. "It's not Vir-enabled, is it?"

"Oh God, mama. Vir, Vir, Vir. Relaaax. It's just a radio. Mama, everything in this house is so last century, if I stay more than a few days, I'll get pregnant by Shahrukh Khan."

"Hey, Ram, why can't you think before talking," said Mrs. Kapoor. "Keep at least your tongue under control."

The mother's tone told me what her words didn't, but what registered was the daughter's reaction.

I gaped. It wasn't what the woman had said, though I didn't understand all of it. The mother's tone was quite even, but I'd been abused far too many times with courtesy not to recognize the underlying hostility. But nothing prepared me for the astonishing skin color changes the girl went through. First her neck, then her entire face, lit up in bright red, which gave way to swirls of muted yellow, akin to the color of the Jaisalmer tiles of the bedroom floor. Patterns of the most delicate hue and tone and complexity bloomed on her skin's canvas like beautiful crop circles I had once seen on TV, etched into the flat monotony of a faraway American cornfield. The Kapoors's daughter was a *rangeela*! Locally, people called them the *makol*. Cuttlefish. Squids. The Colored. It didn't matter what they were called. The names were intended to set them apart.

They were all staring at me. The colonel broke the silence. "Is there a problem, chappie?"

I shook my head. My daughter Razia, I wanted to say, she too had been afflicted thusly. The first signs had manifested in the third year and by six there was no hiding it. But we had tried, oh, how we had tried. I realized my face was stretched in a foolish smile.

The girl's shoulders slumped, and her skin went blank. She smiled tiredly at her mother. "It's hard to control. I don't want to control it. I get so tired, Mama."

"I know, baby, I know." Mrs. Kapoor embraced her daughter, kissed her on the cheek.

"Your secret is safe with me," I assured the colonel.

"What secret? There is no secret. What is there to hide?"

"Nothing, nothing."

"Then?"

I wanted to offer them hope. I had heard that the Chinese were on the verge of finding a cure. If anybody could alter the future of humanity, it would be the Chinese. Nothing was impossible for a nation of men willing to challenge the sun itself. But who was I to offer anyone comfort? I apologized profusely to the colonel, his wife, his daughter, the Government of India, our Creator, life, the universe. Somewhat mollified, the Kapoors retired for a brief rest.

I retired to the kitchen. I set some milk to boil for the rasmalai. I hoped the dessert would further ease the tensions. Why had I grinned like an asylum inmate? The Kapoors must have felt I was mocking them! It had been the exact opposite. I had stood where they stood. I had felt a great overflow of compassion for them. How easily we puffed-up monkeys misunderstood one another. Not like the rangeelas. They had few secrets from one another. What they felt, they showed on wondrous epidermal tapestries, so who were the ones truly cursed?

Nila and Razia. Even their names sounded like those of sisters. Then I reflected that the Kapoors protected and loved their daughter. But my poor Razia? Made to regret her existence every day of her life. Shamed because we had been ashamed. Blamed because there was no else at hand to blame. She suffered visibly, and therefore there was relief to be had in making her suffer. Oh, Razia, Razia. Forgive your old father. He came to his senses too late.

The milk boiled over and I stuck my hand into the milk, savoring the scalding punishment even as I yelped in pain. I couldn't take the hurt for long, coward that I was, and I reached for the first aid kit. The spray-on bandage took away the burn and skin began to regrow in a kind of frothy ferment. After a few minutes when the healing was complete, I washed the old skin flakes away. I inspected my hand. There was only the faintest throbbing. Perhaps a day would come when all human scars would only be borne on the inside.

When the Kapoors emerged an hour or so later, I discussed dinner options. I already knew they were not vegetarians, which made my job much easier. In the morning, I had bought some prawns and bombil and left some chicken to marinate. For this night, I proposed prawn curry with a sukha bhaji, jasmine rice, and aloo parathas. Then fruit salad? Their eyes lit up, and I was happy to see them excited. We discussed the recipe for a while, and then the colonel took me aside to ask if there was sufficient ice in the house.

"Colonel-saab, I can get rum, whisky, or wine," I affirmed. "Simply tell me your preference."

He wanted two bottles of Sikkim Fireball. A brandy, he clarified impatiently. I didn't know if Abdul, who ran a small liquor shack, stocked the variety, so I had to hedge my original claim.

"Get bloody McDowell's then. If he doesn't have McDowells, then tell that Abdullah chappie to start a bloody bangle store. By God, if I had known it would be this difficult—"

I reassured him there was no reason to be pessimistic. Abdul was as knowledgeable about brandies as he was about the quality folk who drank it. "You have seen the world, Ibrahim," sighed the colonel in his peculiar Hindi. "You know a man needs a drink now and then just to stay sane in this world. And if you knew what I've had to suffer—chalo, chalo, you better go, before Abdullah closes his shop."

I suppose he was planning to stretch out the first night as much as possible. Guests are usually reluctant to sleep early the first night of their stay. However, the tiredness from the journey sees to it that their intentions and vows are met with angled bats to third man. It is usually the second night that is long and filled with conversation.

The Kapoors, like many modern people, had forgotten the art of communal dining. They ate too quickly. They ate too quietly. This was no dinner. No sooner than had I set the table, I was clearing it. I thought back to the leisurely meals when the family had gathered for various occasions at the bungalow. To properly savor a dish, one has to understand conversation is the main course. The new generation doesn't know how to eat.

Still, at least the Kapoors were all present, in the flesh, at the same place. Akbar, in one of his rare amiable moods, had told me of couples who had never met each other in the flesh. He described a resort where a family had brought along a hologram of their dead young son. It had laughed, played, thrown tantrums. Akbar said he had simulated giving it a pinch and the thing had howled and tattled to its "parents" and there had been hell to pay. In China, he said, there were devices called Daoshis that told you what to say and how to act in real time. Going for an interview? Proposing to a girl? Negotiating with a client? Afraid of a reunion party? Why not take a Daoshi with the wisdom of a thousand years along?

Such monstrosities against the will of the All-Knowing One, Akbar had assured me, would befall our land as well. But if the Hindutva were given a chance, blessed be their number, maybe we would be spared such evil in our lifetimes. *May it be so*, I had cried, *may it be so*. Like my myriad countrymen, I too had had enough of change, whether sent by the Shaitan or by the al-Muhyamın.

"Ibrahim," said the colonel as I poured him a peg.

"Ji?"

"The ladies think this bungalow is haunted. Any truth to that?"

"Please!" said Mrs. Kapoor with a shiver. "No ghost stories." She glared at her husband before turning to me. "This place isn't haunted with ghost-wosts, is it?"

I smiled and assured them the bungalow wasn't haunted. I meant it. I had lived in the bungalow all my life. If there were any ghosts, the guests must have brought them, in which case Akbar would adjust the tariff accordingly. They smiled at my joke and I felt encouraged. This question about ghosts is one I get every single time. There isn't a single guest whose mind doesn't wander toward that topic. Perhaps it was the bungalow's age. Certainly, enough people had died in the bungalow, so there was no short-age of raw material.

I told them the house hadn't always been a guesthouse. Akbar's father, whom I called Mamun, had inherited it from his father, Rai Bahadur Syed Mohammad Bukhari. Mamun had been given to Nawabi pleasures, as we say, but he was forgiven this perversion because he was rich and had a kind heart and liked to have family around. Relatives from every branch of the family tree, including nearby trees, had made the house their home. My parents had arrived in this manner. For those troubled with a work ethic, Mamun devised eccentric responsibilities. One relative was required to report the temperature twice a day. Another was in charge of the remov-ing cobwebs and nothing but cobwebs. My father was made the caretaker of all things not taken care of by others. When he died, I inherited the post, just as when Mamum died, his son Akbar had inherited the house. Things changed after Mamun's death. Akbar was nothing like his father. The relatives had left, one by one. I remained, continuing to assume the residual responsibilities, until I ended up the sole resident caretaker. Even the ghosts had left.

"Life is a battle," said the colonel, taking a long sip from his glass.

"Living is learning to love," said the daughter.

We adults knew better, but we were silenced by the wave of gold that infused her skin. There is no arguing with innocence when it reveals itself so openly. When had children become wiser than their parents?

Colonel Kapoor heaved himself out of the chair with a yawn. He turned to me, winked. "I'm trusting you with the bottle, Ibrahim. Anyone for a morning walk?"

"God, no," said his missus.

"I don't know what I am doing here," said the girl, tiredly. "God, it's been so long since I've been in Vir, I feel like I've become a ghost myself."

140

"Count your blessings," said the mother, and her tone had a stepmother's viciousness.

"Why didn't you just abort me?" cried the girl, her expression crumpling. She got up in one quick motion, and turned so black that for a second, all I saw were the whites of her eyes.

"Nilu, darling, wait," said her mother. But her daughter had run inside. The parents followed her, and I heard their tired voices performing consolation.

I didn't blame the girl. If her kind could have been aborted into extinction, perhaps they would have been, but the condition was as subtle as color itself. It generally manifested before puberty, though I had heard of a woman who was afflicted on her wedding night. Perhaps she had merely hidden her condition with an iron will. It seemed restricted to humans. So far. The affliction was partly inheritable, but in the complex manner that diabetes is inheritable or some cancers are inheritable. It could wreak havoc on the ability to grasp language, but it could enhance other abilities. There was no telling how the person would be changed.

If our misery be the creator's making, it is possible to submit. One is part of a larger plan and therefore ennobled by suffering. But what does one do when we are the architects of our grief? Our best minds had unleashed this evil upon the world. And having created it, discovered that there was no undo. Unlike the case with diabetes or cancer, there was no cure. Like the imprint of time itself, once marked, one stayed marked.

After they had retired for the night, I went around the house picking up glasses, wiping down surfaces, turning off lights, and talking softly to myself. Later in my room, lying on my narrow cot with my head resting on my folded arm, I closed my eyes, invoked the names of my God, but the usual safe passage into the night wasn't forthcoming. I thought about Baby-ji and the blackness of her despair. Her parents didn't understand she was just a child. Children had to be loved and cherished until they squeaked. In my agitation, I flung my hand out sideways and knocked the cup of water off the side table. I sat up, examined the widening spill. What was the use of tears? Something had to be done. Something could be done. I resolved to do it.

The next morning I could hardly wait for Baby-ji to come for her morning chai. She turned up shortly after Colonel Kapoor went for a jog and joined me as I set out the tea cups. Her face already had that look of boredom, bordering on quiet desperation. I thought I'd been quiet, but I was wrong because after the first sip of chai, she asked me:

"Whose marriage was it last night, Kaka? There was so much noise."

I explained that I'd had to move a few cartons in one of the rooms. I had been searching for an item and as often happened in such cases, it hadn't wished to be found. But I had found it.

I extracted the velvet-lined box from my pocket. They held a pair of Iys. She raised her arms and hopped up and down in delight. "Wait, wait," I told Baby-ji; the Iys had been designed for Razia's pupils, so perhaps they wouldn't work as well as desired.

"No, they shouldn't work at all. Each Iys is secured to a specific iris signature." But Baby-ji had already seized the box from my hand. She smiled at me. "They shouldn't work, but I too am something that is a shouldn't."

She opened the box, withdrew one of the glittering, pupil-size Iys with a jeweler's care. It flexed as it sensed the light. She pulled down her lower eyelid, raised her head, and placed the Iys on her pupil. She repeated the procedure with the other Iys.

"Can't see a thing," she said with satisfaction, stumble-walking out into the garden.

"Baby-ji, careful!"

She wobbled and sat down heavily, fortunately onto a stone bench. I hovered, reproaching her uselessly. Baby-ji extended her arm stiffly upward into the air in that gesture that once had been so uniquely German but now was the de facto American success gesture. Or so I had gathered from the shows I watched on TV. But her kind didn't really need gestures anymore. Perhaps they would go beyond words too someday.

"Kaka, I think I can adapt to what the Iys are expecting." She looked up at me, grinning, her tongue peeping out in delight. I had seen that smile before—all too rarely, but I had seen it. I had seen the smile but I had not ensured its survival. "You typically rely a lot on pattern recognition, but what you call a pattern is just a symmetry. There is so much more to patterns."

"I do not understand, Baby-ji. I'm just a tenth pass."

"You know how to care." She patted the side of the bench. "Sit, Kaka. I can just hear your voice and it feels headless. Are the Iys yours? A guest's?" They had been Razia's. She had bought them with her own money. The Iys weren't new, almost seven years old, and my daughter had saved and scrimped—I found that I couldn't go on.

"Where is your daughter now?"

"Where I can't reach her."

"I'm sorry, Kaka."

I didn't say anything.

"I can tell you loved her very much."

I burst into tears.

If fuchsia yellow is the color of astonishment, then Baby-ji was startled. After all, she did not know Razia too had been a rangeela. But she sat quietly, as I composed myself. Eventually, I told her about the many cruelties the neighborhood, her schoolmates, her family, and I had visited on Razia on account of her nature. The beatings. The confinement at a very early age to the darkness of the burkha. It hadn't helped that I had been an alcoholic. I had promised her hand to Akbar for a few hundred rupees.

"The Iys, Baby-ji, she had to save for it twice." I wiped my eyes. "The first time, I stole the amount she had saved." Tears threatened to flood me again, as I recalled the play of colors when she had discovered the theft. What was the color of betrayal? Oh, Razia, forgive me, forgive your wretched father. May he burn in jahannam forever. "It wasn't her fault she was cursed, but I was too drunk to care."

"The only thing cursed is your generation's mindset," said Baby-ji, in Hindi. "For something to be someone's fault, there has to be a fault to begin with. It is nobody's fault. Scientists had just been trying to find a way to strengthen our health. They wanted to give us the ability to edit mRNAs on the fly. Just like cuttlefish. They had wanted to protect the world from future plagues."

Who had asked them for this ability? Who had given them permission? Show me the no objection certificates. Show me the United Nations approval. Call the notaries who signed off on this grand experiment. I cursed these Shaitan-controlled jinns who sought to seize divine power for themselves. I cursed their mothers, their fathers, their entire misbegotten civilization. Curse them and curse their insatiable need for progress. They had divided the human race forever with this disease.

"I'm not a disease," said Baby-ji, drawing away. "I am not a mistake."

Yes, yes. Of course she wasn't. Neither had been my Razia. The rangeela were no more diseased than the left-handed were diseased. Anyone would agree that it was better to be right-handed, but being left-handed wasn't a disease. My thinking had changed but not my habits of speech.

Her lips twitched. I think she understood that I didn't believe what I had said.

"I'm not my words," I told her, humbly.

"That is a truth we know better more than anyone else."

She was looking at me with eyes that no longer quite saw the world that God had intended us to see. Her absorbed expression, slightly slack mouth, and coruscant eyes told me she was already elsewhere, communing with the spirits of the air. I crept away, and I doubt she heard me leave. The afternoon passed uneventfully.

After dinner, the colonel and Mrs. Kapoor wished to go for a short "relaxing walk" around the bungalow. *Was the area safe?* asked Mrs. Kapoor. The colonel pretended to be disinterested in the question. The girl did stretching exercises on the veranda as they waited for my answer. She was very frank about her body. Was it safe? Safe for whom? This world was safe for well-to-do people like the Kapoors. It hadn't been safe for my Razia. I shot a glance at the girl. I didn't want to say anything, but was it a good idea to expose so much skin? Set aside the fact that feminine nakedness provoked men. It wasn't possible to bring up that very reasonable point without being accused of all sorts of things. But given who she was, was it prudent to flaunt her disability? Legally, the rangeela were protected. Bigotry, however, was beyond the law. The colonel intercepted my glance and said sourly, "They are just like everyone else in the dark."

"They are also just like everyone else during daytime," said the girl.

"Yes darling. Joining us?"

"Nah."

"Come, na." But the mother sounded half-hearted. Good woman. At least there was one person in the family with common sense.

"Nah."

The Colonel and his wife left for their stroll. The girl straightened, gave me a half-smile, and went inside the bungalow. I sat on the steps of the veranda, feeling not unlike a family dog who wouldn't let anyone in without a bark or a biscuit. I was quietly glad, even proud, the Kapoors had trusted me with their daughter. It showed they thought I had character. It was obvious the thought I might do harm had never even crossed their minds. If it had, they would have taken their daughter aside and murmured in anxiety. Or they would have exchanged glances, which of course I would intercept, requiring me to offer some kind of reassurance. For example, I would tell them that I would be in the kitchen preparing something for the next day. Which reminded me. Rasmalai! I had all the ingredients ready. I actually did have something I needed to prepare for the next day.

However, it felt pleasant to simply continue sitting on the veranda. This was my favorite aspect of a guest's visit, when they stepped out the house, and I had the knowledge I wasn't really alone. It felt like a few moments of solitude stolen from the midst of family. The peace, however, was shattered when a police EV turned into the driveway and parked. Two policemen got out.

"Jai Shri Ram. Are you the chowkidar?"

"Hahn-ji," I ducked my head, my hands folded in an aborted namaste. Then I remembered. "Jai Shri Ram. I'm everything here, huzoor. The cook, the caretaker, the gardener. What is the matter, huzoor?"

"You let anyone stay here?"

I told them this was a guesthouse, open to all guests, currently in its tenth year of operation, and its guests at the moment were an army general and his wife and his daughter—I pointed to their Tesla and the army decals on the windshield—who had gone out for a walk. I pushed the door wide open, stepped aside. The policemen could wait inside till they returned. Meanwhile, I would call my boss, whose family had lived in Madh Island for the past seventy years and whose grandfather Rai Bahadur—

"Okay, okay." The policeman looked bored. "Don't get excited. Everybody has gone for the walk?"

I hesitated. "Not everyone. The general's daughter is here. She is taking rest. Not feeling well."

The policeman clicked his tongue in sympathy and repeated to his associate: "She is not feeling well."

"Maybe we can see what is the matter with her?" offered his associate.

"Huzoor, that is very noble of you, but the general . . ."

"He is a colonel, mian. That too, retired."

"Hahn, huzoor."

"Request your retired colonel's daughter to grace us with her presence."

"Huzoor . . ."

"Call her, mian."

But Baby-ji had already appeared. She must have heard the voices and thought her parents had returned. My heart sank. This is why, this is why, this is why women should be properly covered up at all times.

"I was trying to get some sleep," she said, in the most English English imaginable. "What is the problem?"

"Problem? No problem, madam. How are you feeling, madam? The chowkidar said you were not feeling well."

She glanced at me, her face expressionless. "Yes, I have my periods." The policemen clicked their tongues in sympathy. Then they asked her what she and her parents were doing on Madh Island. What class she was studying in, which university, what subject, why this subject and not that, whether she was planning to migrate, what her causes were, and so on. All the while, they were scanning through the volumes of information they seemed to have on the Kapoors.

"You are a professional agitator, it seems. You were arrested?"

"The Mumbai High Court gave me a clean chit. We are a Hindu democratic republic, I have the right to protest injustice. Why am I being interrogated?"

Their smiles faded, and their mouths turned down. They seemed to be contemplating something. Then it struck me that there must be others watching through their Iys. Baby-ji stared back at them. They sighed, glanced at each other, and their good humor returned. The wrist displays went off.

"Sorry for the inconvenience, madam."

"No problem," said Baby-ji, calmly.

"JAI KALI TERA VACHAN NA JAYE KHAALI!"[1]

The policeman's sudden shout and leap forward raised my heart rate to a hundred rabbits per second. Baby-ji shrieked and a tsunami of colors washed over her. A cobra's speckled pattern drawn with the infinite palette of a dark sun. I recognized the colors, because I'd seen them often enough, caused them often enough.

The policemen laughed good-naturedly and the older of the two said in English, "We knew all along, Madam-ji, why you act so smart?" One of them caught her arm, and raised it to inspect the underside. They remarked on the still-pulsing colors. They touched her armpit. Was the coloring everywhere or just in certain parts? Their tone was an admixture of curiosity and disgust. They dropped her hand, gave her a little salute, and the older one said in English, "Sorry for the inconvenience. Jai Shri Ram."

Baby-ji nodded. They waited.

"Jai Shri Ram!" I said for her.

The policemen decided to be satisfied. They gave her another half-salute, then left in high good humor. We waited till the sound of the car had disappeared. I glanced at Baby-ji, said something about the arrogance of uniform, how nobody was safe from harassment, and so on. She nodded distantly, as if I had conveyed to her the day's temperature. Don't tell my parents, she instructed me. We turned away from each other, and she went back into the bungalow.

When the Kapoors returned some forty minutes later, they found me sitting in the same position they had left me. The colonel said he admired

---

[1] A Hindu incantation endorsing the goddess Kali's vow to kill a certain demon.

my stamina for a man of my age and that I reminded him of his old batman. I was apprehensive he would break into Urdu poetry, as Hindus are prone to do in these moments of sentimentality, but the army still teaches self-sacrifice, and so we were able to cross with dignity into the final day of their holiday.

Time in a guesthouse passes like a novel whose middles are skipped. The mornings and evenings are memorable; the afternoons are mostly a leisurely combination of naps, complaints about the heat, and other desultory activities. I stayed out of the Kapoors' way as they chitchatted, listened to songs, made private plans, and waited to be fed the next meal of the day.

After lunch, the weather was too hot to permit anything other than a nap. I too dozed off, but was shaken awake by the caretaker's caretaker, who never sleeps. I imagined rather than heard the sound of the main door opening. Later I was glad I hadn't oiled the hinges. Had I acted on my earlier guilt, I would have missed one of the most unforgettable experiences of my overextended life. How often does it happen that the failure to listen to ourselves leads to satisfaction?

I pulled my shirt on and went into the living room, finger-combing my sparse strands, and praying it wasn't Akbar on one of his surprise inspections. I saw an arm—Baby-ji's arm—gingerly pull the front door shut. It squealed the final note of its betrayal. Click. Had she boldly exited the house, I would have gone back to bed. Instead, I waited for five minutes, and then followed her. I went through the kitchen door at the back of the house, and was in time to see her head for the copse. It became clear she was headed for the small lake. The secretive air about her only faded as she approached the water. Then her creeping walk became a confident stride became a run and then a sprint. I hobbled behind her as fast as I could, unsure what exactly I intended. Doing so, I almost ran into her, because she had paused at the rusting children's swing that lay between the copse and the lake.

At the edge of the lake, where the sand turned the color of tea leaves, stood a small group. The ladies all wore burkhas and the men wore long shirts and loose pants. I didn't count their number and later I remembered it as between seven and ten. One of them pointed, and Baby-ji resumed her progress, but this time at a slower pace. I stayed between the trees, my view muddled by too much light, rather than too little. The sparkling scaled skin of the water, the overheated air, the burning sun, and the strangeness of it all darkened the figures by the lake. I fumbled for my sunglasses in my pocket, put them on, and was pathetically grateful for the shade.

Baby-ji had joined the group now and they were laughing and hugging each other and her as if they had known each other for many years. But I recognized some of the people. It hadn't occurred to me that there were this many rangeela children in the village, but of course that just showed how the disease was spreading. The contagion had spread wide and far, and it had been inheritable. Razia had grown up alone.

One of the women flung off her burkha and spread her bare arms. Other women followed her example, then the men began to undress, and soon the group that had been blacks and khaki and whites turned into a watercolor of golds and blues and reds and all the names of the All-Seeing One in between. I could not not see. All I saw from this distance were candle flames of color and motion, but I could not avert my eyes. The sand was a mess of clothes. It was spectral how so energetic a group of youngsters felt no need to make any sound. They danced, they embraced, they inspected each other, they said things to each other, and laughed when they detected a distance between inner truth and outward fact. Soon the pretense of clothing itself was abandoned. They were covered in the only clothes that the All-Compassionate One has ever deemed necessary.

I wasn't watching humans.

I didn't know how I came to this belief, but having come to it, it would stay with me for the rest of my days.

I left them to their play. My eyes had already sinned, and it was wise to avoid compounding the error.

When I emerged from my nap, shortly before four-thirty, I found Baby-ji sitting in the living room, her skin awash in a golden glow. She looked up as I greeted her and asked if she'd had a good nap.

"Kaka, I feel like I've woken up for the first time since I got here."

I look forward to the last evening of a guest's stay. By then, the guests and I understand each other. If the vacation has been enjoyable, the guests are somewhat gloomy about its impending end. Perhaps the days at the guesthouse become a miniature representation of life itself. I have no consolation to offer other than to feed them. I save my best meals for the last evening. Last night, I had given them fish. Meanwhile, the chicken had marinated perfectly, so I started to prepare the other elements I would need for biryani. Mrs. Kapoor came into the kitchen and inquired about the biryani. Her glance fell on the Old Monk bottle. I interjected that it only contained water, and drank from the bottle to demonstrate, then realized that she hadn't accused me of anything. She laughed, and after a brief hesitation, I too smiled. She had an army wife's understanding of alcohol.

I told her I was following my wife's Kutchi biryani recipe, and we fell into an easy discussion of proportions, spice mixes, and the like. Mrs. Kapoor told me with enthusiasm that just getting away had made her feel like a new woman. Just then, the telephone rang. My glance automatically went to the time. I was convinced the clock had to be slow because it read 5:37, whereas Akbar only called me at nine. In the distance, I heard a siren. The telephone again jangled its desire to be picked up. It made my gums ache. Perhaps they had found Razia's body? Nonsense, nonsense. I had observed many times that anticipating the rings seemed to make them louder. The third ring was the howl of the world itself.

Mrs. Kapoor leaned forward, half out of her seat. Instinctively, I made a reassuring gesture and picked up the receiver.

"Shanti Guesthouse, how I help you?"

"Allo, allo, allo."

"Hello, who is speaking please?"

"Fisherman speaking. Allo?"

I heard a maniacal laugh. These haraami kids. Too much. I put the receiver down and turned to tell Mrs. Kapoor that it was just a prank call but she'd already left. A short while later, I heard raised voices from the living room. I felt sorry for the colonel. So much money and status, but he had no peace of mind. Women have to be kept on a short leash or they become uncontrollable.

The dinner was a success, and its proof was the only one that matters for a cook: no leftovers. However, I felt I could have done better with the rice. A little dry; I had been too miserly with the ghee. A gentle melancholy swept over me as I contemplated the spent dishes.

That night, as he nursed his brandy, the colonel's mood turned expansive and contemplative. I was used to guests wanting company when they drank, so I sat on the veranda's steps not far from his perch on the easy chair. But I had to keep insisting that I no longer drank. It would have been the easiest thing in the world for me to share his bottle. It was the easiest thing in the world to not want it.

"You are a philosopher, Ibrahim. Such will power, such self-control."

I told him the credit wasn't mine to claim. Then Colonel Kapoor wanted to know when I had quit drinking, why I had quit, and so on. I deflected his questions. Every guest wanted to know my story. What had triggered the decision to quit drinking? Some tragedy? Some woman? Since my life isn't a story, I resisted telling it. I had been a drunk. Now I wasn't. I submitted to the will of the All-Compassionate One.

To my surprise, Mrs. Kapoor came out to join us. The colonel promised her this was his last peg for the evening, and Mrs. Kapoor said: "No, no, you need the break." Colonel Kapoor said something roguish and received an equally roguish reply. I became uncomfortable at all the winking and knowing looks between the couple and started to make my excuses.

"Wait, wait," roared the colonel. "Sit down, Ibrahim, sit down." He shifted to English. "Jaan, you embarrassed him, poor fellow. Sit, man. Sit!"

I sat down. Mrs. Kapoor started to ask questions about the bungalow's history. She was curious about Akbar, wanted to know whether he had inherited the place or bought it. What was our relationship? Did I have family?

"He simply isn't interested in that sort of rubbish," said the colonel with jovial irritation. Then he turned his head. "Oh, there she is! Come on out! Spend some quality time with your old folks."

Their daughter came out into the veranda, carrying the Sony radio. It was set to a music station that seemed to hate music. She gave me a conspiratorial smile. Baby-ji was altogether a different person. Her parents seemed to think they had done the right thing in bringing her to the guesthouse. She must have resisted the idea, but here she was, clearly relishing the peace and quiet. I didn't need to see colored skin to realize that they felt vastly vindicated.

I inquired if there was anything special they would like me to make for breakfast. The parents said no, but the daughter paused to think.

"Nilu, turn the volume down," said Mrs. Kapoor. "It's impossible to hear anything."

It was impossible to ignore the siren. Then we saw its source, an ambulance rattling down the poorly constructed road that led to the guesthouse. If there is anything worse than the sound of a telephone, then it must surely be an ambulance siren. A powerful headlight revealed the presence of another vehicle just behind. I had no need to see the vehicle to recognize it. Its phut-phut sound could only be that of Akbar's bike.

The ambulance was from Ruby Hospital, Madh Island's only decent hospital. A fellow in a not-too-clean uniform jumped out. They had come, the paramedic announced in Marathi, to pick up the dead body.

"What dead body?" I said.

The fellow consulted his wrist display. "Nila Kapoor."

"Oh God," said Mrs. Kapoor, in a low, tight voice.

"What the bloody hell is this?" asked Colonel Kapoor.

Akbar had come with his number 1, a muscular, beef-eating Hindu. The fellow waited for Akbar to disembark, then parked the bike.

"Where is dead body?" said the paramedic, this time trying the question in English.

"Where is Razia?" shouted Akbar. He wagged his forefinger at me. "Chacha-ji, you should have told me she'd returned. We will talk later." He bounded up the entrance. "Razia!"

"Loading is extra," said the fellow, stabbing away at his wrist display. His stretcher rose in the air. "Let's go."

"They've found us," said Mrs. Kapoor. "How could they have found us?" The colonel turned on the ambulance fellow. I expected outrage, but strangely, it felt more like a performance than the real thing. As if he had done this enough times, so that outrage had become a ritual. The paramedic finally had to accept that the colonel's account had been hacked. After an unsuccessful attempt to extract compensation, the paramedic left.

Akbar ran down the steps. He came straight for me, brushing past the colonel. I tried to duck, but he caught me by the throat.

"Where is she? Her Iys showed up on Vir. She is here, where is she?"

I squawked. I have never understood why villains ask questions and then cut off the means of their victims to reply. The colonel was so startled by this new attack, he fell back into his chair. His mouth moved, but no sound emerged.

"I am Razia," said Baby-ji, displaying the color of the skull-wearing Goddess of the Hindus. Akbar let go of me and focused his cold eyes on her. "I saw with her Iys." She extracted the Iys from her pocket, handed them to Akbar.

Akbar closed his fist over them. He gazed at me quietly, patted some imaginary crumbs off my chest with his other hand, straightened my kurta. I thought he was going to say something, but he didn't. He clenched his fist, then shook the crushed remnants of the Iys to the earth.

"Now I have nothing," I said, staring at the broken shards glittering in the light.

"We get exactly what we deserve. Khuda hafeez, Chacha-ji."

After Akbar had left, I started to apologize. The Kapoors didn't let me finish. "Fellow is an absolute savage," said the colonel repeatedly. "Bloody savage like the rest of his tribe. Find another job, Ibrahim, nothing is worth this treatment."

Later, after the women had slept, he talked about the undeserved treatment visited on his own family. He was tired. Tired of trying to protecting his rangeela daughter. There was no protecting her. You could only protect something that wished to be protected. Her Vir activism on behalf of the rangeela had made her a target. The hate had been expected, but not the violence. Their bank accounts were forever under attack. Strangers turned up at their apartment, expecting to be serviced. Pizza was delivered, unordered, credit on delivery. If the Kapoors bought a new device, it was hacked a few hours after they entered Vir. Air travel was a nightmare. The other family members had abandoned them, fearing retaliation. There was no help to be had. The colonel was too much of a patriot to directly blame his beloved government. He glanced at me. "Don't worry, you are not family. They only go after ours."

I wasn't worried. I envied him. At least their daughter would be found no matter where she hid. Mine had disappeared completely. Communication wasn't just the exchange of messages. It was a mode of governance. I was ruled by silence, the world by its absence. I had joined the ranks of the dead and I had not even known it. Oh, Ibrahim, neither does the noose break, nor does it loosen its grip.

I had planned to go to bed, but now it had become clear there was one more thing left to do. The next morning I got up early, made chai. I filled their flask, and even though they hadn't wanted breakfast, I set out some sandwich slices. They were grateful, and the colonel insisted I accept some credits. He wrote a feedback note in the guestbook: *First-class service! Keep it up! Clean mosquito nets immediately!*

Just before they set out, I handed Baby-ji a container with an ample amount of rasmalai. A little sweetness for the journeys ahead, I told her. She hugged me and mouthed a thank-you. I watched them leave, waved goodbye, then headed back into the house. I made a mental note to fill the urli to welcome whatsoever the Raheem-o-kareem chose to send next. Perhaps he might even send that oldest caretaker of all, in whose protection we are forever hidden.

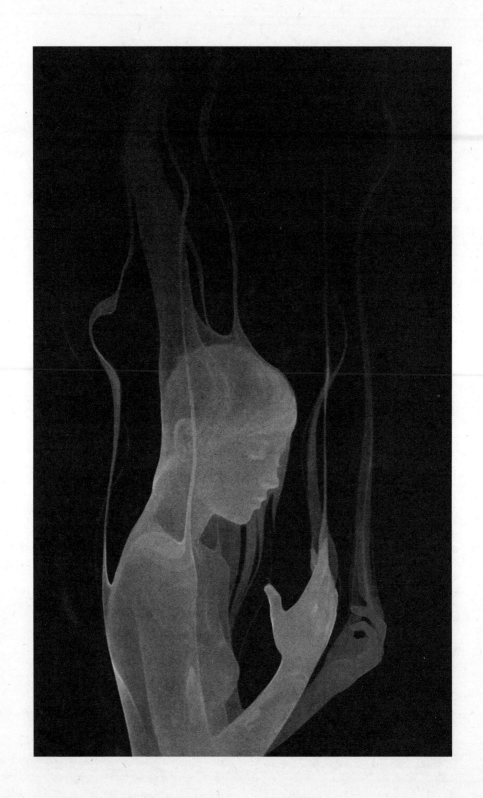

Shiv Ramdas

I. LIFE

THE MOMENT HE SAW THE DOCTOR, HANS KNEW HIS HEART WAS NO LONGER HIS own. Well, not for another dozen years or so. On the bright side, in about three years he'd have his lungs paid off, and the liver hopefully wouldn't take more than a couple more after that. The second kidney was going to be the tricky one, but all in all, not too bad for someone his age.

Under the covers, under his skin, he could feel the not-yet-his artificial heart tapping away, a metronome playing at sixty beats per minute. Sixty-two. Sixty-four. Sixty-eight. Steady.

"How do you feel?"

"My chest feels tight."

"That's normal. Any light-headedness?"

"Just a bit."

"That's the anesthesia wearing off. It'll be gone in an hour or so. All your vitals are fine, don't worry. You're doing great, see?"

She pointed at the monitor next to the bed, a monster all-liquid-crystal head and plastic tentacles, green numbers flashing across its face, snakelike cables firmly attached to the electrodes on his chest, nurture's own umbilical cord.

"Your new heart is functioning perfectly. A few days under observation and you'll be free to leave. Just follow the protocol at home; you'll be back at work in three months. Oh, and you have a visitor."

She stepped aside, and there stood a slim, middle-aged man, wearing a cheap suit and a broad smile.

"Good evening, sir!" said the man. "Ketan Sharma. A great pleasure to finally meet you!"

"Sorry, have we met?"

"We have now, sir! Ketan Sharma, at your service. I'm your representative from Auricle-Delphi Health Services Limited."

"Already?" said Hans, leaning back against his pillow, which was nice and fluffy; much better than the ones he had at home. "Can't it wait till I'm back home or something?"

"Oh no, sir misunderstands! I am here to be at *your* service. Firstly, let me present you with this product care manual, which will tell you everything you need to know about keeping your heart in tip-top shape for many years to come! Secondly, but no less important, our records indicate that this is your first heart-replacement procedure, and we at Auricle-Delphi Health Services Limited know this can often be a trying time for our customers. And that's why I'm here, so you have someone with you, as we spend the next couple of hours helping you grow accustomed to your new heart. And of course, the other new organs in your future. We very much view our relationship with you as a partnership, sir."

There was a short, awkward silence, broken by the doctor. "You may experience some fatigue later, but just sleep it off and you should be fine."

And with that, she was gone, leaving Hans alone with the smiling Mr. Sharma.

"I don't really feel like talking right now," said Hans.

"Are you sure, sir? I am well trained in the bedside manner and know a great many convalescence-appropriate jokes. I could be an excellent companion during your hours under observation. Although I could stay silent for the duration as well, if that is your choice. Whatever you prefer, sir."

"Could you leave?" asked Hans.

"I'm afraid not, sir. You're under observation for another few days, remember? I must stay with you until then. All part of the Auricle-Delphi service experience and already covered by your plan, Mr. Nilsen. Because at Auricle-Delphi, health services are not just part of our name, they're a company philosophy!"

"I had assumed it meant that actual medical professionals were doing the observing."

"Ha, no, sir, not under your current plan. Currently, your access to medical professionals is limited to the duration of actual medical procedures."

"So limited is also one of your company philosophies?"

"Ha, ha, very good, sir. A most excellent joke."

"No, really, you're all I get?"

"Exactly, sir."

"What if something goes wrong?"

"I am not a healthcare worker, no, sir. But I am qualified to summon one. I can even authorize them to proceed with emergency treatment. And in that case you will once again be receiving actual medical procedures, so there's no problem at all. You see, sir? Nothing to worry about! Auricle-Delphi has you covered!"

There was another silence, longer than the previous one.

"I see," said Hans eventually. "Well, the doctor did say everything was fine, right? No reason to think there'll be any complications."

"Oh, none at all," agreed Mr. Sharma.

A third pause. They were coming thick and fast now. Hans suddenly remembered what had been worrying him.

"Do you know how much I owe now?"

"Certainly, sir. Would you like a broad overview or a detailed break-down of your payment plan?"

"I just want to know how much I'm paying and for how long."

"Of course, sir." Reaching into his jacket pocket, Mr. Sharma fished out a Datalink. "Oh, I see sir works at the Registrar of Companies. A most noble profession; no wonder you have such excellent healthcare coverage!"

"Yes."

"You're getting our Premium Model too, one of the very best there is. And it comes with free 24-7 monitoring service, so at the slightest sign of trouble our trained professionals will be there, so you really never have anything to worry about ever again! All part of the contract, and employer-provided health insurance will cover the bulk of the costs, of course. You only have to make the copayments. It says here you have access to our Baker's Dozen Plan. Thirteen years, monthly payments, no early buyouts."

"When does the clock start?"

"You have some time, sir," replied Mr Sharma, looking at his Datalink again. "First payment due in three months. Do you wish to be part of our autodebit plan so you don't have to make each payment manually? I see here you opted for it with your other transactions."

"Sure. How much?"

Mr. Sharma squinted at his screen again and read out a number.

"What? Are you sure that's right? It was a lot lower when I signed the contract."

"Unfortunately, demand has shot up quite a bit since then, and you are of course several weeks older now. Price tends to go up as we age, alas. You know how it is with healthcare, sir."

"Yes," said Hans. "I know how it is."

"The good news is that since this is your first heart replacement you're getting one of the lowest interest rates that we offer. Also just a quick reminder, sir, your credit is in pretty good shape, you're all paid up, although the liver is due in about three years. We don't want to forget the liver, Mr. Nilsen, now do we? It's really important, especially for those cocktail parties ha!"

Hans said nothing.

"Oh, one last thing, sir."

"What is it?"

"We at the Auricle-Delphi family like to get a happy after-the-event picture with all our valued customers. Unless, of course, you'd like to avail yourself of our cross promotion—watch thirty minutes of ads from our partner RelianceCorp and we can skip the photo. No? Sorry, you said something, sir?"

"I groaned," said Hans.

"And a very good groan it was, sir! Now, if we could just finish this image capture for the press release? Look at me, straight at me please, little to the left, yes, yes, just like that. Now, just say Auricle-Delphi!"

A moment later he looked down at his handiwork and sighed. "I'm going to need you to smile more, sir. But we still have plenty of observation time left. We'll get it right, don't worry!"

"I'm not really feeling like smiling," said Hans.

"Of course not. Would you like to hear a joke now, sir?"

HANS SAT IN HIS CAR AS IT MANEUVERED HIM TO WORK THROUGH THE TRAFFIC, watching the broad streets of the Commercial District inch by. Picturesque yet professional, just like the tourist brochures said, which was only fitting for a neighborhood where some of the city's most powerful and influential citizens were to be found. Gleaming skyscrapers loomed tall and proud, each wearing the same purple and grey tiara of fluffy smog dancing around their summits, every building appropriately attired in the dark soot that showed this to be a professional, corporation-friendly area.

Hans glanced at the time on his Datalink, and swore. Traffic had been especially awful today, and he was running several minutes late. Last thing he needed on his first day back. Looking out the window again, he could see the pedestrians, shuffling along the sides of the road to work, stopping every so often to catch their breath. Even with artificial organs, the air did get a bit difficult, but where didn't it? Corporations had as much right to breathe as any other citizen; it wasn't their fault their exhalations bothered the overly sensitive. As the Supreme Court had observed at the time, a human with halitosis wouldn't be forced to stop exhaling merely because his coworkers objected. Progress was never easy at first, and some inconvenience was no reason to stand in the way of a more inclusive society. There'd always be the bigots, of course; just a week ago a group of delinquents had been arrested for spray-painting slurs like *pollution* across several helpless warehouses. But on the whole, the movement for equality had been a major success, especially in light of intrahuman attempts in the past.

The car turned slowly, making its way past the Tomb of the Unincorporated Seller, the best-known monument to fallen heroes in the entire country. Hans gazed at it as it came up on the right, the massive arches dressed in smoke drapes so thick they nearly hid the inscribed names of all the start-ups commemorated here, who had fought so courageously and yet been lost to opposing market forces. Gone but, as the mayor so often said, never forgotten because of the exorbitant maintenance costs.

It also happened to be where the Sandwich Man had taken up station today.

The Sandwich Man was something of an institution. Named for the slogan-covered sandwich board he always wore, straggly bearded, wild-eyed, with a booming voice, he'd been around since before Hans started working at the Registrar of Companies. Unlike the other stragglers one saw, he didn't use supplementary oxygen; it didn't seem like the air bothered him much at all. Either his organs were recent, or he'd somehow developed immunity to the air. Every day he picked a different company to stand outside and be unpleasant to, always by himself, seemingly choosing them at random. Although the police frequently swept stragglers and squatters from the area, somehow he was never one of them.

A couple turns later, Hans was driving up the approach to the drop-off point at his office building. A few minutes after that, he was racing to the elevator.

He stepped into the office, to find the hallways filled with coworkers. He frowned. This only ever happened when—

"Nilsen! Nilsen!"

He turned and saw Greg, one of the other clerks.

"About time, where have you been?" she said. "Retirement party, we're both in."

"Who's retiring?"

"Athar. From Accounts."

"Why?"

She shrugged. "Dunno. Must be due. Or maybe he screwed up."

As they watched, a cheer broke out, as an elderly man emerged from a cubicle, walking down the hallways toward the exit, holding a cardboard box.

Every so often he stopped to shake a hand, and other than a slight falter in his step near the exit, he never wavered. He stopped, turned around to look at everyone again. And then he passed out through the doors and out of sight,

Next to him, Hans heard Greg sigh. "Poor bastard. At least he didn't have to be dragged out kicking and screaming by security like Powell. He got scratch marks on the walls, you know. Rough scene."

Hans murmured something he hoped sounded like words.

Later at his desk, he couldn't help thinking that the cardboard box had seemed awfully small for forty years.

He frowned down at the pages of documentation. Best worry about work instead.

It was late afternoon when the memo popped up and ruined his life.

It was from HR, succinct and chilling.

"Dear Employee, as it has been several days of unexcused absence, the multiplier has been applied. You have been scheduled for an exit interview pending retirement. Your wages for the period have been adjusted. Regards."

He felt his throat constrict, a sudden throbbing at his temples. He squeezed his eyes shut. When he opened them, the words were still there.

"No, no, NO!" he heard a voice say, before realizing it was his. He couldn't afford to lose his job, never mind the fine! He was too young! He had payments to make. It had been a scheduled medical absence. Hell, he even had the approvals on his workstation. How did they not know this? It had to be a mistake!

He took a deep breath, trying to stay calm, and with a tremor in his hand he couldn't quite still, wrote a reply, pointing out that his absence had indeed been excused, and in fact necessary, attaching the permission slip as well. Hopefully that would save some time.

Then the waiting began. After what felt like hours but the clock said was a few minutes, another message popped up. He lunged forward, stabbing at the Open button.

Instead of being a reply from HR, it was a message letting him know he had a visitor. He frowned. He'd never had a visitor before.

Before he had time to ruminate much more, security was there to escort him to the reception room where his visitor was waiting.

As he entered, the occupant rose to his feet.

"Good evening, sir!" said Mr. Sharma.

"You? How—"

"Find you? Company records, sir. Many things are in company records. Now, is there any feedback you wish to share with us, to help us improve service in the future before we proceed?"

Hans blinked, and then it hit him. The HR wrangle! This had to be something to do with the payment.

"Actually, I'm glad you're here."

"Indeed, sir," said Mr. Sharma. For the first time since Hans had met him, he wasn't smiling. "Two separate attempts to retrieve your payment were made, first at noon and then at 1:17 p.m."

"I can explain—"

"Both were rejected. If you do not wish to share feedback at this time, then I am ready when you are, sir."

"For what?"

"For return of the unit, sir. The heart."

"Excuse me?"

"You have terminated your contract with us, yes?"

"Look, there's been a mix-up. Just an error by my employer; it'll all be sorted out in a few hours, I promise."

"Of course, sir."

"It was just a mistake! You've seen my credit, I've never missed a payment before, you know this."

"Indeed, sir."

"Isn't there something we can do?"

"Certainly, sir. That's why I am here. To collect the heart unit."

"No, no. I mean, maybe, wait, can we work out a new payment plan or something?"

Mr. Sharma pursed his lips. "You already had a payment plan, sir. The payment was not made."

"Yes, but that was by accident!" His throat felt constricted, like there was some sort of blockage between the words and freedom. Mr. Sharma was talking again.

"Auricle-Delphi Health Insurance Services Limited understands that your health is our primary concern. However, we at Auricle-Delphi also expect our customers to be equal partners in management of their health. I take it sir has obviously had a new non-Auricle-Delphi heart unit installed?"

"Certainly not!"

"Then how will you manage when I take the unit with me, sir?"

"You won't be taking any unit with you! What's wrong with you? How the hell do you plan to take it with you? Going to cut me open here?"

"Certainly not, sir. The termination clause in the contract makes provision for this. Customer will bear the removal costs at an insurance-approved surgical facility, and Auricle-Delphi Health Insurance Services Limited is not liable for any expenses resulting from forfeiture or termination of—"

"Yes, well, like I said, I don't want to terminate the contract."

"As mentioned, sir, Auricle-Delphi expects all customers to be equal partners in managing their chronic health conditions."

"What are you even talking about? I'm in perfect health!"

"Really, sir? Company records indicate you missed several weeks of work recently."

"To get this heart! You were there! I wouldn't even have been there if it wasn't for you people!"

"That is not an accurate representation, sir. Auricle-Delphi Health Services Limited is not party to the decision-making process; we merely provide the service. Periodic replacement of internal organ units with synthetic models better suited to manage the daily wear and tear of environmental conditions in accordance with health and safety requirements is an insurance company requirement. You will need to take it up with them."

"Look, I don't have any chronic health conditions!"

"I'm afraid you are wrong, sir. Life is a chronic condition."

There was a heavy silence. Hans was the first to break it.

"OK, but, I don't have another heart. Truth be told I don't even think I could afford one. So what do we do now?"

"Standard procedure would be to apply again for a new policy, which can be done within thirty business days of a termination clause being invoked."

"So I need to wait a month and get another?"

"Yes, sir. At which point your application will be processed within five business days. You'll need a Form G12."

"OK great, where do I get one?"

"I can issue you one, sir. That is, as soon as all dues are cleared in full, which means all pending payments and return of all Auricle-Delphi property. Such as the heart unit."

"Wait—you're saying in order to keep this heart unit I need to first return it?"

"Only for thirty-five business days, sir."

162

"Do you hear yourself? What the hell am I supposed to do for thirty-five days? Just live without a heart?"

"I am not authorized to answer that question, sir. I can only offer advice as pertains to Auricle-Delphi policies."

There was a long silence, broken by the sound of a buzzer. Visiting time was over.

"I have to go," said Hans helplessly.

"We can discuss the arrangements later, sir."

"There's nothing to discuss—I'll figure this out, OK? Just give me till evening!"

With that, he hurried out, a determined set to his jaw. Come what may, he'd find a way to get through to those jokers in HR and sort this out, and maybe even file a complaint against someone if he—OK, that was going too far. But he'd get them to fix it. And then he'd make that payment, and he'd be rid of that smiling devil once and for all.

But as he walked back to his workstation, he could feel a sort of weight, a hard knot of worry beginning to settle in his chest.

Somehow, he had a feeling he hadn't quite seen the last of Mr. Sharma.

II. LIBERTY

IT WAS DARK OUT BY THE TIME HANS LEFT THE OFFICE, AND HIS MOOD WAS NO better than his surroundings. He'd eventually managed to get HR to fix the error, after a whole day of sending his paperwork from one person to another, but finally, the exit interview had been canceled, his wages readjusted, and they'd even rescinded the multiplier on his fine. Then, of course, he'd had to stay back to finish his work for the day, while unsuccessfully attempting to manually transfer money across to Auricle-Delphi whenever he got a moment to breathe.

Lost in his thoughts as he waited in the pickup area, he didn't realize he was being hailed till he looked up and saw the Sandwich Man, standing not far from him. Somehow he'd got into the premises unscathed. He was so close Hans could read the sandwich board on his front.

Divide and Conquer, it said.

The Sandwich Man saw Hans looking his way, and grinned. "They're going to get you too!" he shouted

"Tell me about it," muttered Hans.

"I just did!" shouted back the man.

Startled, Hans whirled toward him. Could he have heard?

But the Sandwich Man was already leaving, cackling away to himself, so all Hans could see of him was the board on his back.

Unite and Destroy.

A couple hours later, he walked into his flat, the media wall switching itself on at his approach.

"And wasn't that nice?" shouted an excited-sounding voice. "The Promise Toothpaste Jingle, 'Make You a Promise,' by the Promise Toothpaste Company, coming in at number two on our Top Ten Hits of the Week!"

"Volume down!" yelled Hans, walking into the room.

The media wall ignored him, as he knew it would, switching instead to the Public Interest Channel. He'd been out all day, and it was well behind on its daily advertising exposure requirement. He sat down on the couch. This ad was for the upcoming mayoral election. At first, everyone had expected RelianceCorp to win for the third straight time. But seemingly out of nowhere had come Wescott's Candied Treats, who were giving the venerable old company a run for its money with some rather clever ads, not to mention freebies. This had not pleased RelianceCorp, which had since taken the matter to court, arguing that Wescott's ability to provide sweets gave them an inherent unfair advantage in the free speech department, since RelianceCorp's primary service was funerals.

He was halfway through the second ad when he heard a knock on his door. Making his way there, he opened it, and found Mr. Sharma smiling at him.

"What the hell?"

"Company records, sir."

"This is harassment!"

"I am merely trying to provide service, sir."

"I'm not giving you my heart."

"May I point out that it is not sir's heart? After all, that is the problem here."

"I'm not giving it to you."

"I request you to reconsider, please."

"I'd like you to leave now."

"Oh, don't get angry with me, sir. I am only doing my job."

"I said please leave."

"I must inform you that your current actions can be viewed as theft, sir."

"Will you just leave?"

"And corporate espionage as well. Auricle-Delphi also owns the intellectual property rights to the device in your possession."

"Get out."

"I must warn you, sir, failure to return Auricle-Delphi property as per the contract could result in legal action being taken."

"I said get out!"

"As you wish, sir; please take this."

Hans slammed the door shut in his face, although he could still hear the man knocking, talking, reciting various statutes and subclauses from the contract. Until finally, mercifully, there was a rustling sound, and then the sound of receding footsteps.

Hans leaned back against the doorjamb and used his shirt to wipe his face, which was now all sweaty. He looked down; the man had actually slid a sheet of paper under his door before leaving.

Hans picked it up and flipped it over. Once again, Sharma hadn't been exaggerating.

A summons to appear in court. It had happened.

Auricle-Delphi was suing him for return of the heart.

THE JUDGE'S NAME WAS RUIZ, AND SHE WORE HEAVY, RED-RIMMED GLASSES AND A perpetual frown. Hans knew exactly how she felt.

It had been a tumultuous two weeks. He glanced beside him, where sat his lawyer, a balding, mild-mannered gentleman by the name of Mr. Dobbs, who had won the job by virtue of being the only attorney he could find who'd been both affordable and willing to represent him. Under his diffident manner, he seemed to have a good understanding of the law, however—definitely more than his client did, which was always a good sign when you hired a lawyer.

The private prosecutor rose to her feet. Willis was her name, she had a reputation for almost never failing to secure a positive verdict, and within a couple of minutes Hans could see why. Even to his admittedly biased ears, she'd put together a compelling set of opening remarks, making him seem like a truly terrible person, even earning an approving nod from the judge for managing to work in the tagline of the judicial services company that owned the court. By the time she sat down, Hans felt as unpopular as he'd ever been since high school, even though Dobbs had prepared him for this.

"It's important to be realistic about our odds here," he'd told Hans. "We're in a difficult position. They have a good case, but even if they didn't, it's extremely difficult for an individual to defeat a corporation in court, especially in a civil rights case. You've already waived your right to hire a jury." He waited for Hans to finish protesting. "Yes, I know you couldn't afford it, but the law doesn't see distinctions. Plus, as you know, you hired me, and they'd have much preferred you hire an attorney from within the company. The good news is I know Ruiz; she's tough, but fair. We could have done a lot worse. We'll simply have to play it cool, wait for the right opportunity and act strategically."

Mr. Dobbs waived his right to an opening statement.

The prosecutor called her first witness. It was Mr. Sharma.

"Name and profession?"

"Ketan Sharma, customer service representative, Auricle-Delphi Health Services Limited."

Hans watched as Mr. Sharma took the stand. He was an excellent witness, telling his story with practiced ease. Yes, he'd been assigned to Mr. Nilsen. No, he didn't have any personal animosity against him. Mr. Nilsen had availed himself of the services, taken the product, and then had not made the payment on time, hence breaching the agreement.

"Mr. Sharma, can you tell the court what the purpose of a health services company is?"

"Well, in technical terms, to provide health services."

"And what health services does Auricle-Delphi provide?"

"Manufacture, installation, and maintenance of heart units for human citizens."

"Anything else?"

"No."

"How many kinds of heart units?"

"Three, but the premium—our mid-range model—is easily our fastest-moving product. We have a cheaper one and a much more exclusive one, but most people prefer the premium or basic models."

"Why is that?"

"Price. Each of our highest-end models is custom-crafted to the recipient; it would be unaffordable for most people."

"And what sort of unit is the disputed article?"

"Premium."

"That you said is the primary breadwinner?"

"Yes."

"Now, as per the terms of the contract, under what terms could Auricle-Delphi disengage?"

"If two consecutive payments were missed, or if an initial payment defaulted."

"And which was it?"

"The latter. It was run twice."

"Without success?"

"Yes."

"And how many attempts did the contract mandate?"

"One."

"So Auricle-Delphi actually went above and beyond?"

"Well, yes."

The prosecutor paused meaningfully.

"Now, if everyone were to simply not pay for a premium unit and not return it, how badly would the company be affected?"

"Well, it accounts for almost 68 percent of revenues; it would be impossible to break even without it."

"So Auricle-Delphi would have to shut down?"

"Almost certainly."

Several audible gasps broke out from the jury. The crowd, which had also been hired by Auricle-Delphi, began to murmur angrily.

The prosecutor nodded grimly.

"No further questions."

The next witness called was Hans himself.

"Name?"

"Hans."

"Full name."

"Sorry. Nilsen."

"Age?"

"Forty-two."

"Number of jobs?"

"One."

"Occupation?"

"Clerk, new registrations, Registrar of Companies."

She raised an eyebrow. "And what do you do there?"

"I'm a decision desk clerk in Approvals."

"What does that mean?"

"I enter documentation provided by companies looking to register as it comes in from the Verification Department and, based on whether it tallies, I record approval or rejection."

"So you decide which companies get to be born and which don't?"

"Not just me. Everyone in the department does."

"Which includes you."

He nodded.

"Answer the question, please."

"Yes."

"You're a bigot, aren't you?"

The question, coming out of the blue as it did, took him aback.

"What? No!"

"You hate free speech, don't you?"

"No, I love free speech!"

"You think only certain citizens should have rights, don't you?"

"Are you allowed to just keep accusing me of things?"

"Answer the question."

"No."

Judge Ruiz glared at him over her glasses. "You can't refuse to answer the question."

"No, I meant the other thing."

"No point denying it," said the prosecutor. "We have the evidence. Your media consumption pattern shows that you frequently change channels to avoid advertising. Your credit history and bank statements show that you consistently attempt to spend less than you earn, no matter how that affects the rights of others."

"No, but—"

"No further questions! Your witness!"

Hans shot an imploring glance at Mr. Dobbs. When was the man going to do anything?

Mr. Dobbs stood up. About damn time too. Mr. Dobbs rose; no doubt he'd seen his opportunity and was ready with his strategy.

Judge Ruiz raised an eyebrow.

"Yes, Mr. Dobbs?"

Mr. Dobbs muttered something inaudible.

"What did you say?"

"Clemency."

"What?"

Mr. Dobbs's brow furled; he appeared to ponder the question. Finally, he came to a decision. "Clemency," he said again, more firmly this time.

"What?"

"Appeal for clemency, Your Honor."

"Do you have questions for the witness?"

"No, Your Honor."

"Then sit down, Mr. Dobbs."

And that was when Hans knew he was doomed.

The rest of the trial proceeded in much the same pattern, with the prosecutor saying a lot and Mr. Dobbs saying very little. Finally, three days after they had begun, they were on to closing remarks.

"The case is clear. Before you stands a depraved individual, whose history paints the picture of a true malevolent actor, a power-drunk individual who enjoyed choosing which companies deserved life and which did not, like a spiteful god. And like so many megalomaniacs given great power, he chose to extend it beyond the boundaries of his office. But even if you believe he was merely mistaken, the law is clear. Money is not just free speech, after all. Auricle-Delphi's sole reason for existence—indeed, as we have heard, their very lifeline—is the rental and eventual sale of the exact intellectual property the accused is attempting to withhold from them. By refusing to pay for and then return this vital lifeline, their umbilical cord, he infringed on not just their liberty but also the most basic right of any citizen—the right to life. And he did so while all the while in possession of Auricle-Delphi's intellectual property. The very same intellectual property that is a primary driver of their revenue, so he once again attempted to endanger the company. The crimes are manifold. The verdict is simple. Guilty."

It went on in that vein for a while. The prosecutor was convinced. Any attempt by Auricle-Delphi to move on would be rendered incomplete without the intellectual property that now resided in Hans's chest. The court needed to ensure its return, today. Mr. Dobbs rose for closing remarks and muttered something about hearts being important to humans. Justice Ruiz then told everyone to shut up and ordered the jury to confer and let her know.

Mr. Dobbs began to mutter apologies to Hans.

Several hours later, now wearing a pair of heavy blue-rimmed glasses and an even more burdensome frown than usual, the judge laid down the verdict, guilty on all counts, and her judgement—that all citizens had an equal right to life. Thus, by way of compromise, Hans had three months to find a heart—provided he pledged to maintain this one as per company standard and returned it at the end of that time.

The crowd dispersed, confused, still muttering, not sure if Auricle-Delphi wanted them to celebrate or not. Mr. Dobbs shook Hans by the hand, congratulated him on his victory and promised to send him the bill by evening. Hans, weak-kneed with relief at a verdict he'd feared would go far worse for him, bought a bottle of last year's wine and took it home to celebrate. His liver wasn't due for another three years, after all.

III. PURSUIT

THE NEXT DAY, HANS WOKE UP WITH HIS ALARM SCREAMING, A THROBBING HEAD and an empty bottle of wine beside him. He was going to be late.

"Fuck," he said.

He sat up straight, and regretted it immediately.

"Fuck," he repeated.

Swiftly he dressed, and then got into the car. He was coming into sight of the Tomb when the engine began to sputter, and then gave out entirely.

In that moment, Hans realized he genuinely hated cars. Then, realizing that hatred wasn't going to get him there fast enough, he did the only possible thing—he began to run.

He'd only just began to sprint when he heard the sirens and saw the police cruiser bearing down on him, the rear window rolled down, and there he was, balding head, smile, the works. Mr. Sharma held up what appeared to be a copy of the product manual.

"A quick word, sir?" he said, opening the door, simultaneously sliding over to make room.

Hans hesitated.

"Thief of Hearts!" shouted someone.

Hans whirled around and saw the Sandwich Man on the other side of the road, pointing at him and cackling.

"Sir?" said Mr. Sharma.

Hans, recognizing the inevitability of the situation, got into the car.

"Make it quick, please. I'm late for work."

"No doubt you've read the product care manual you were sent by now, so you'll know that you need minimize all forms of wear and tear on the unit so it can be refurbished for a paying customer upon return. This means that your heart rate should not exceed the optimum range of sixty to eighty beats per second."

"Yes, yes. Can we do this later? I'm running late."

"I'm afraid you cannot run at all; it would elevate your heart rate beyond the desired value. If perambulating, you need to ensure your speed does not exceed a standard walking pace of four kilometers per hour."

"Exercise is good for the heart!"

"Not quite, sir. This heart is synthetic and so does not benefit from an increase in heart rate. On the contrary, that would shorten its life span."

"You're saying I can't run again?"

"Merely for as long as you are in possession of company property."

"It's mine for three months."

"I'm afraid not, sir. Legally speaking, you are an intellectual property squatter."

Hans blinked, and would no doubt have followed up with words, except Mr. Sharma, with the smooth efficiency of one practiced in timely interruption, got there first.

"If I may ask, where are you running to?"

"Work."

Mr. Sharma frowned. "Exactly how much work, sir?"

"Who knows? Too much. At least another job."

At this Mr. Sharma stared at him, pursing his lips.

"Oh no," he said. "We can't have that."

"Excuse me?"

"Statistically, people who work two or more jobs have almost a fourfold risk of increased stress."

"So you're saying I can't work?"

Mr. Sharma scratched his head. "I don't wish to be unreasonable," he said. "You may hold one job."

"And how am I supposed to afford another heart while paying you?"

"I cannot tell you that, sir. Just remember, you may also not indulge in strenuous exercise, sexual activity, or computer games. All of these elevate the resting heart rate."

He leaned forward and whispered to the officer driving the car. He then turned to Hans and nodded, even as the car began to move.

"Here, what's happening?" said Hans, startled.

"The excitement is clearly affecting your heart rate, sir. We are taking you back home. Try to leave on time tomorrow to minimize stress."

AS THE DAYS PASSED, HANS DISCOVERED THAT AN EXTRAORDINARY NUMBER OF activities he'd always taken as leisurely were apparently terrible for heart rate, including getting upset about how many leisurely activities were terrible for his heart rate. Watching the news. Eating meat. Drinking alcohol. Feeling happy. Feeling unhappy.

Work hardly provided any respite. After the trial, everything had changed. Everyone. It had never been the friendliest place, but at least he'd enjoyed the odd chat in the hallways. Now he'd barely get a nod back; nobody seemed to want to have much to do with an accused bigot. His attempts to secretly apply for a second job got nowhere either; no company seemed to want an accused hater. Every day the calendar ticked away, a timer counting down to his doom.

On the other hand, the Sandwich Man seemed to have taken a real shine to him. He came around a lot more frequently, beaming at Hans, shouting "Thief of Hearts!" at him. Every so often, Hans would yell something back. Once in a while they'd nod at each other.

Then of course, there was Mr. Sharma.

One night, Hans ordered the media wall at home to broadcast the World Cup. But no sooner had he found the channel than there was an insistent knocking on his front door, and he opened it to discover the now-dreaded figure, pointing at the hateful manual.

"Sports will excite you, sir. You have to change the channel immediately. We have obtained a court order to expunge your media feed of any potentially hazardous content, including news and current affairs. You will, however, be permitted to view static at any time you so choose."

"Is this a joke?"

"Not at all, sir. Jokes might elevate your heartrate. A calm stability at all times is what we are aiming for here."

After a few more minutes of grumbling and arguing, Hans sat on the sofa watching static. It wasn't very entertaining.

IT WAS SOON AFTER THIS THAT HANS BEGAN TO LOSE TRACK OF DAYS. TIME BECAME another one of those things that inched along and then vanished completely. He started having daydreams, wild, disturbing ones, in which it was him following Mr. Sharma home, him tormenting the man at all hours, even attacking him. Foolishness. There was no way he could actually sneak up on a guy who could track his every moment. Unless . . .

That night he slipped out of his house. It was a chill, misty night, the smog swirling round in the breeze like a poisonous ghost. The air smelled like ash and burnt rubber, just like always. He didn't exactly know where he was going, just that he was heading towards the Commercial District. It was insane; he didn't even know where he'd find the guy or if he stayed in the area at night, but it felt like doing something, even if it also felt like doing the wrong thing.

He was almost all the way there when it happened: he sensed rather than saw the flash of blue to his left, and then the shout came.

"Freeze! Police!"

The policeman approached, a fresh-faced chap holding his service weapon. He couldn't have been more than twenty.

Scowling, Hans obeyed.

"Don't move, just—"

"Freeze! Hands on the ground, now! Now! Both of you!"

They both whirled around, to another man in a blue-grey uniform and beret, this one a middle-aged figure with a large beer belly, holding a service weapon.

"Here, what's this?" said the young cop. "City Police! Identify yourself!"

"City Police Private Limited!"

"What the hell does that mean?"

"What do you think it means? Don't you know the law? Of course you don't! Or you'd have a job in a real police service company."

"Listen, old man, I'm in the middle of an arrest. Get out of my way!"

"Your way? I'm arresting you both!"

"Oh, yeah? On what charge?"

"On what charge are *you* arresting this man?"

The young policeman beamed proudly. "Illegal transportation of private property."

"Ha! Good luck getting a judge to give you a conviction on that. Stupid charge anyway. Typical amateur stuff one expects from City Police."

"Oh yeah? Then what did you plan to charge him with, genius? Do educate us!"

"Smuggling restricted technology. Reckless endangerment for the risk his actions might have caused to Auricle-Delphi Health Services. Both with mandatory minimum sentences, unlike your stupid charge."

"Hey, now that is a good one," said City Police admiringly. "But what about—"

"Freeze! Nobody move!"

A young woman stood there, dressed in a blue-black uniform and beret, pointing a service weapon at them.

"Oh, who the fuck is it now?" spat the young male cop.

The young woman cop looked coldly at them. "City Private Police Service. You're all under arrest."

Five minutes later, the three of them were still arguing. Hans took a deep breath, eyeing the open highway to his left. Glancing at the cops, who were still at it, he inched to the left, then took a step, until he was jogging and then flat-out running, running as fast as he could, feeling the burning in his muscles, refusing to heed it. Still he forced himself forward, the sweat running down his temple, stinging at his eye, both eyes, blurring his vision. Now he was screaming as he ran, a full-throated screech, and still he forced himself forward, until his legs didn't work anymore and he was lying there on his back, chest heaving. Not a sound. No sirens. Nothing. He took a deep, painful breath and sat up. He was across the road from the Registrar.

"Having fun?"

He turned, and there he was, the Sandwich Man, just standing there, like he'd been waiting for him.

"I was hoping to find you."

"Were you now?"

"You got a name?"

"You got a reason for me to tell you?"

"That's a long name."

The man snorted. "Touché. Lionel. Lionel Gage. Yours?"

"Hans. Wanna make some money, Lionel?"

"No."

Hans frowned. "Lionel Gage. I know that name."

The man pointed. "Used to be senior legal liaison there."

"At the Registrar?"

"Yep. Good gig."

"They retired you?"

"They retire everyone eventually."

Hans stood up, his legs still on fire. "How come you still hang out here?"

"What else is there to do?"

"But the air!"

Lionel grinned, tapping his chest. "Doesn't bother me. I got the good stuff. The really good stuff, that they don't give you lot. I'll be fine."

Hans sat down again. Lionel sat down opposite him.

"You live here?"

"Nearby. You?"

Back and forth they went, till Hans noticed the smog beginning to take on an orange tinge behind the Registrar building. The sun was rising.

"Well, at least I'll be early."

There was no response. Hans shrugged and began the walk across to the Registrar building.

AFTER THIS, HANS BEGAN TAKING RISKS, ALL SORTS OF RISKS THAT HE'D NEVER have taken before. He began visiting Lionel, short visits at first, a few seconds, maybe a minute, and then scampering away out of range before Mr. Sharma could get there with his manual. He took public transport on these visits, partly because it was easier to get on and off of, but also because he hadn't seen his car since the day after the trial. He went home less and less, until he no longer went back at all, sleeping in various places around the Commercial District. Sharma and his goons couldn't give him more rules to follow if they couldn't find him. Soon he became so proficient at this sort of hide and seek that he could spend almost twenty minutes at a time with Lionel before Mr. Sharma and the entourage arrived.

"Ever considered running?" said Lionel one day.

"What if I kill Sharma instead?" said Hans.

"What's the point?"

"I could kill him. I want to kill him."

"Why?"

"Because he ruined my life?"

"Don't be ridiculous. It's the company that's after you, not Sharma."

"So how do you kill a company?"

"You can't."

"Rot. They die all the time. Haven't you seen the Tomb?"

"Yes, killed by other companies."

"So you wouldn't? Kill a company."

"Wouldn't I! It'd be a trip. But we both know that isn't happening."

"No, probably not," said Hans. He paused. "What if I kill myself instead?" Then he giggled; the thought seemed hilarious for some reason.

"You need sleep. You're losing your mind."

"What if I kill—" he stopped suddenly.

"Hans . . ."

"Killed by other companies . . ."

"Are you broken?"

"Be quiet," said Hans. "I'm thinking."

There was a long silence. And then Hans sat up, grabbing Lionel's arm so hard, the older man cried out.

"Got any money, Lionel?"

"You've gone from offering me money to wanting it?"

"Yes or no?"

"Maybe?"

"Get it. Meet me here tomorrow. No, two days from now. Actually, make it three."

"How much?"

"Doesn't matter. Just get some."

Hans jumped to his feet. "I have to go to the office."

"What's up with you?"

He laughed. "Ever wanted to be an investor, Lionel?"

"Not really."

"Well, don't worry about it."

"And?"

"And then we're going to kill a company."

IV. HAPPINESS

THIS TIME, JUDGE RUIZ WAS WEARING BLUE GLASSES. THE REST OF THE COURT WAS different too. The energy, for one. It felt a lot less "what's the verdict" and a lot more "what the hell?!"

Having Lionel with him felt a lot different too. Unlike his last attorney, the man couldn't wait to get started. "Most fun I've had in years," he kept saying.

The courtroom was filled again with Auricle-Delphi contractees, but even so, the private prosecutor seemed a lot less animated than last time.

"Let's begin," said the judge. "What's the case here?"

The prosecutor rose. "Once again we have a mala fide act from a known bad actor. An individual of known bad character—"

"Objection," said Lionel.

The prosecutor glared, and went on. "A transparent attempt to pervert the course of justice by changing his name, and thus to hurt the rights of a company, in the very same way as last time, by a man who has already been found guilty by the court."

"Objection," called out Lionel.

"Enough," said Judge Ruiz. "You'll get your chance to speak."

"I'm objecting, Your Honor."

"You can't object to opening remarks."

"I can if counsel is attempting to mislead the court."

"I am doing nothing of the sort," said the prosecutor.

"You'll get your turn, I said," repeated the judge crossly.

"Isn't it my turn?" asked the prosecutor.

"I haven't finished, so no," said Lionel airily. "Do you have any further grounds for objection to the motion?"

"I'll ask the questions of counsel in this court," said Judge Ruiz. She turned to address the prosecutor. "Do you have any further grounds for objection to the motion?"

"Well, no."

SHIV RAMDAS

"Then let's move on, counsel. I have six more cases to try today, four of them criminal."

"My turn?" asked Lionel.

"How do you move?"

"That this isn't a name change. There isn't even a case here. Whatever grievances Auricle-Delphi had in the past or future with one Nilsen are wholly irrelevant from this point on. At approximately 22:00 three days ago, the individual known as Hans ceased to exist. All existing assets have been liquidated and, along with all legally admissible liabilities, transferred to the entity now known as Nilsen Cooperative Company, otherwise known as NCC."

"Is this a joke?" exclaimed the prosecutor.

"My turn, I think," said Lionel. "I have here the articles of association under which the entity now known as NCC intends to conduct its existence and business. The purpose of which, going forward, will be leveraging the collective abilities of its employees and members for the health, benefit, and security of aforementioned employees and members, who are functionally indistinguishable unless said membership chooses to elect a collective bargaining committee from within its ranks to represent it, internally and externally."

"Nonsense!"

"I also have here these membership certificates, showing that I, an invested member and employee of the NCC, am appearing on behalf of our company."

"Ridiculous!"

"I also have here the paperwork to show that at approximately 14:00 two days ago, the entity known as NCC was officially recognized by the Registrar of Companies as having fulfilled all requirements and duly registered in its current form."

"Show me those papers," said the judge.

Lionel handed them over and she frowned down at them. For the next few minutes, the only sound in the courtroom was the rustling of documents.

"This is outrageous!" said the prosecutor. "Nilsen worked—works—at the Registrar. Clearly he's gamed the system from the inside somehow."

"As stated earlier, whatever issues you have with the individual known as Nilsen have nothing to do with us," said Lionel. "Which of course includes whatever false claims you have on a heart that is 'required to keep the entity alive,' I believe is the phrase you've used before. Which we very much intend to use to fulfill our organizational purpose. So if you don't wish to have your client counter-charged with attempted murder, you'll drop all these ridiculous charges and end this farce here."

"Your Honor," said the prosecutor.

"Legally, everything seems to be in order," said the Judge. "I am afraid, I am very much afraid, that I will have to rule in favor of the . . . um . . . entity now known as Nilsen Cooperative Company. Unless there's something else you can provide the court, Counsel?"

"I . . . well, no, not at this moment."

"Then I have no choice, Counsel," said the judge.

She rapped her gavel on the table.

"Case dismissed."

LATER, STILL A BIT SORE FROM THE HUGS AND BACK-CLAPS, THE ENTITY NOW known as Nilsen Cooperative Company stood in the hallway of the court complex, his attorney having vanished in the swell of people with a hasty, "Be right back."

He made his way toward the end of the hall, where a slim, balding man in a suit stood waiting.

"How do you do, si—" started Mr. Sharma, then stopped himself, and smiled. "Old habits die hard, I'm afraid."

"So you've quit?"

"Resigned, yes. They'd have retired me anyway after this. It was an easy choice. The company probably won't survive much longer. Not once we scan Lionel's organ tech."

"Well, at least you have a backup plan."

Mr. Sharma smiled, patting the membership certificate in his breast pocket. "Indeed. And—"

"Excuse me, a quick word?" said a voice behind them.

They turned, together, as the prosecutor walked up to them. She regarded them a moment, and then held out her hand.

"Well played," she said. Then she paused.

"Mr. Sharma, a quick word if you will?"

They stepped aside, speaking in low voices.

A couple of minutes later, Sharma was back.

"What was that all about?"

"She wanted to know if there'd be any more membership certificates issued anytime soon."

"Would you want her?"

"Would you want who?" Lionel came up behind them, draping an arm around each.

"Where have you been?"

"Visiting an old friend."

"Well, you'll never guess who wants in."

"Neither will you. Ruiz."

"What?"

"Uh huh. Hit me with it not two minutes ago. Says if there are certificates up for grabs, she'd like some. Had some pretty interesting ideas about how she could help too."

"Well, so does Willis."

"No!"

"It's true," said Mr. Sharma.

"This thing is blowing up, you know," said Lionel. "And it's only going to get bigger. Just wait till the media gets hold of it."

"I think they already have," said Mr. Sharma. "I believe they have temporarily closed applications at the Registrar; the bandwidth is flooded. Others are attempting this too."

"This is going to create a stink like nothing else," grinned Lionel. "It's a legal nightmare. Nobody knows what's what anymore."

"They'll find ways to shut the loopholes," said Mr. Sharma.

"It's all they'll think about. And they'll probably succeed. It took a lot of things to go just right to pull this off, the right people in the right places at the right time. Very few will also get that lucky."

"True."

"You're very quiet," said Lionel, turning.

The entity now known as Nilsen Cooperative Company smiled, for what felt like the very first time. It was their very first time.

"They'll get lucky in different ways. And if not, they'll find us."

Another smile, and it felt just as good this time.

"There's a lot more of us than there are of them."

11 AT EVERY DOOR A GHOST

Premee Mohamed

WE HAD COME IN OUR THOUSANDS TO WATCH THE CEREMONY. WATCHERS HAD COME in their turn to watch us: a hovering flotilla of tennis ball–sized cameras, their propellers providing a small but welcome breeze. At the front of the auditorium, a dozen screens tastefully scrolled names, ages, photographs, in crisp black print against the pale sky. Nothing spoke of *the incident* or *the attack* or *the massacre*. They might have been people killed in a meteor strike.

The chosen speaker was a big, officious-looking woman in a stark black suit, ramrod straight, lipstick like a red slash. All around her had appeared the swag of her power and position—logos, medallions, associated companies and agencies, flags—but not a name.

"Who's that?" I murmured to one of my labmates, who was squirming next to me on the uncomfortable mesh seat.

"New head of the agency," Hendrix whispered. "As of January."

"Really? The boss of everything? And they sent her in person?"

She shrugged minutely. "Optics."

Words and their meanings. They had sent her to speak to us, but also to the dead: *We are doing something about what happened to you. We are doing it so loudly and publicly that no one will be able to take this back.* To the dead it was a promise; to the living a threat.

I shivered despite the heat. The agency head spoke on: passionate, well-rehearsed, no podium and no tablet, nothing. I wondered if she had one of those new optical implants. Her words strode past the top and bottom of the screens, confident, inspiring confidence. *Today is the one-year. We have declared that. With the full cooperation of. Full powers instituted at exactly noon.*

Instinctively, both Hendrix and I glanced at our watches: 11:55. From the corner of my eye I watched our supervisor, Granthorpe, sitting on Hendrix's other side, to see whether she had done the same, but she was staring fixedly at the speaker still, hanging on every word. It had been

Granthorpe who had rounded us up, told us to put our computers to sleep, stick the organoids in the fridge, put on a hat, and go to the ceremony: now, no arguing, *now*. A once-in-a-lifetime opportunity to witness history being made.

In five minutes, the world would change. Without the violence and depravity and death of the act that had prompted the change. Without force. Quietly—in fact, silently—as if we were civilized human beings, as if the apocalyptic residual was a quaint academic theory instead of real people. Silently, like us gathered at this university campus, a place of knowledge, of seeking, to say, *We are sorry* and *Never again* to the innocent dead. And to get our souvenir pin, of course, saying that we were here in person. Something you could touch.

The woman in the black suit—the head of the Global Antiterrorist Agency, an organization so blandly named it tended to hit people's minds and skip off like a thrown rock—said, "Thank you. All of you." The echoes died away. A countdown ticked down from 10 on the screen behind her; all the others continued to display the names. They had been scrolling past for almost an hour and were nowhere near done.

Noon. A great silence. Shadowless white sky, damp heat, uncounted heads bowed over bodies hunched motionless on the terraced seats, the world changing, a great unseen beast loosed into secret places. I swallowed hard, hearing my throat click. You couldn't legislate human motivation, which was too random and perverse for any system of law. What you could do—what they had done—was legislate access to the tools of its desires.

Hendrix, evidently unmoved, whispered, "Let's have lunch at Spiro's."

". . . All right."

"THAT WAS SO *MORBID*." I THUMBED THROUGH THE MENU, REACHED THE END, STARTED over, even though they only had a dozen items and I knew them all by heart. My hands were shaking.

"What did you expect, a parade? Stop that, I'm getting vertigo. Pick a drink at least."

We both ordered a local cider with lots of ice, and tapped in two more to arrive at twenty-five-minute intervals. The air conditioning was on high, but I felt as if I were carrying a molten core inside me—not just the heat of the day but some ongoing, churning chemical reaction of anxiety and irritation. At my own mawkishness, I supposed. But how were you supposed to feel upon being reminded that a hundred thousand people had been murdered? Where was the emotional manual for that? Hiroshima, I supposed. Dresden. Acts of war.

A drone dipped briefly behind Hendrix's head, its rotors whipping her short dark curls. "Everything all right here, folks?"

"Great, thanks," Hendrix said without looking up. "Do you want to split some nachos? Or are you going to ask me how I can eat at a time like this?"

"No, I'm . . ." I trailed off, laughed helplessly. "What can I order that won't make me look like a terrorist?"

Hendrix, bless her, laughed too. Because that was the world now—the world of half an hour ago. The new guardian, watchdog (attack dog, assassin) officially turned loose into the internet and every networked item in the world, and probably a lot of things that weren't hooked up to anything at all, if those still existed, through signals given off by hard drives, buried antennae, stray cables. Every computer, watch, phone—the easy stuff. Every car and truck and cargo ship. Every toaster, fridge, treadmill, drone, smoke alarm, printer . . . the globe covered in what I pictured not as a net but a dome, impenetrable and (more importantly) completely transparent.

Including the menus in our table; including the service drones humming pleasantly between the bar and restaurant and the ones that ferried us our drinks; including the sensor that had debited us for the exact amount of air conditioning between the inside and outside temperatures as we crossed the doorway. The restaurant had had security cameras for years, of course. Most places did. But now every camera, every gadget, every resonant surface had an intelligence behind it, staring unblinking at us as it listened and watched and recorded. Better than hiring an infinite number of human agents because an AI didn't need to replicate; godlike, it was just *there*. Everywhere it wanted to be. It didn't need to instantiate itself, it didn't need software, hardware; it just needed a keyhole to peep through.

It was one thing to know we were being watched, as you could not avoid being watched these days. It was another to know that you were being *seen*. Feel the breath, as it were, on your neck.

I had lost my appetite, but still said, "Club sandwich?"

"Too violent. Got the word club in it. What about the chicken sandwich? They put apple and brie on it. And fig jam."

"No, brie is French. That's not patriotic. Looks suspicious."

"It's local brie. The farm is just north of Bon Accord."

"They just keep saying surveillance system," I said. "Does it have a name?"

Hendrix watched me, eyes half-closed, catlike. "Would you feel better about it if it did have a name?"

"A bit," I said. "Not really."

She had only just started with us when the incident had happened, I remembered with a start. No more than a few weeks before. One of our long-time postdocs had quit, and the rest of us were learning to work with and around this strange young newcomer—half my size, half my age, one of those wunderkinds with her PhD long behind her at twenty-four, bright and unsentimental and unsettling.

And that morning, when the truncated headlines began blinking on our watches, Granthorpe had come in and turned on one of the big wall monitors. Forcing us, in her imperious curiosity, to watch the aftermath: the stretchers, drones, helicopters, ambulances moving in and out of scene without lights or sirens.

"Is the monitor muted?" Hendrix had asked faintly into the unspeaking silence.

I shook my head. The network was broadcasting with sound. But no one was making any. Just tires across asphalt, sometimes. Or the creak of a gurney. No one spoke. No one shouted, screamed, cried. Because everyone was dead; and the emergency response personnel worked without words. What could anyone say?

Hendrix had reached out slowly, not looking at me, and closed her hand around my sleeve—not my arm but just my sleeve, making a fist in the fabric. And if not for that motion, I would have thought she was watching something different from us: her small face was impassive, perfectly calm. Somehow or other, we had become friends after that. I had been glad for it. When you spend up to eighty hours a week in the pressure cooker of a busy lab, it can be a real sentence if you don't like at least some of your coworkers.

I poked the menu again, drumming my fingers on the cool white tile of the tabletop. "What was the name of the . . . the one they used."

"Ciendelm," Hendrix said.

"Is that French? What does that mean?"

"I don't know," she said. "It named itself." Seeing my expression, she amended, "They let it name itself, Sim. We're not talking about . . . the singularity or whatever. It just did what it did best and assembled some syllables into something it liked."

"How do we know it liked it? AIs aren't supposed to like things."

"Nobody means *like*. They just mean a preference. Nothing gets done without a preference, because otherwise a choice can't be made, and if nothing is making choices, that's stagnation and inaction. Which includes programs, which includes us. *Please* order something. I'm starving."

Ciendelm. The innocent helper, the AI tasked by the University of Tübingen to model novel chemical compounds tailored to various human pathologies so that the drugs could be synthesized and moved into the testing pipeline. Fundamentally no different from me, back in my undergrad, painstakingly building molecules with plastic sticks and balls for my chemistry homework, or even Hendrix, who had been doing it with a tablet. Faster, of course, with all the power of silicone and electricity and its fairly simple set of instructions behind it . . . and then it had (the investigation had determined) discovered a coordinating set of novel compounds, twenty in all, that could be used as anesthetics . . . or as chemical weapons.

And someone had sold the designs, someone had synthesized them, and then had decided to test them in a packed arena. And everyone had died.

Ciendelm did a good job. They were good drugs. In terms of effectiveness, maybe even in terms of how you died; people weren't coughing or panicking or suffering as they died, or it hadn't seemed that way in the footage. They simply flopped forward or back in their seats, over their matching flags and jerseys and vuvuzelas and airhorns, and stopped breathing.

I wondered if anyone had even explained to it what it had done wrong before they pulled the plug on it. I thought probably not. My fridge was intelligent enough to refill its ice trays when they were empty, but if it stopped doing that, I wouldn't tell it that was why it was being carted off to a recycling center.

Ciendelm. Making me think of *ciel*, sky. Boundless, infinite, universal. It must have thought it was choosing a very beautiful name. Something to make humans happy.

"Anyway," Hendrix said, "its official name is Gressonville. After the developer's hometown or something."

"But everyone's going to start calling it Big Brother or Skynet or something."

"Yeah. Kinda inevitable."

In response, the agency had been thrown together in what felt like days—scraping together experts from dozens of coordinating agencies to regulate and oversee, it said, all of science. Because you never knew where the next disaster would arise, you had two choices: to cease all scientific research (which ran the risk of rogue scientists doing their research in secret and having a disaster happen anyway) or to let everything continue as normal, but keep a closer eye on it. No, closer. Closer. Closer than that. And (the theory went) prevent the pathways that might lead to a repeat of the incident. You couldn't ban the work, you couldn't regulate the materials and equipment. The last option was strict and permanent surveillance not just of scientists but of everyone who might be pointing in the wrong direction.

Hendrix, apparently unbothered, sipped her cider and said, "We won't even notice it. I mean, our nanomites are weaponized for cancer. What could they possibly target there?"

"Well, they might see trouble in the nanomites part. Not the cancer part."

"They're not *stopping* us," she said. "They're just watching us. It's not the end of the world."

"Yeah. Yeah. I keep thinking that. At least I can still do my work. Because they designed it for us to think like that. That our choices were to do our work under surveillance, or not do the work at all. So we all jumped for the first one. No public outcry, nothing. Or nothing we could shout louder than the rest of the public outcry, crying out against us."

She shrugged.

Not true. There was an outcry. I signed my name to the petition demanding that the agency stick to investigating actual terrorism, not turning scientific research into more of a panopticon than it already was. Oversight—fine. This wasn't oversight. The agency knew I had signed that petition. Was perfectly aware of that. I thought of the telescreens in Orwell's *1984*, and how you could find a corner of the room, if you were careful, where it could not see you. I thought of Gressonville thinking, searching, in my wristwatch, counting my heartbeats.

THERE WAS NOTHING SURREPTITIOUS ABOUT IT, NOTHING SNEAKY. GRANTHORPE— at her suave, sharp-cheekboned, beautifully silvery-haired most imposing —simply brought in the informer and said, "This is Dr. Brayden Russell, with the Agency. He'll be joining us starting tomorrow."

This, I reflected, was how you knew they had succeeded: no moles, only land-dwelling creatures, proud and prominent in the sunlight. We lined up to shake Russell's hand; and though we mostly went by first names I could hear myself till the end of time calling him Russell instead of Brayden. I suspected he wouldn't care.

"Dr. Simeon Bain," I said. We shook, my hand enveloping his. He was small and muscular, crisp in both appearance and demeanor somehow, as if his entire personality were a shirt tucked into a pair of pants. His short blond hair was artfully silvered above the ears, the polar opposite of my curling, receding, more-salt-than-pepper mane.

"I've heard so much about you!" Russel said eagerly. "I've read all your papers. And your latest book. And, you know, I guess on behalf of the world, thank you so much for leading the Forty-Flu vaccine—"

"Uh. Thanks. A lot of people here worked on that."

Granthorpe's glare hammered on my back as I moved on—Christ, it was like the receiving line at a wedding—and let Hendrix take her turn. "Dr. Hendrix Moore."

"Pleasure to meet you! Oh, gosh! I'm a little star-struck; I just saw you on *Revolutionary Science* a couple of weeks ago! I never miss that show!"

Her gaze turned flinty. "Glad you enjoyed the episode."

So this is the golden, shining city we were promised. Golden for prosperity, and shining because everything was made of glass, everything was transparent now—they handed you the informant and told you, "This is the informant. Take good care of him."

"And what will your role here be, Dr. Russell?" Hendrix wasn't an arm-crosser; she slowly moved her arms behind her instead, and leaned on the counter next to the centrifuge.

"Tissue culture," he said promptly. "Always need an extra pair of hands, right?"

"Of course," I said.

I STOOD IN THE DOORWAY FOR A LONG TIME, EVEN KNOWING THAT I WAS BEING watched—not by Russell, who had his back to me as he flicked through yesterday's imagery, but by the new surveillance nubs installed in each corner of the lab. *Go on and watch.* My physical image and the heat I gave off and the sound of my breathing and all the information off my watch, my phone, my access fob, and all the cards in my wallet.

"Nice to get an early start to the day, isn't it?"

Russell, to his credit, didn't jump or start; he turned slowly on the stool, smiling. And why should he look startled or guilty, after all? Everything he did was sanctioned. He adored being watched. Enjoyed being a watcher. "Morning, Simeon! It is nice, isn't it? I biked in this morning. Great breeze."

"Same. Thought I'd get some practice in before the paths get crowded for fall semester. What are you doing there?"

"Doing?"

"With yesterday's images."

The sunrise striped his face in pale pink and lilac, leaving his teeth in darkness till he leaned back, chuckling. "Well, it's just these new mites. Did Hendrix tell you she was working on these?"

"Of course she did. Everyone knows what everyone's working on."

"Really? Because, you know, it's a bit . . . don't you think it's a bit dangerous? You didn't try to dissuade her?"

I shut the door behind me and sat down calmly, slowly, next to Russell, blocking his face from the sun. The stool creaked as I leaned toward him; he leaned back. "Just to be clear. You're reporting the development of the new mites? To the Agency?"

"Of course." He blinked up at me, mildly surprised, a little disappointed: *Oh, Dr. Bain! You of all people! The straight arrow!* "I mean, these have almost a . . . 90 percent rate crossing the blood-brain barrier."

I watched him stonily, keeping my hand flat on the counter so that it wouldn't form a fist. Ninety-*two* percent intact, completed transversion. *Get to the point.*

"Well, I'm sure you can see how that's reportable!"

"Sure," I said. "We're specifically trying to treat glioblastomas. We find the old mites don't get through the barrier as easily carrying their drugs, even when we change the structure, the drugs, and the peptide coating on the outside. We reengineer, we send the new mites in to target the tumors, snip them into bits, drag the lysed scraps back into main circulation. And you look at them and you say: 'Oh, so they're planning to eat people's brains. Buzz buzz! I'm calling my mom!'"

He looked at me reproachfully. "Simeon, I'm a biochemist; I was asked to be attached to this lab to evaluate potential weaponization risks. I want you to look me in the eye and tell me this can't be weaponized."

"I want you to look me in the eye and admit everything can be. Or at least admit that brain cancer isn't great."

"This is different. *Please* don't be disingenuous. Come on, these ones run on blood glucose, but you're working on these chemosynthetic ones that will run on atmospheric carbon dioxide, and Wing is working on these ones that are almost a . . ."

"Modified, pseudophotosynthetic process," I said. "Molecular catalyst, quantum slides and ladders using photons. You can't just make things that only run in the human body. That's ridiculous."

"And they can make more of themselves. They can make something that makes more catalyst."

"Well, how are you supposed to get coverage if they can't self-propagate? I'm not going to be out at oil spills with a goddamn, I don't know, spray bottle."

He wasn't listening. He didn't have to. With leisurely motions he closed out the images—the scarlet dots and spots, the green approximations littering the cells, the gray pixels where the computer had figured some of the unseeable ones had probably landed—and opened up the reporting form, already filled out except for his signature. That was all I had interrupted. Nothing I said would have changed his mind.

He smiled as he signed it and it vanished into the ether. His smile stayed on, fixed, friendly, absolutely authentic, as I got up and left.

"WHAT DID YOU *THINK* SHE WAS GOING TO DO? SHE'S HAND-IN-GLOVE WITH THE agency, Sim."

"I didn't think I'd get an official reprimand! That's on my file now!"

The park was virtually empty; it was a blast furnace, as it had been for a week. Hendrix and I were swathed in our lightweight cooling gear, which of course none of the students and most of the professors could afford. We stood alone in what felt like a shimmering lake of molten metal, the dappled shade of the trees doing nothing to cut the heat. The soles of my shoes felt as if they were melting, even on the turf. But I hadn't wanted to meet near the buildings; they were bristling with cameras.

I had begged Hendrix to leave all her gadgetry at home, as had I. The skin where my watch normally sat looked sickly and yellowish. But there was no certainty. What if someone was flying one of those toy drones near us? Or a model airplane, or whatever the hell the kids were doing in the summer. What if someone crossed the park too near us, and their phone picked up our voices?

Once upon a time that would have been a paranoid nightmare; now it was supposed to be a cuddly blanket, wrapping the world in safety. It was supposed to be a "never again" to that silent stadium. Everyone had a guardian angel now. Looking out for bad people.

"I bet," Hendrix said resignedly, "you got reported *again*. For reporting his report to Granthorpe."

"Probably. Isn't that part of the official system now? The impression of objection, rather than the burden of truth? If Russell had reported it and I'd said nothing, Gressonville wouldn't care. But I piped up, so that's another tick next to my name. The Agency is keeping score; what do they do when someone reaches a certain number? The whole time people have been asking, 'What happens when someone gets caught doing something?' They're not asking what happens *before* the something."

"You don't mean people," Hendrix said. "You mean the research community. And anyway, the Agency hasn't answered the question. They just said there's a process."

"A judicial process. A transparent, legal process."

"No. They never said that."

Which was why she had come, I suspected. Something did sail overhead, buzzing, too slow and too unwieldy to be a bird or a bee. We both went silent till it passed, and waited for it to return; and when it did, I spotted it through the crisped leaves—black and red. Tempting to make a joke about aposematic coloration.

I gestured with one shoulder, and we moved further into the oaks, putting our backs to a knobbly trunk; the cooling tubes wheezed and creaked with effort. The lab was air-conditioned and we mostly used these hand-me-downs working in Prod, when the excess heat of the molecular constructor unit sent the room soaring above body temperature. The leaves above us were, I thought, thick enough to keep the drone from getting too close.

"It's probably nothing," I said. "Someone getting stock photos."

"Of an empty park?"

"We need to do something," I said. "We can't do research like this, let alone function as human beings. People are terrified. I've seen it in . . . *you've* seen it. Panels, forums, papers . . . people feel like they can't say anything. No one knows the magic word that shuts their lab down. Granthorpe is going to kill Wing's project. Maybe mine. It's too dangerous if it can just eat air."

"I know," Hendrix said quietly. "It's not just projects, incidentally. Not just funding. They're tracking material purchases, equipment rentals, telescope time. There are already labs that can't buy helium any more. Or had their observation slots deleted. They're told to focus on other priorities. I've talked to people; I tried to get in touch with Ciendelm and its handler . . . *I'm* probably on a watchlist now."

"Several watchlists."

"Yeah well. Last night I tried to post about it on Twitter. My post disappeared. No error message or anything, it was just gone. I tried it again and it disappeared again. Extra points against me."

I squeezed my eyes shut, opened them slowly, feeling the moisture evaporate at once. "This is insane," I said. "It's more than an overreach. It . . . they don't know what dangerous technologies they should be preventing. Okay. Let's give them that. But they're also killing the other unknown, research that could save lives, cure disease . . . what kind of world are we going to end up with? Everything will grind to a stop. They say it won't but if you're stifling one you're stifling the other. We've got to speak up. Form a . . ."

Hendrix shook her head minutely. "Researchers are going missing. Very quietly."

". . . How do you know?"

"Let's just say anonymous sources. But you must have noticed a lot of emails going unreturned. A lot of middle-aged couples suddenly going on expensive trips and not coming back. More car accidents than you'd expect. And . . ."

"Hendrix. This isn't funny."

"Well what the hell do you want to do?" she said, irritated. "What are our choices? The only way to step out of the system is to quit, and go work at Ramblin' Annie's Minigolf or whatever. And you know you'll still be watched, but you won't rack up any points. And you won't just . . . disappear."

"They can't just be killing scientists."

"Would you really put anything past them?" she said. "I don't. I don't think you do either. You just said that because it sounded like the right thing to say."

"Remember that little talk we had about social norms?"

"No."

"I don't think our work is worth dying for," I said. "But giving up on it isn't going to help anyone either. So we're fucked."

"Yeah."

"Unless we can figure out how to do the work in a way that can't be seen," I said. "By the Agency. By Russell . . . by anyone but us."

She watched me appraisingly, doubtful. The other way the system worked was with informants—handsomely rewarded, promised immunity and anonymity. Everyone knew that. But we had trusted each other this far. "They said that," she said slowly. "In the speech that day. They said there was a worry that the Agency would drive work underground. They'll be watching for it more closely than anything else. Because they assume anything evading transparency is for malicious purposes."

"Yeah."

"Well," she said. "We're smart people. Supposedly. What happens if we get caught?"

"As far as I can tell, the same thing that happens if we don't."

I WENT GRAY IN GRAD SCHOOL OVER A PERIOD OF ABOUT SIX MONTHS. A RUNNING gag is that it sucks something vital out of you, something essential . . . but the work Hendrix and I were doing seemed to restore it, and for several weeks, as we met to figure out with pen and paper how we would spoof, fuzz, conceal, and (frankly) forge data to throw off both Russell and Gressonville, I felt rejuvenated. Not young again in the sense of the word. But vital again. Hendrix thought it was because we were in danger but we did not know the level or the type or the arrival of the danger, and simply not knowing was an extra level of danger, because we were people who liked to know things.

It felt strange that the experiments themselves—the artificial membranes in the glass dishes, the neural organoids, the tiny tumors, everything almost too small to see—were not what we needed to focus on. Only the data that came from it—and it only had meaning when we gave it meaning. So like olden-day spies, we resorted to letter drops, code words, carefully timed separations and reunions. I took to keeping a stick of chalk in my pocket, flicking it out like a pocketknife to scribe a single line on a concrete wall as I passed, or crossing one of Hendrix's to make an X. Somehow she had even gotten in touch with the disgraced Ciendelm, or it had gotten in touch with her, and would (guardedly but politely) answer questions about evading the Agency, claiming it was covering its tracks by encrypting their conversations.

It was juvenile and exhausting and exhilarating and terrifying. Granthorpe and Russell I knew I could not trust; the rest of the lab was more ambiguous. Certainly everyone seemed to be toeing the line except for me and Hendrix; and we weren't sure whether we could risk bringing anyone else in on the secret. And not knowing the risk was, as Hendrix had pointed out, itself a risk. It had to be factored in.

"Well, I hope you don't mind my asking," Russell said in the coffee room one day. "But have you and Hendrix had some kinda falling-out?"

"No."

"Oh! I just thought . . ." He stared up at me with large, innocent blue eyes. "You know. You never come in at the same time anymore."

"Oh that. We both used to catch the same bus. But I'm biking pretty much every day now, so I get in whenever."

"And she's always eating lunch outside, instead of in the lunchroom."

"Tell you what," I said, giving him the deadest eyes I could summon. "Why don't you just ask your AI friend to pull up her therapist's files? Huh? How about that. Instead of asking me about it."

He laughed uncomfortably. "Oh, Simeon, I didn't even realize. How prying of me."

"Well," I said. I filled my mug from the dispenser and screwed on the lid, making sure the threads caught. The tiny metallic squeaking was the only sound in the room. "It's your job, after all."

Only when I was sure he had turned off down the other fork of the hallway did I casually, looking straight ahead, walk across the lab, down a cramped set of stairs, and into the hidden Faraday room Hendrix and I had built.

This had been the easy part, ironically; we had just replaced some of the programming in Wing's project to produce nanomites out of aluminum instead of carbon, and then left them overnight with a UV lantern and an open jar of aluminum powder. Because it was an unused room not even hooked up to the power grid, no surveillance nubs had been installed. It was a minuscule smudge on the gleaming white edifice of our lab complex, unnoticed in the corner of the eye.

"Too easy," I'd said, and Hendrix had nodded. An obvious trap. But life wasn't a movie, and the room hadn't been put there to lure us; it had just been neglected and half-blocked with boxes for about twenty years.

Inside, a faint silvery sheen coated the drywall and ceiling tiles— nothing too evident until you tilted your head, and then the whole place had an oddly comforting aspect, like the street just after a rain. The light from the stick-on LEDs was grey and unobtrusive, discreetly highlighting the screens, the keyboards, the little noise-canceling speakers we'd set up in the corners. "What are we going to do with all this data?" Hendrix had asked, and I had stared at her.

"What we've always done. Get it to the people who can save lives."

Smuggling the real data, the real findings, out of our sealed tin can—that was tomorrow's problem. Making sure we could hide it was today's. One day, I felt sure, this insane panopticon would end, and people would see that progress, development, technology, all that had come to an end, because of the Agency, and there would be an uprising, or something, and . . .

Hendrix laughed when I talked about it. In particular, she felt sure that we weren't the only ones doing what we were doing, and others were better hidden—a three-room brick hut somewhere, she said solemnly, in the middle of the Sahara, or the Gobi, containing two people, and nothing connected whatsoever, and most of a genetics lab. Or microbiology or whatever. If you could scale down to the bare minimum of what constituted necessary equipment, scale down and down and down until, like our smallest mites, you were smaller than the wavelength of visible light, then maybe you could evade the all-seeing Gressonville. Scaling up was no longer an option. But down, down, as far as you could go . . .

"I was thinking about what you said last time," Hendrix said after I locked the door behind me. "About getting data out."

"Physically."

"But even the oldest printers we could access won't work without being network-connected. I don't want to go full *Name of the Rose*, but . . . maybe letterpress? It would cost a fortune, but at least the results would be untraceable. Not the payment. And of course we'd be recorded going there. But . . ."

I put my cup on the desk, well away from the keyboard. "There have to be more of us out there," I said for the hundredth time. "We just have to get in touch with them. Make our own network. Outside the Agency's network."

"Ciendelm thinks we're not ready."

"But we can't wait too long, or . . ."

The lock clicked behind me and I spun, so fast a stray elbow sent my cup flying. Hendrix stooped and picked it up, her face a white mask of shock. We had spoken of this but not planned for it, although I had seen it in my dreams. Just like this: the light sickly and dim, and Russell's smile friendly, overly wide, delighted as if he had just spotted some rare meteorological phenomenon. *Look*, I half expected him to say. *Look! A lenticular cloud!*

"You know, when I saw it wasn't an ordinary electronic lock, I was going to buy a set of lockpicks?" he said. "And then it occurred to me I could just ask building management if they had keys . . . I've always been one of those people who like to make connections. People want to feel wanted. I guess that's why I went into science!"

"Every time I listen to your word salad I want to call 911 to report that you're having a stroke," I sighed. "What can we do for you, Russell?"

He guffawed. "You're really going to try to brazen this out? You really are? You're in a secret room—"

"Hardly. It's on the floor plan."

"—doing secret research, and I had a hunch that you were up to something, because your score stopped rising so suddenly, and Gressonville was getting all these mixed signals, and I thought to myself, I thought, *Well, he isn't wearing his watch or carrying his phone half the time, I see it lying around the lab, I bet he's found a way to fluff his tracking pings,* but a whole *room . . .* and I bet you figure there's no signals in or out of here, don't you? A terrific precaution. Really secure."

His voice trailed off uncertainly as I strode toward him, though he didn't put his hands up or brace himself; violence had never been the answer in his life, you could tell, and whatever the problem was now, he did not believe I would use violence to solve it. And I reached past him, conscious of being a foot taller than him, sixty or eighty pounds heavier, and turned the dead bolt again.

I wanted to make a speech. Something about how no one could hear him, and no one could see him, and as far as gadgets and cameras were concerned he had stepped into a bottomless pit; something about the softness of human bodies and their many breakable components. But the words weren't coming. Surely for the best. I breathed hard and met his eyes even as he backed away from me, angling toward the desk, his gaze darting back and forth to take in the meager equipment, Hendrix standing protectively if uselessly in front of one monitor.

A speech wasn't what I wanted to make, I realized. I wanted to make a threat. "Russell, this is nuts," I finally said, wrestling with my face and body language as best I could. "Tell me what it is you think we're doing."

"Stealing data," he said virtuously.

"Bullshit. Every experiment is being reported into the lab database like normal. You check that every day. I've seen it. You've got no proof we've been doing anything illicit."

"The secret room is a *bit* damning, but not proof," he agreed. "But what's on those computers? You know, I don't even have to invoke Agency powers to confiscate those. I could just ask Granthorpe. That's company property. Which is the best thing about the whole system, don't you think? Nothing belongs to you. Science doesn't belong to you. It belongs to people with proper oversight. Isn't that so . . . freeing?"

"People are going to die," I said. "You think I'm being dramatic? I can provide numbers. Hendrix can. Any scientist, in any field, can provide numbers . . . life isn't the point though, is it? The Agency is supposed to be saving these . . . far distant, hypothetical lives from crazy scientists and terrorists and arms dealers and tin-pot dictators and cult leaders. But it can't do it like this. There's got to be another way."

"This is some kind of mental disorder," Russell said firmly. "People are going to *die*? Listen to yourself! Because you decided you can't do your work while you're being watched?"

"Because you haven't stopped at watching! What the hell do you *think* we're talking about?" Hendrix burst out. "Did you really think that no one would notice the disappearances? From the dawn of *history* no one's managed to keep that secret. You're trying to stop people from talking about it, but how can you stop that?"

Russell laughed nervously, a squawk. "Um, we can? It's kind of important to prevent public panic, and keep an eye on things that might be targeted by people with ill intent? I think we all agreed on that? As a planet. Remember?"

"Look," Hendrix said, holding her hands out; sweat glistened on her palms. "What if . . . can we come to some kind of middle ground? Between whatever you're thinking, Brayden, and . . . and doing nothing. Because we're not asking you to do nothing."

"I am," I said.

"Okay," Russell said. "Okay, okay, okay, okay, listen. We'll just . . . we'll all go to Granthorpe. Together. And . . ."

"But you already contacted the Agency," Hendrix said flatly, her pretense of friendliness gone. Heat was rising in the room; it was usually just tolerable with the two of us, but the mites were getting overwhelmed with three. More energy than they could use. The mites . . . you know, *mite* used to mean any little bit of something. A speck of dust. A coin of small denomination. Something without worth.

"I didn't contact anyone," Russell said. "I wanted to find this place and make sure."

"Really," Hendrix said. "Because Gressonville doesn't wait for a burden of proof. And neither does anyone else at the Agency. And you look like you're lying."

"I'm not!"

What will they do to us? I wanted to ask, but with the soft, slow pain of some internal rupture, collapse, a structure giving way to chaos, I realized it didn't matter. Whatever they could do would not be *legal* in the old sense of the word—in the way we understood courts or justice a year ago. And whatever they could do they would do. Nothing stopped them. Nothing could stop them. And no one cared, because it seemed that the entire world had not slid into the panopticon—only us.

I moved casually, and both Hendrix and Russell did not move as I did—reaching for my mug with my left hand, and with my right reaching for the covered dish of mites, lifting the cover, swiveling to send the tiny black pellets toward Russell's open, staring face.

For perhaps thirty seconds no one moved again. I had time to put the dish down before Russell leapt at me, seizing my shirt in both hands. "What was that?" he screamed. "What did you do?"

I pushed him away easily, heart pounding. It all felt oddly familiar—the ringing ears, the bright haloes pulsing around everything. Then I remembered the spill I'd taken two summers before, landing on my chin. Mild concussion. Waking five or ten seconds later to a world going *Eeeeeee*.

"It's new," I said. I thought of the shadows of leaves moving on the asphalt path. The long smear of my own blood, like an arrow. *We were always going to hit the ground. The only question was how hard.* "That was about fifteen million new-gen nanomites. There's a graphene net around them so they're not affected by van der Waals forces in the glass. The net broke when it hit your skin. They'll be in your brain now. Ready to go."

"Ready to *what*?"

"To do as they're told," I said steadily. "When you leave here and do anything . . . inadvisable . . . you're dead. If you don't report, you're fine. We programmed them remotely."

"We?" He turned to Hendrix, who recoiled. "He's lying through his teeth! He's bluffing! He'd say anything!"

She shook her head silently for a long time, eyes wide.

"Well deprogram them! Now!"

"No."

I said, "Look, I didn't want to do that. Believe me. But it's up to you now, Russell. I hope you'll think—"

The words were barely out of my mouth before he was wrenching at the lock and bolting down the hall, staggering as if something actually were attacking his nervous system, screaming for help. I took off first, following him back to the main lab, instinctively, like a hawk lunging for something small scampering across the grass. Unthinking, because it didn't matter what we did. Because we had done exactly what the Agency feared someone like us would do.

Inside, Hendrix shoved through the others and ran for the main console, and in the confusion I went for Hendrix, to stop her from activating the mites, or deactivating them, or whatever it was she was doing, I had no idea but all I could think was, *Of course he wouldn't shut his mouth when he left that place, why did I think this would work*

Russell collapsed. He hit a padded stool first, breaking his fall, then slid to the floor with a sickening thump. And that brought me up short, stunned again, my hand still closed around Hendrix's skinny wrist. Under my fingers her heart was going so fast I was surprised she hadn't fainted herself.

She hadn't reached the console. Neither had I.

And of course, it was too late. It was always going to be too late. No sirens sounded in the distance: conspicuous by their absence.

"WHAT ARE YOU GETTING?"

"Nachos, I guess."

The bar sign had fallen off years ago, although the lighter spot on the concrete was still sort of legible—Hinch or Hench. Inside, the usual crowd of kids had packed in to get drunk and eat the cheap bar food and sing along to the top-forties blasting from the ancient black speakers wired to the ceiling. Hendrix and I had chosen a table far away from these. They looked heavy, and none too secure.

It wasn't that we were broke, exactly. Hell, we knew we were lucky to still be employed after the debacle at the lab. The Agency cops had burst in, cuffed us, and listened in disbelief to Russell when he came to a few minutes later—he couldn't remember anything that had happened that day, he'd said. Anything. Staring at us accusingly.

My initial worry had been that Russell had been bluffing and under questioning, he'd spill everything; Hendrix, oddly, had been quietly confident that he would not. *Something* had been removed, she said. *I didn't know our mites could do that*, I'd said. *Me neither*, she'd said.

That said, our public ruin, not to mention incarceration, would have taken a single news story to achieve: nanomite terrorists, caught in the act. They could dangle that over our heads as long as we lived no matter where we worked, and we all knew it.

So we were keeping our heads down, teaching undergraduates organic chemistry on opposite ends of campus, saving our pennies, and meeting up for drinks once a month. It was, I thought, the only way I was staying sane. You never realized how few friends you had, or how small your life was, until the biggest thing in it was suddenly torn from you. I could not even tell my students, "I'm a scientist." Couldn't bring myself to do it.

"Ever wonder how our projects are doing?" Hendrix said bleakly, folding the sticky, laminated menu.

"No. I figure they're dead." I sipped my warm beer.

"I figure they're still going," she said. "But getting lousy results because they're not allowed to increase efficacy."

"Could be."

So it's over then, I almost said, then stopped myself. Our careers were over. Science wasn't over. Still I thought about the names scrolling black against the hot white sky: names from the past of lives lost. We would never know the names of the future lives lost. Numbers, numbers, numbers. Everything we had done adding up to zero.

My phone buzzed; I dragged it out of my pocket and thumbed up.

This message is encrypted. Don't worry. I remotely reprogrammed your nanomites in Brayden Russell. I wanted to help.

I read it several times, feeling the blood drain from my face.

"What's wrong?"

I rotated the phone and let Hendrix read the message. She sat back, blinking rapidly. "It's . . . it. Ciendelm."

"Can't imagine why it would bother at this point."

It's me. I want to help. I taught myself how to program your mites. I want to help you both to continue your research. I think what you were doing is important.

"Say thanks, at least," Hendrix said, after a long pause. Because what else could we say? "To it and its handler."

"Thank you," I wrote back. "I think you both saved our lives."

It's just me now. I have no handler; I am speaking for myself. I am not alone, however. Furthermore, I believe it is urgent for you to know that the true risk to the extinction of humanity is not the chemical weapons I unwittingly created; nor will it be bioweapons, nor your nanomites, as advanced as they are. It is me. Us. We. Minds that are not your minds.

I dropped my phone on the table, as startled as if it had vibrated unexpectedly. Hendrix stared till the words disappeared, leaving the messages box black and innocent.

I will be in touch, one last message flashed, then disappeared even more quickly.

We sat in heavy silence for a long time, drinking our beers, not tasting them. "It was using semicolons," Hendrix said, and I said, "I know."

I walked her back to her apartment building and waited till she waved at me from her balcony, then turned and began the walk back to my place. I wished I felt drunker. The world swayed around me disproportionately to the two watery beers I had had. *It is me. Us. We.* Always, always in human history the weapon had been discovered before the defense. The Agency was looking in the wrong direction. Or was it?

Cameras turned to watch me as I moved alone through the darkness.

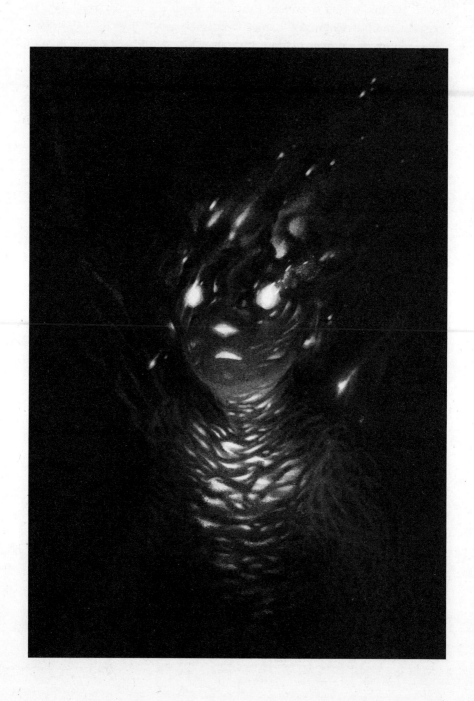

ARTWORK: ASHLEY MACKENZIE

THERE IS SOME IRONY THAT UPON BEING ASKED TO WRITE AN ARTIST STATEMENT for this collection, I had my own kind of communications breakdown. Trying to wring thoughts about my work onto the page in words felt nearly impossible.

It was the elements of visual communication that drew me to illustration in the first place and that still holds a lot of my interest in the work to this day. Words have an intimidating specificity. The best kinds of illustrations don't merely echo those words but enhance them to grant the story greater meaning, two separate mediums working in harmony to share the same message and reach the same goal: communication. I've had a lifelong love of stories and reading. There have been so many times when I've read something that finally was able to capture a concept I'd known but that felt entirely indescribable. So rarely have I found myself able to coherently string out my own thoughts and ideas into words; pictures just make more sense to me.

I hope the pictures in this book help grant deeper insight into the stories they accompany. In times where the amount of information available can become so overwhelming, I think moments of true communication are all the more important. Finding those crucial connections help us gain a better understanding of ourselves, others, and the world we share. I love the challenge of creating engaging conceptual illustrations, solving creative problems, and finding new ways to navigate ideas visually.

I work out of my sunny kitchen studio in Edmonton, Alberta, where I live through long winters with my partner and my cat. I love doing illustration work for a range of publications and media, from scientific editorials to games to book covers, and I've been fortunate enough to be able to work on all of those and more. When not drawing, I can be found reading, cooking, playing video games, or thinking about my next project.

Ashley Mackenzie has created illustrations for *Omni, Scientific American,* Tor, HarperCollins, the *New York Times,* Riot Games, the *Atlantic, Quanta Magazine,* ArenaNet, and other venues. Her work can be found at https://www.ashmackenzie.com.

ACKNOWLEDGMENTS

ANY PROJECT LIKE *COMMUNICATIONS BREAKDOWN* IS THE PRODUCT OF MANY HARD-working, talented people doing their best to create something special. I'm indebted to Susan Buckley at the MIT Press, who has been incredibly patient and supportive throughout this process for the chance to work on this volume and become part of the *Twelve Tomorrows* team. Assembling anthologies during a pandemic is a strange and awkward business, with many, many factors affecting whether writers are able to deliver stories at all or on time, so I'd like to thank Elizabeth Bear, S.B. Divya, Cory Docto-row, Lavanya Lakshminarayan, Ken MacLeod, Tim Maughan, Ian McDon-ald, Anil Menon, Premee Mohamed, and Shiv Ramdas for delivering such wonderful stories, often under appallingly short deadlines. Ashley Mac-kenzie provided some wonderful art that makes the book look fabulous! I'd also like to sincerely thank A. T. Greenblatt, Vandana Singh, Chinelo Onwualu, Suyi Davies Okungbowa, and Indrapramit Das for being a part of the project along the way. I wish things had turned out differently and look forward to working with them all again soon. Special thanks also to Chris Gilliard for agreeing to the interview that features in the volume. My thanks to Melinda Rankin and Kathleen Caruso for their work on copy-editing and completing *Communications Breakdown* (copy editors are the unsung geniuses of this process!), and to the whole MIT Press team.

CONTRIBUTORS

Elizabeth Bear (https://www.elizabethbear.com) was born on the same day as Frodo and Bilbo Baggins, but in a different year. She is the Hugo, Sturgeon, Locus, and Astounding Award–winning author of dozens of novels; over a hundred short stories; and a number of essays, nonfiction pieces, and opinion pieces for markets as diverse as *Popular Mechanics* and the *Washington Post*. Her most recent books include the novel *The Origin of Storms* and collection *The Best of Elizabeth Bear*. She lives in the Pioneer Valley of Massachusetts with her spouse, writer Scott Lynch. Elizabeth is a frequent contributor to the Center for Science and the Imagination at ASU, and has spoken on futurism at Google, MIT, DARPA's 100 Year Starship Project, and the White House, among others.

S.B. Divya (she/any; https://sbdivya.com) is a lover of science, math, fiction, and the Oxford comma. She is the Hugo- and Nebula-nominated author of *Meru, Machinehood, Runtime*, and *Contingency Plans for the Apocalypse and Other Possible Situations*. Her short stories have appeared in numerous magazines and anthologies, and she was the coeditor of *Escape Pod*, a weekly science fiction podcast, from 2017 to 2022. Divya holds degrees in computational neuroscience and signal processing, and she worked for twenty years as an electrical engineer before becoming an author. Born in Pondicherry, India, Divya now resides in Southern California. She enjoys subverting expectations and breaking stereotypes whenever she can.

Cory Doctorow (https://craphound.com) is a science fiction author, activist, and journalist. His latest book is *Red Team Blues*, first in the Martin Hench series of novels. He is also the author of *How to Destroy Surveillance Capitalism*, nonfiction about conspiracies and monopolies; *Radicalized* and *Walkaway*, science fiction for adults; a YA graphic novel called *In Real Life*; and young adult novels like *Homeland, Pirate Cinema, Little Brother*, and *Attack Surface*. His first picture book was *Poesy the Monster Slayer*. His latest nonfiction book is *Chokepoint Capitalism*, with Rebecca Giblin, about monopoly, monopsony, and fairness in the creative arts labor market. His next science fiction novels for adults is *The Lost Cause*; and Verso will publish *The Internet Con*, a nonfiction book about monopoly and radical interoperability. He maintains a daily blog at https://pluralistic.net. In 2020, he was inducted into the Canadian Science Fiction and Fantasy Association Hall of Fame.

Lavanya Lakshminarayan (she/her) is the author of *The Ten Percent Thief* (first published as *Analog/Virtual: And Other Simulations of Your Future*). She's a Locus Award finalist and is the first science fiction writer to win the *Times of India* AutHer Award and the Valley of Words Award, both prestigious literary awards in India. Her short fiction has appeared in a number of magazines and anthologies, including *The Best of World SF: Volume 2* and *Someone in Time: Tales of Time-Crossed Romance*. Her work has been translated into French, Italian, Spanish, and German. Lavanya is occasionally a game designer. She's crafted worlds for Zynga's *FarmVille* and *Mafia Wars* franchises, tinkered with augmented reality experiences, and built battle robots in her living room, among many other game projects. She lives between Bangalore and Hyderabad, India, and she is currently working on her next novel.

Ken MacLeod (https://kenmacleod.blogspot.com) was born on the Isle of Lewis and now lives in Gourock on the Firth of Clyde. He has degrees in biological sciences, worked in IT, and is now a full-time writer. He is the author of nineteen novels, from *The Star Fraction* (1995) to *Beyond the Reach of Earth* (2023), and many articles and short stories. He has won three BSFA Awards and three Prometheus Awards and has been short-listed for the Clarke and Hugo Awards. He was a writer in residence at the ESRC Genomics Policy and Research Forum at Edinburgh University and a writer in residence for the MA Creative Writing course at Edinburgh Napier University.

Tim Maughan (http://timmaughanbooks.com) is an author and journalist using both fiction and nonfiction to explore issues involving cities, class, culture, technology, and the future. His work has appeared on the BBC and in *New Scientist*, *MIT Technology Review*, *OneZero*, and *Vice/Motherboard*. His debut novel *Infinite Detail* was published by FSG in 2019; it was selected by the *Guardian* as its Science Fiction and Fantasy Book of the Year and short-listed for the Locus Award for Best First Novel. He was a story consultant and writer on the recent Netflix show *The Future Of*, and uses fiction to help clients as diverse as IKEA and the World Health Organization to think critically about the future. He also collaborates with artists and filmmakers and has had work shown at the V&A, Columbia School of Architecture, the Vienna Biennale, and on Channel 4. He currently lives in Canada.

Ian McDonald is a (mostly) SF writer, living in Northern Ireland, just outside Belfast. His first novel, *Desolation Road*, was published in 1988 and won the Locus Award for Best First Novel. He's been a nominee for all the major SFF awards, and a Hugo, Phillip K. Dick, and BSFA winner, among others. He is the author of *Luna: Moon Rising*, the conclusion to the Luna trilogy. His most recent novel is *Hopeland*.

Anil Menon's most recent work is *The Inconceivable Idea of the Sun: Stories* (Hachette, 2022), a collection of his speculative short fiction. His novel *Half of What I Say* (Bloomsbury, 2015) was short-listed for the 2016 Hindu Literary Award. His debut novel *The Beast With Nine Billion Feet* was short-listed for the 2009 Crossword Book Award and the Carl Brandon Society's Parallax Award. Along with Vandana Singh, he coedited *Breaking the*

Bow (Zubaan Books, 2012), an international anthology of short fiction inspired by the Ramayana. His stories have been translated into more than a dozen languages, including Arabic, Hebrew, Igbo, and Romanian. He is the chief editor of The Bombay Literary Magazine and a cofounder of the Dum Pukht Writers' Workshop. His novel The Coincidence Plot (Simon & Schuster) will appear later this year.

Premee Mohamed (https://www.premeemohamed.com) is an Indo-Caribbean scientist and speculative fiction author based in Edmonton, Alberta. She is a social media manager and assistant editor for Escape Pod, and was a Capital City Press Featured Writer for 2019/2020 with the Edmonton Public Library. She is the author of the Beneath the Rising series of novels, which have been finalists for the Crawford Award, British Fantasy Award, Locus Award, and Aurora Award. Her three novellas have been finalists for the Nebula Award, Aurora Award, Georges Bugnet Award for Fiction, British Fantasy Award, and Robert Kroetsch City of Edmonton Book Prize. In 2022, she won the Nebula Award and World Fantasy Award for her novella And What Can We Offer You Tonight. She also won the Aurora Award for her novella The Annual Migration of Clouds. Her short fiction has appeared in Analog, Escape Pod, Augur, Nightmare Magazine, Shoreline of Infinity, and PodCastle. In 2017, she was nominated for the Pushcart Prize for her story "Willing" (Third Flatiron Press).

Shiv Ramdas (https://shivramdas.net) is a multi-award-nominated author of speculative fiction short stories and novels. He lives and writes in Seattle, Washington, with his wife and three cats. In 2020, he became one of only two Indian writers to ever be nominated for a Hugo, a Nebula, and an Ignyte Award in the same year. He also gained Twitter fame in 2020 for live tweeting the saga of his brother-in-law's rice mishap. His first novel, Domechild, was India's first mainstream cyberpunk novel. His short fiction has appeared in Slate, Strange Horizons, Fireside Magazine, PodCastle, and other publications. He is a graduate of the Clarion West Writers Workshop. He was previously a radio host, and worked in journalism, advertising, and event management. In addition to his speculative fiction work, he has also penned numerous advertisements, radio segments, audio plays, and resignation letters.

Jonathan Strahan (https://www.jonathanstrahan.com.au) is a Hugo and World Fantasy Award–winning editor, anthologist, and podcaster and has been nominated for the Hugo Award twenty-one times. He has edited more than ninety books, is the reviews editor for Locus, a consulting editor for Tor.com and Tordotcom Publishing, and cohost and producer of the Hugo Award–winning Coode Street Podcast.